Deanna Cooner, PhD

ii
Profane Dragons
Copyright © 2020 by Deanna Cooner, All rights reserved

Stones in Clay Publishing
P.O. Box 1302
Newcastle, Ok 73065

Living stones, being built up as a spiritual house for a holy priesthood, to offer up spiritual sacrifices acceptable to God through Jesus Christ. 1 Peter 2:5,
But we have this treasure in jars of clay, to show that the surpassing power belongs to God and not to us. 2 Corinthians 4:7

Cover Design and Graphics by Mindi Stucks
Book Design by Gary Cooner
Edited by Jeanne Marie Leach
Published in United States of America
ISBN: 978-1-7337093-0-9
Young Adult Fiction / Religious / Christian / General
2020.02.10

*Mammon led them on—
Mammon, the least erected
Spirit that fell From
Heaven; for even in Heaven
his looks and thoughts Were
always downward bent,
admiring more The riches of
heaven's pavement, trodden
gold,
Than aught divine or holy
else enjoyed In vision
beatific· By him first Men
also, and by his suggestion
taught, Ransacked the
centre, and with impious
hands Rifled the bowels of
their mother Earth For
treasures better hid· Soon
had his crew Opened into
the hill a spacious wound,
And digged out ribs of
gold...*
    *Paradise Lost,
    by John Milton
    published 1667
    Book i, 678-690*

> "NO one can serve two masters; for either he will hate the one and love the other, or else he will be loyal to the one and despise the other. You cannot serve God and Mammon."
>
> *Matthew 6:24*

Other Books by Author

The Dragon and the Mask

A Gathering of Dragons

A Cursed Dragon

Estrangement: A Word that Spells PAIN

Contents

1

Last Kiss

"And death will be chosen rather than life by all the remnant that remains of this evil family, that remains in all the places to which I have driven them," declares the LORD of hosts.

Jeremiah 8:3

THE HARD METAL of the fancy wrought iron fence pierced Rance Troye's hand with cold and his soul with the bittersweet memory of his last kiss. Jenny had shivered after that kiss and said yes to his proposal. He wrapped his arms around his bride-to-be and held her tightly against this same gate. Jennifer Anne Gowan would soon be Jennifer Anne Troye.

"I love you more than you can imagine, Jenny Gale." Rance whispered in her chilly ear.

"Why Gale?" she asked him.

"Because you create a wind gale of love in my heart," he answered.

She giggled and put her gloved hand on his chest.

The gate evoked intense, paralyzing fear in him. He took a deep breath, pushed his hands further into his coat pockets, bowed his head, and approached the front door of the house for the first time since that last kiss, five years ago today.

Rance pushed on the door even though it creaked in protest. He stood there gazing at the contents of his broken heart—the house held the image of their last night together. Except, it felt cold, not just from temperature but from the absence of souls.

Rance gasped as a sparkling green shadow moved in front of him. With racing heart, he inched his way into the house. He thought he saw the shadow fade into the wall. He took a deep breath and tried to shrug it off. *You idiot, there's nothing in here.* A faint sound like a voice reached his ears. He hesitated. The memories he and Jenny made in this house had a life of their own and this . . . something invading his mind was not the happy memories of Jenny.

He removed his gloves. "You're just being silly." He scolded himself with his childlike fear of the monster under the bed. He touched the stone wall of the fireplace. In spite of Rance's dismissal of something in the house, the monster stood beside him shouting for his attention. Rance felt the monster but didn't hear or see it. He focused his attention on the cold gray bed of ashes in the fireplace.

"My heart!" he gasped and grabbed his chest. He ached with loneliness being fed with memories. That last night he and Jenny warmed in front of this fire. *Those ashes . . . were the same logs which warmed us?*

They had to be. The house remained empty since that night. He pulled the few logs left in the storage bin. Logs he cut five years ago. He placed them on the fireplace and the fire roared to life. Light and warmth whooshed through the empty house. He held his hands in front of the flames, not because they were cold but he wanted to pull in the memories of that last night to calm his anxious spirit. He looked into the living room and his lips turned up in a weak smile at the sight of the still-decorated Christmas tree. An artificial green tree with decorations and lights still on it with unopened packages piled high from that fateful Christmas. "Ah, that's what I saw." He said with some relief. The monster roared, "No, it was me, you idiot!" Rance continued in his solitary reverie.

"Oh, Jenny Gale, we had the whole world to conquer."

His eyes filled with a wet mist. He'd learned to suppress the tears and the grief, but in this environment, the grief overwhelmed his stoic emotional control. The fire warmed the place and made it appear as if Jennifer would come waltzing out of the hall door to greet him as she had done so many times in the past.

The monster whispered words and memories into Rance's ears. "Go on, wallow, you pig."

Another shadow passed in front of the hallway door. He took a deep breath, shook his head, and wiped his face. "Get it together old man!" He scolded himself.

He forgot the hallway and stared at the Christmas tree. He couldn't help himself. With the delight of a child, he pushed the light plug into the socket. The tree lit up with a myriad hues of red, green, and blue sparkles on the aged tree. The lights reflected off the foil-wrapped packages with the promise of glee. Rance saw green sparkles beside the tree, instead of on the tree. He turned his head away from them.

The joy the Christmas tree promised magnified the lie. No happiness of any kind was left in the house, at least not until Jenny Gale returns.

Rance looked up at the ceiling, "Where is she?" He screamed. "Bring her back to me."

"Never!" a deep guttural voice answered.

Rance jumped.

The voice had come from the packages under the tree. The warmth of the fireplace didn't penetrate the cold fear creeping up his spine. He wanted to run, at the same time he felt hopeless to leave. He needed to be here. He needed to remember Jenny Gale. Her visible beauty faded from his memory to be replaced by the grotesque faces of models positioned for maximum gross sexual images.

It started when he heard the television news reporting the disappearances of young women by human traffickers. Women being forced into the sex industry. Strangely, it gave Rance hope he could find Jenny Gale. He bought every girlie magazine he could find. At first, they repulsed him. He only looked at the faces. He soon learned the hair and makeup hid the natural beauty and innocence of the girls. He shook his head, willing the image of Jenny Gale he knew in this home to return to him.

His eyes fell on the small blue package he'd carefully and secretly placed there that Christmas morning of 1991. He took the small package that contained the engagement ring he planned to give to Jennifer that day to make it official. That morning was the happiest of his life, and the evening, the most miserable. And in this fancy blue box sat the little trinket evoking both feelings.

He sat on the couch with the little box in hand and rubbed the seat cushion next to him as if the action could make her appear. He held up the package and said, "For you, my love, there will never be another, even if you exist only in my memory." Then he opened it—the diamond he wanted her to have.

He smiled as he imaged her reaction. The deals Rance made and was making for the community of Church Creek Falls easily paid for the ring. It sat under this tree without Jenny Gale ever seeing it. He wondered what might have been, how many children would be running through this house, how many gifts would be piled up under a new, bigger tree. Rance could now buy anything his heart desired except the location of his beloved.

He took notice of the other packages and decided to call his sister Barbara and ask her to come help him unwrap them. He would donate the goods to her crisis pregnancy center.

When Barbara entered the house, she shuddered. "Are you alone?"

Rance nodded and led her to the living room. "Why?"

"I feel . . . it's just that . . . never mind. I'm just imagining things," she stammered and sat next to Rance. "What are we going to do?"

"Unwrap them all and you will find suitable homes for them."

"It's not going to be easy," she said.

"Sure, it is. Just rip the paper. We're not going to keep it."

"I know that silly, but to see . . ." Her voice drifted off without completing her thought. She didn't need to, they both understood.

Some packages were for Barbara and her family—toys for her two boys and two girls. Hannah was still a little girl at the time. She held up the little dress Jennifer had purchased for Hannah.

"Look at this. Isn't it darling? Jennifer sure knew how to pick out presents."

Rance was in his own world of memories and sorrows. He held up a shirt purchased for her dad. "She sure did. Max would've looked great in this."

For the next hour the two of them opened and sorted packages.

"There's one more." Barbara pointed. "Who's name is on it?" she asked.

Rance sighed, "Mine. It's from Jenny Gale." He stared at the handwriting and rubbed his fingers over it. "It doesn't look like her handwriting." He pulled his hand away from the package as he said it.

"What's wrong?" Barbara asked.

"It's hot!" he said and held it out for her to touch. She pulled back her hand. "Yikes!"

Rance tore into the package and found a handsome shirt and sweater. "I guess the lights heated up the foil wrap, it's not hot inside." He pulled the shirt out of the box and admired it. "She must have bought this for me to wear at our wedding. She told me her wedding dress was unusual so maybe this wild shirt was to complement the dress." Rance smiled at the memory of their shopping together a few days before Christmas. "We knew we'd marry, but she had no idea I already purchased a ring and placed it under her Christmas tree. She knew me so well." Rance wiped a tear from the corner of his eye.

"I wonder how her dress looked if this is what she wanted me to wear."

"I know."

"What?"

"I know about her dress," Barbara responded. "Her mother made it for her. It was a bit unusual, but when you see it, you'll understand why she wanted you to wear that shirt."

"I'll never see it now." Rance wiped his cheek.

Barbara rose from the floor. "Come on. I'll show you." She headed toward Jennifer's room, opened the closet, and removed a garment bag. She laid it on the bud, unzipped it, and displayed the dress for Rance.

The muscles of his throat tightened and stopped any words, but the mist now flowed in tears with gut-wrenching sobs. Barbara placed it on the bed and wrapped her arms around her brother's chest.

"I don't understand. It doesn't look like a wedding dress; it's pink and red."

"Technically, its Magenta and blush." Barbara squeezed him.

"Why would she want those colors? Did she tell you?"

"Yeah, she said they would go perfectly with the diamond bracelet you bought her."

Rance gulped and nestled his head on her shoulder. "Sis, I can't quit looking for her."

When the two of them regained their composure, Barbara replaced the dress in the closet, and they returned to the living room where they sat on the furniture instead of the floor.

Rance picked up the box with the shirt and sweater. He opened the card and a loud thunk came from the box.

"What was that?" Barbara asked and rose to see.

"Stop!" he said firmly and held up his hand toward her. He fingered something inside the box and grimaced.

"What is it?"

"Sis, I'm so sorry," was all he could say. "I'm so sorry," he repeated again.

Barbara stood and walked toward him and peered into the box. Her hands went over her mouth, and she screamed, "You were supposed to get rid of it!"

"I know, but it's high quality diamonds. Do you know how much it's worth?"

"Right now, I would say it cost Jennifer's life."

"No! please God, No!" He moaned and fell to his knees. When he did the object in the box fell to the floor.

Barbara stepped away from it. "Do you know what I went through?" she shouted at Rance.

"Michael and Daniel brought you back, and you handed it to me."

"Yes, to get rid of it, not to keep it."

"It didn't do anything."

"Yes, it did. There's a spirit of evil in that vile thing. It's an idol."

"What? why?" Rance groaned. The two of them stared at the floor.

Sparkling in the dancing light of the fire lay the magenta and blush diamond-crusted bracelet in the shape of a dragon.

2
Trouble Brewing

"Do not listen to the words of the prophets who are prophesying to you. They are leading you into futility; they speak a vision of their own imagination, Not from the mouth of the LORD."

---Jeremiah 23:16

"GREED PLANTED INTO the heart of a man causes insanity. Greed devours and consumes all that gets in its way." The guttural voice said as it came out of the shadow and into the center of the living room. The clawed hand retrieved the bracelet from the floor. "And greed brought me to you, Rance Troye."

Rance stood frozen in front of the green, scaly dragon with a head covered in spikes, each throbbing with heat. Even though he couldn't see the beast, the dragon allowed him to hear his growling roar and feel the heat of his distaste.

"What's your name?" Rance stood tall in front of him, demanding an answer.

"It's easy to be brave in the face of terror when the terror can't be seen," the dragon drawled. "You've grown brave over the years."

Rance stood firm, the dragon's words lost in the droning sound of the refrigerator motor. He whirled around as if searching for the dragon. The dragon laughed. This human knew they could change form and hide in plain sight and was trying to act as though a puny man could defeat him.

"Leave us!" Rance demanded yet shivered and looked like he was bracing himself for a slash of sharp claws.

"Us?" The dragon shifted his cumbersome head around the room. "I only see a sniveling little rat shaking in his boots," the dragon responded.

Rance heard the sound as if a distant conversation carried on the wind. Then he heard the dragon laugh and saw the filth of burning sulfur rise in the air. The words came clear and concise. "My name is Mammon."

He could see Barbara next to him, but apparently the dragon couldn't. He made a small hand motion for her to leave.

"He can't see me, but I see him clearly," she responded. "And I'm not leaving you alone with this beast."

Rance didn't say anything but smiled to express his gratitude she wasn't leaving him. He wondered if Barbara knew the beast had no visible form to him.

"What are you smiling at?" The beast roared and slapped Rance across the face with his claw.

It stung. Rance wanted to cry like a baby and crawl up in a ball. Seeing Barbara kept him strong. He retrieved the bracelet from the floor and slipped it into his pocket. "This time I will get rid of it." He whimpered to Barbara. The dragon snickered, "No you won't. It's my leash on you." Neither Barbara nor Rance heard the monster announce his claim on Rance.

Rance slid to floor in a heap and ducked his head. One question raced through his mind. How did Jenny get the bracelet?

Merilee Troye grabbed her robe and pulled it on before she answered the door. When she saw a red-faced Barbara and a drunken looking Rance standing there, she forgot about the robe and reached out to her children.

"What happened?" She wrapped her arms around her son and helped him to the bed.

"Rance," she answered.

Merilee smiled. "I think I need a little more." She left her son in his old room and walked to the kitchen and poured them both a cup of coffee and set them on the table.

"Do you remember that horrid bracelet?" Barbara said as she sat down and wrapped her cold hands around the hot cop.

Merilee blew across the hot brew and shook her head.

"My friend Teresa—the one who died of an abortion—you remember?" Barbara rambled.

Merilee nodded and set her cup on the table, giving her daughter her full attention.

"She gave me the bracelet, quite expensive, I think. It's filled with diamonds and rubies. I thought it was beautiful until I realized it represented the dragon, it was even shaped like a dragon and wrapped around my arm, but I was too stupid to notice." Barbara moaned.

Merilee didn't have enough information to understand so she nodded and listened.

"Did you see it?" Barbara asked her mother.

"No, I wasn't there, remember?"

Barbara jumped up from her seat and went into the room where Rance lay sleeping from the sedative Daniel had given him. She remembered seeing Rance put the bracelet in his pocket. She pulled it out and dropped it when it felt like a bee sting in her hand. She grabbed a towel and picked it up again. She carried into the kitchen where her mother sat confused but patient.

"After Michael and Daniel rescued me from that monster, I took the bracelet off my arm and handed it to Rance, I told him to get rid of it." Barbara dropped the bracelet on the table. Merilee gazed at it.

"I'm guessing he saw dollar signs instead of danger."

Barbara nodded, tapped her nose and took a drink of her coffee. She stared into space for a few seconds.

Merilee interrupted her pensive thoughts. "Where did you get it?" She looked at the jewelry, it truly was exquisite. Merilee felt that same quickening in her spirit she felt when she gazed at the mask in the store. It's design and purpose was to enslave the spirit of the beholder. Before Merilee could take her eyes off the bracelet Barbara groaned.

"Mom. Oh, Momma." Barbara began to sob. "We found it."

"What do you mean, you found it?"

"Rance and I were at Jennifer's house. He wanted me to come help him unwrap the presents so we could put then in the pregnancy crisis center."

"I didn't think Rance went into the house."

"He didn't. But he's thinking about selling it, so he wanted to see what was left and how much repair work would be needed."

"Humm?" Merilee responded.

Barbara nodded. "It was hard on him," she said. "But when that bracelet fell out of Jennifer's package to him, he flipped out. I did too."

"How did it get in the package?"

"I don't know, but we both have a good idea it has something to do with Jennifer's disappearance."

"How so?" Merilee gave an involuntary shudder.

"Look at it, it's the image of the dragon. Since Rance didn't get rid of it, the dragon followed him." Barbara pondered.

"I still have that old mask, but it doesn't bother me." Merilee said.

"It seems to be pretty impotent now, doesn't it?"

"Yes, it's totally without power, but as soon as I put it back in circulation, that demon spirit will inhabit it again. As long as it sets in the bottom of my incinerator with no one to see it, it has no power."

"I guess it's the same with the dragon bracelet?"

"Could be." Merilee said. "So how did it get in that package?" She turned the conversation back to the bracelet. She smiled at her daughter and pushed a strand of hair behind her ear. "It's evil, honey. It'll do whatever it has to do to destroy people. Remember Jesus said in John, chapter eight, the devil is a liar and a murderer. He even went on to say, "I tell you the truth, but you won't believe me.""

"We are pretty stupid." Barbara twisted her napkin into knots.

"We rely too much on our imagination." Merilee rose and retrieved the cookie jar. It was time for crunchy snacks with this conversation.

"Mom, you have something on your mind." Barbara smirked.

"Why do you say that?"

"You got the cookies out, and that only happens when there's about to be a serious talk."

Merilee smiled and patted her on the hand. "You know me too well."

"What are you thinking?"

"I'm thinking the dragon may have been with Rance all along."

"Why?"

"Why did it show up on our farm, why does your dad suffer every day because of one of those monsters?"

"I haven't ever asked those questions." Barbara took a bite of cookie, feeling much better and secure in her mother's presence, yet embarrassed to discover she hadn't considered her parent's trials with the dragons.

"You would if it was one of your children." Merilee smiled slightly.

"When do you think the dragon came after Rance?"

"The same time it came after your daddy."

"I don't understand." Barbara set her cookie down and wrapped her arms around herself with a shiver.

"Do you know what it says in first Peter about the dragons?"

"Is that the one that says their leader, the devil, walks about the earth looking for us?"

"Pretty much, but there is more to it than that." Merilee sighed.

Barbara raised her cup and took a drink while watching her mother.

"There's another verse in Psalms that gives more meaning to that statement. You know Psalms is the short version of the Bible." Merilee smiled.

Barbara laughed. "You mean; the Psalms is a good place to go for meaning."

"The best." Merilee patted her daughter on the shoulder.

"What does Psalms tell us about Peter's statement?"

"In the tenth Psalm, it describes a wicked one."

"Well, that describes a dragon," Barbara snickered.

"Yes, it does, and it isn't a pretty description. It says the greedy curses and spurns the Lord."

"Yikes, that describes Rance."

Merilee nodded with a mist forming in her eyes. She tried to speak, but the words became tangled in the tightness of her throat and couldn't escape.

"Mom." Barbara took her mother's hand to comfort her.

With that action Merilee is able to continue. "The description is hard to take when it is so close to home. It says the greedy will rely upon his own ways and will prosper. It says his mouth is full of deceit and oppression. He kills the innocent."

"Mom, that's not Rance, he's a kind, caring man."

"It's hard to see the wickedness in someone you love."

Barbara nodded and read the next verse from Merilee's Bible. "He sits in the lurking places of the villages; His eyes stealthily watch for the unfortunate. He lurks in a hiding place as a lion in his lair; He lurks to catch the afflicted: He catches the afflicted when he draws him into his net. He says God has forgotten; He has hidden His face; He will never see it."

"I don't understand how this relates to Rance." Barbara stared into her mother's eyes.

Merilee wiped her eyes with a tissue and took a deep breath. "I've thought this for years, but this is the first time I've expressed it."

"What? Mother?" Barbara urged.

"I think Rance may be involved in the disappearances of our friends and neighbors, including Jennifer."

"What are you saying?"

"I think Rance may be selling something illegal."

"You mean drugs?" Barbara's eyes widened.

"Could be since I think he's selling people."

"No! That can't be!" Barbara stood and turned her back on her mother. She put her arm on her hip. "How can you even think such things about your own son?"

Merilee wept openly now and shook her head.

Barbara stomped around the room. After a few minutes, her daddy came into the room with a stack of papers.

"This is why." He handed a document to Barbara.

"Where did you get this?"

"Michael found it."

"But it doesn't prove anything. We all know he started a hedge fund several years ago."

"Look closely." Buster buried his head in his hand.

Barbara read the words. "This only proves that Rance bought some kind of commodity named Tender Expressions and sold investments on it. It doesn't mean he's selling people." Barbara raged at her parents.

"Look at the initial investment he used to start the fund." Buster pointed to a small print line listing assets. It read, "Jewelry, diamond and ruby encrusted bracelet "5.4 million."

Barbara leaned back in her chair, "he. . . he didn't." A tear trekked down her face.

"He doesn't know." Merilee whimpered through her sobs. "He saw opportunity, not evil."

Buster leaned closer to Barbara and handed her a picture. "He found this a few days ago."

He pursed his lips and handed a picture to Barbara. She gasped. "That's Peggy Strand."

Buster nodded.

Barbara fell onto her dad's waist. He put his arm around her shoulders. "What do we do?"

Merilee opened the Bible Barbara left on the table.

"The last verse of this Psalm says, "The Lord has heard the desire of the humble; He will strengthen their heart, you will incline Your ear to vindicate the orphan and the oppressed, so that Man who is of the earth will no longer cause terror."

"I'm more confused than ever." Barbara sat down

Buster pulled up a chair and rested his elbows on the table. "My sweet, the wicked is not referred to as human, he is addressed separately from the greedy man."

"I don't get it?"

"The wicked is the dragon. He plants his desires into the heart of one who doesn't believe in God."

Barbara sat down across from him. "Rance doesn't believe?"

"Now you know." Merilee sobbed.

"But . . . he really wants Jenny back." Barbara argued with the idea set before her.

"I don't think he intended for Jenny to go."

"Do you think he knows where Jenny is?" Barbara asked her daddy.

"I think he has a good idea, and that's why he spends so much time—" Buster stopped talking and choked. He couldn't finish his sentence.

"So much time looking at pornography." Barbara finished his thought.

Merilee nodded.

"Do you think he found her?" Barbara asked.

"I think he found Peggy," Buster said, pointing to the picture of Peggy. "She would never dress that way, and he knows if Peggy's there, Jenny can't be far behind."

Barbara stared at the photo of Peggy with heavy makeup, short skirt and low-cut, see-through blouse. "No, she wouldn't."

Merilee stood and embraced her daughter. "We have to pray for all three of them: Rance, Peggy, and Jenny. At least we know Peggy and Jenny belong to the Lord, and as it says in the Psalm, "He will defend the oppressed."

"But it also says, he will judge."

Buster took Barbara's hand in his own, "It says; so the man of the earth will no longer cause terror."

"I don't understand." Barbara said.

"The man of the earth is directed by a dragon to cause terror, but once the dragon is judged, both the victim and the man used to inflict the terror will be set free by Jesus's death and resurrection," Buster assured his daughter. "It took all of us to rescue you from that wily demon and dragon. This time your part of the rescue team for your brother."

Barbara kissed her daddy's hand and smiled at him, "It ain't gonna be easy."

"The first thing we have to do is get rid of that bracelet," Merilee said.

Barbara shuddered.

"That dragon wants more." Buster smiled and patted his daughter's hand.

"What's more than taking over my body?" Barbara asked.

"You were in rebellion, but you belonged to the Lord, and He fought for you through your family."

"What's the difference between me and Rance?"

"Rance already belongs to the dragon."

3

Mammon

My son, if sinners entice you, Do not consent. If they say, "Come with us, Let us lie in wait for blood, Let us ambush the innocent without cause; Let us swallow them alive like Sheol, Even whole, as those who go down to the pit; We will find all kinds of precious wealth, We will fill our houses with spoil.

Proverbs 1:10-13

THE SWEET SIREN call reached the black spirit of Mammon, the dragon of greed. The monster spread his wings and flew toward it, looking for the bracelet, his lost idol. The precious gem of deception that could claim a soul with a mere glimpse. The weak call moved through the air, searching for its master.

Mammon settled on a housetop, waiting for the call to come again. The wisp of noise reached Mammon's ears. The muffled sound came from the house. The whimper of humans drowned out the call of the idol. Diving into the house, the dragon saw one of the master's servants, Rance, holding the precious gem. Not actually holding it but a box in which it lay. The beast stepped toward Rance and noticed him talking. Mammon looked around the room but could see no one. Turning back toward Rance, the beast lifted a single claw and scrapped across Rance's face. The action allowed him access to the thoughts of his servant. He blew a little puff of flame onto Rance when the beast saw the anguish in his soul.

"Very good, my faithful servant." The beast whispered into Rance's ear with a snicker. Rance didn't respond.

"Why can't you see me?" Mammon roared.

At that moment Mammon felt ... a strange sensation. It wasn't one felt often, but it was easily recognizable. The beast turned in all directions around the room. There were no other warm bodies in the house, yet he felt that sensation of Him, the Holy One. The only one Mammon feared. Facing the direction to which Rance spoke, the beast lowered its head and squinted its eyes but still didn't see. The beast knew Rance didn't harbor the Spirit. The spikes on the beasts' head tingled with fear, and there's only one thing a dragon fears—Jesus!

The stifling pressure of the Holy One drove the beast of greed out of the house with a whoosh. The idol image of the brute rested in the box on the floor. It could be retrieved later. Mammon headed for the sand dunes.

Once Mammon curled in the safe place where the sounds and sights of people carrying the Holy One could not disturb, a stream of fire came out of his mouth. Why were there so many of those impossible people around?

Mammon heard another roar, one that caused him to tremble but with a different kind of fear. Nisroch arrived and shook the hill with the landing.

"What are you doing?" Nisroch roared in the face of Mammon, leaving his green face blackened with smoke.

"The servant Rance can't see me," Mammon moaned.

"He saw me, why can't he see you?" Nisroch clearly didn't believe Mammon.

"His family?" Mammon answered and shrunk back into his sand cave.

Nisroch calmed a bit and sat on its haunches. "You know you have to get that bracelet?"

Mammon nodded, staring at the ground.

"If the harvest is coming, we have to have it."

Before Mammon thought about the words in the mind of the beast, it blurted out, "What about the mask?"

Nisroch lay flat on the ground and breathed heavily, letting the dust fly. "I know where it is." Nisroch said.

"Yeah, but can you get it?"

"No need until the harvest."

"Aren't we ready?"

"It's been delayed by that . . . Troye family." Nisroch spit the words out with distain.

"What's the plan?" Mammon hoped to change the mood of his superior before the blast of fire would turn his comfy sand cave into shards of glass.

"The seed was planted in Donnigan."

"Well that one is gone." Mammon mocked Nisroch with sarcasm.

Nisroch didn't notice. The higher ranking beast continued, "It's time for the harvest."

"I've heard that line before, then came Michael and Daniel delaying it. Now what?"

Nisroch turned his long snout and looked at Mammon with a piercing yellow eye. "The harvest will come; the question is how big will the harvest be?"

"How much do you expect?"

"More before that dreadful Robert Troye started praying. Now four generations down, and we still get needled by that blasted Troye family."

"Do you have a suggestion?" Mammon asked Nisroch.

The bigger dragon turned, almost slapping Mammon in the face with his tail. "Yeah, I do. Let's get his younger sister Alyssa and take Rance on a wild ride."

"Sounds good. How?"

"Use Matt . . . get Alyssa away."

"Why Alyssa?" Mammon wondered out loud.

"She's a girl, easy deception," Nisroch growled.

"Is that why the master went after the woman in the beginning?" Mammon purred.

Nisroch nodded. "And with all their feminism, they are easier to manipulate than ever."

The two dragons roared with laughter.

The plan to capture Alyssa wouldn't be easy because she did belong to the Holy One. But she was still such an infant and would be easier to capture than Hannah, Barbara's daughter. Hanna still lived under the protection of her parents as their child. Alyssa knew of Him more than knew Him. She went to church and all the activities, and she even went to a weekly Bible study but never opened her Bible. Her sword lay dusty and dull. While ten-year-old Hannah couldn't be reached through her parent's prayers.

"Alyssa has a fascination with bad boys. Tell Matt to start wooing her and get her trust. We'll use him to bring her to us." Nisroch said. "You can work out the details."

Mammon smiled. "I know how to do it. What about our servant Patti Paulsen at The Honey Tree?"

"She abdicated to the other side."

"When?" Mammon grunted.

"Back in Burleson. With three little words, the Holy One swooped her out of my stable."

Mammon shook the beastly head, "Hurts doesn't it?"

Nisroch raised his serpent head and twisted it at the sound penetrating the cave.

"What's that?" Mammon grunted. "Belial?"

"I think so. Come on." Nisroch declared.

"Why?"

"When Belial calls, you go. You don't want to keep the head dragon waiting."

The white dusting of ice crystals stirring wildly, told Nisroch and Mammon that Belial was not in a good mood.

The two monsters approached a throne covered in eyes staring at them through aborted baby body parts.

Nisroch spoke. "Yes master."

"Are the girls ready for their final baptism into my kingdom?" Belial roared.

Mammon ducked his head. Belial saw the action and bellowed with full force, "Idiot! What have you done?"

Mammon crouched on the icy hot ground and hissed. "Master, my servant can't see me."

"Then why do you call him servant?"

"Sometimes he hears me, and he always follows my lead, his heart is hard and filled with love for money."

"Obviously not or he would see you."

Nisroch hid in the darkness. "Are you teaching this one?"

"Trying master." Nisroch moaned.

"I need my harvest." Belial shouted with an elongated hiss.

"Master?" Mammon spoke and Nisroch kicked his protégé.

Belial turned his gaze on Mammon and bore through him with eyes of hate so sharp, not even a dragon could stand. Without warning, a powerful force caused Mammon to crash to the ground with his head melting into the fiery hot ice.

"Ugh!" Mammon cried out in pain.

"Shut up, you fool." Nisroch whispered.

Belial rose from the bloody throne and walked around the pinned dragon. "How dare you speak to me."

"I'm—" Mammon started to plead before Belial.

Instead, Belial spewed a plume of fire and brimstone on him.

Mammon yelped with a loud, painful hiss.

"Get out of my sight!" Belial roared and turned away from the two dragons.

Nisroch went the other direction and left the icy hell before Mammon could get his claws beneath his scorched and pain-filled body.

Mammon heard Belial call to him in the distance, "Get the girls ready. Soon! "

4
Peggy and Jennifer

If you see among the captives a beautiful woman, and have a desire for her and would take her as a wife for yourself, And it shall be, if you have no delight in her, then you shall set her free, but you certainly shall not see her for money; you shall not treat her brutally, because you have humbled her.

Deuteronomy 21:11,14 (NKJV)

MAMMON STOOD IN front of a favorite token. The young girl hadn't changed any since the day she became part of the monster's collection over two years ago. With a sharpened claw, he stroked the cage and laughed.

"You will not fail me. Your boyfriend found the bracelet," Mammon growled at Peggy.

With no response coming from the frail, emaciated girl, Mammon roared. It hurt his burned body. The monster needed this girl to feel the burn of skin. The monster swallowed, looked at her and blew his fiery bile on her. She still didn't move.

"You better not be dead." Mammon roared.

Peggy could see the emerald-green scaled claws standing in front of her and feigned unconsciousness. She couldn't stand to look at that horrific face she sadly knew so well. For seven days a week, her body and soul were in servitude to this vile creature. Human feet stood beside the claws of the dragon. It didn't matter, this human was as much a creature as the dragon. The overseer delivered the blows to her body and the words of destruction to her soul that the dragon demanded.

She closed her eyes. Whatever they were saying, it wasn't good, and she no longer cared. She wanted to die, even being in hell would be better than in this nightmare. Peggy inched her body in front of Jennifer and spread her arms to provide a wider hiding place. Jennifer curled up behind Peggy, trying to be invisible.

The man possessed the soul of cruelty and the mentality of a possum. As soon as Peggy covered Jennifer, the man would forget Jennifer existed. The monster of a man didn't realize there were two of them.

The monster man yelled, "You'll be cut loose soon."

A smile lit upon Peggy's lips. She didn't care if they were referring to freedom or death. To be away from them would be enough. Then she heard something that gripped her heart with an untold fear,

"Someday, Rance Troye will stand here and observe his lady love." The words were followed by a wicked laugh and a slight scratch across Peggy's face as the monster's claw lifted her chin. She willed her heart to stay calm and her eyes closed. Peggy couldn't see the dragon as clearly as Jennifer could, and she didn't want to see it, smelling it was bad enough. She could feel Jennifer's body trembling and hear her whimpering. A low, rumble growl came from Peggy's chest.

"He remembered you today." The monster slightly pierced her skin leaving a small red scratch. Not enough to break the skin but enough to hurt. This monster knew how to wound the soul without marking the flesh.

"No, he didn't, you liar." Peggy snarled.

At the shout of defiance, the monster pierced her skin. "Careful!" he snickered. "I have a plan you won't be able to refuse."

With a final evil snicker, Mammon flew to Rance's apartment and settled in, waiting for him to return. It would be a fun night pouring memories mixed with imaginations into his soul. Now the fulfillment of Rance's role in the kingdom of evil could begin. Mammon licked his claw in anticipation of the fear Rance would feel and show. He felt the cold eyes of Belial on him, which increased the tenderness of his skin under his charred scales. This human creature would feel ten times the pain.

The young people shivered as they were led back to the group prison where they would have a few hours of rest. Even the cold of the concrete walls and floors felt warm. They took their thin blankets and wrapped themselves up in them.

Peggy scooted next to Jennifer. She felt her head still burning with fever. Their jailers remained unaware of Jennifer's presence, as were most of the other girls. Jennifer became ill the first day, another lifetime ago. Her illness came and went. Peggy felt they would kill her if they knew she was there, but she wasn't sure how much longer she could hide her. But she wouldn't give up.

She pulled Jennifer's blanket over the two of them and scooted up as close as she could to her. She hated that at that moment she felt grateful for Jennifer's fever. It kept her warm. She heard Jennifer mutter the same words she muttered every night, "Dear Jesus, don't let him give up. Keep us alive." Then she fell into sleep.

Peggy soon fell into a restless sleep. The exhaustion never leaving her bruised and abused body. A slight clicking noise on the floor caught Peggy's attention. She saw a rat skittering across the floor. The noise pulled her out of a light sleep. She threw her boot at the cat-sized rat. She hit it. The rat lay dead in the floor. Another girl picked it up and skinned it, throwing the refuse in the one lone trashcan which also served as a toilet. With a little help from a couple others, she built a small fire in the middle of the concrete floor, using hair clippings, clothing, trash; whatever they could find for fuel. They used an old coat hanger which they kept hidden to skewer the rat and hold him over the fire, letting the meat roast. It actually smelled good.

When the girls tore the meat from the bones, one of them handed Peggy a bite.

"Thanks for the dinner." Peggy nodded and started to eat the meat, she stopped and looked at Jennifer, deciding whether to give the bite to her. Jennifer was sleeping, Peggy ate the bite of rat meat and felt grateful for it. The problem she found with finding extra food was not that she was eating a rat, but that it kept her body alive to suffer another day. The little bit of food calmed the gnawing pain of hunger in her stomach. She fell into a more restful sleep.

Peggy was awakened by a flash of light and then screaming. She jumped up and saw the doors to their prison open. She saw smoke coming down the hall. The little fire used to cook the rat grew into a big flame.

Peggy stood and helped Jennifer up. She whispered in her ear, "This is our chance to escape. Can you run?" Jennifer nodded and came alive. "Thank you, Jesus," she said.

Getting out of the burning building was easy. Even though their cells were made of cinder blocks, the surrounding area buildings went up like kindling, and the comforts of blankets and books given to the guards served as fuel.

Jennifer leaned over to Peggy and said, "He won't give us more than we can bear without a way of escape."

"You're right, he'll give us a way to escape," Peggy repeated, but not feeling it. *God, I hope she's right. Please show me the way.*

The two women stayed together, while the others went in different directions. Heavy footsteps sounded behind Peggy and Jennifer. There weren't in a hurry, but they continued to come closer. The long stride of the deformed tall man beat down upon them like the sound of a timpani drum. The cold air burned their lungs as they inhaled deeper with each footfall. Peggy held Jennifer's hand. She would slow down before she let go of her. She could hear Jennifer breathing, but it wasn't the wheezing she expected. Jennifer's breath came in long deep draws, just as her own.

"Look!" Jennifer said between gasps.

Peggy saw the little alcove ahead covered in brush and barely visible in the dim light of the early morning. The daylight crept upon them faster than the jailer. "Let's go for it," she said to Jennifer.

The two women headed for the brush and the little space within the thorny bush. This was going to hurt, but it would harm them a lot less than the punishment the jailer would administer if he caught them.

They huddled in the space, clinging to each other and trying to control the gasping noise of their lungs screaming for air. They saw the footsteps of the jailer stop in front of them. They both held their hand over their mouths, willing their frantic heartbeats to slow.

Jennifer pointed.

Peggy looked and saw the clawed feet of the monster. Peggy could see the horror on Jennifer's face which reflected her own. She smelled the stench of Sulphur and smoke and held her nose, the smell so strong it burned.

Jennifer continued to stare with her mouth agape and her eyes wide and wild. The two women held to each other. Their bodies shivering, more with fright than cold. Peggy looked around to find a better hiding place, but Jennifer wasn't moving. She shook her head and pointed to the ground. They would stay there.

Peggy wiped the sweat from her forehead. They'd be roasted alive by that fire-breathing monster. As a second thought, she let the corner of her mouth raise in a smirk. At least they would have some warmth. She shivered, feeling the cold for the first time and realized their breath made little clouds of identification. She put her hand back over her mouth. The two women looked like a tattered rag, neither of them dressed for the cold and both shivering like flags blowing in the wind.

"I know you're here," growled the monster. He released a little puff of smoke. "Here's some heat for you. Bet it feels good, huh?" He roared.

Jennifer prayed almost indiscernibly, "Dear Lord, send a warrior angel to hide us."

Peggy heard the prayer, and even though she believed in God, she'd long ago given up her faith, especially any faith for rescue.

Jennifer never gave up. She prayed daily and always the same prayer, for their protection and for their rescue. Her most fervent request came when she prayed for Rance Troye, her long-lost fiancé.

Peggy knew Rance from school. They became good friends. Mostly because he was the only boy in her class bigger than she. Peggy grew to six feet by the time she was twelve. She hated her height, and Rance made her feel smaller. They shared a love of the outdoors and adventure. They built a friendship on mutual trust, so when her cousin Jennifer Gowen moved to Church

Creek Falls, she introduced them. Rance fell hard for her. He never had eyes for anyone else.

The monster moved closer to them. It even appeared to look at them. Jennifer didn't move, and Peggy held tightly to her hand. With each advancement of the monster, more of its physical reality came into focus, even though it stood as a dark shadow with the rising sun behind it.

Slime dropped from the spiked maw onto the ground in front of them. The mucus smoked the brush in front of them.

The closer he came, the more globs of phlegm fell and burned their only cover. He would see them soon. Their backs up against a brick wall and the disappearing brush in front of them, they could take a chance and run for it, but Jennifer knew the monster would reach out with one clawed foot and rip them open where they stood. The goo coming from the mouth of the monster stuck of rotten fish and old blood.

Peggy felt something move behind her. She didn't question it but grabbed Jennifer's hand, and the two women moved with it. They felt warmth, even in the musty smell of the dark. Waiting for their eyes to adjust to the darkness, they stood still holding on to each other.

"Here," Peggy said and pointed to the left.

Jennifer followed her down a narrow brick corridor with a dirt floor. Jennifer held Peggy's hand and watched the walls pass.

Peggy stopped, "Look!" She pointed to the end of the corridor. There a green door slightly opened, offered light. They watched the door and noticed a shadow cross in front of the narrow crack. For a second, a flash of green came from the area.

"What is it?" Jennifer whispered.

"I don't know, but stay back until we know," Peggy answered.

Jennifer hid behind Peggy and held tightly to her hand.

The minutes ticked by with little activity in the room. "I think there's only one person in there." Peggy said. The two women inched closer to the door, hoping to be able to inspect inside.

Suddenly, the door swung open.

Alyssa dropped by Rance's apartment after work, bringing a bag of burgers and fries.

"How'd you know I was hungry?" Rance said as he greeted her and motioned for her to come inside. "I hope you brought enough for both of us."

She nodded.

Rance loved his adopted sister more than his own life. From the first moment twenty-five years ago when he picked up her tiny body covered in the blood of her mother, and she wrapped her arms around his neck, a bond formed. He cared for her and Jason, but it was Alyssa's attention to him that bound his heart so closely to her. In the last twenty-five years, that hadn't changed. She was a beautiful young woman with a heart of gold, and he knew she loved him.

"What's the occasion? I thought you had a date tonight." Rance opened the bag and pulled the burgers out.

"I did, but I cancelled it. I don't like the way he's treating me."

"What do you mean? "Rance asked then took a big bite of his burger.

"He wants to tell me where to go and when to go and who to go with." Alyssa took a sip of her drink and opened her burger.

"I can't imagine anyone getting away with that." Rance snickered. "Not even me."

"You're right. I don't need a man to tell me what I can do." She hesitated before taking a bite of burger and said, "Unless it's Daddy."

Rance smiled. "Or me?"

"Maybe." She flashed a coy smile at her beloved older brother.

"I thought you liked him."

"That's the problem, I do like him."

"Where'd you meet him?" Rance asked.

"The Honey Tree. Patti introduced him to me. She said he was from Burlington Heights."

"Did he move here?"

"I don't think so; I can't get a straight answer. He says he's here on temporary assignment."

"Maybe he's working on the new government base being built at the sand dunes," Rance offered.

"Could be, but when I ask him how long it would take, he answered that it depended on me."

"What did he mean by that?" Rance raised one eyebrow.

"I didn't ask."

Rance reached out and took Alyssa's hand. "Be careful, my sweet. Trust no one."

"I know, but I'm going to eventually have to trust someone besides you."

"You can't. No one is trustworthy. Everyone is looking out for themselves."

"Even you?" Alyssa said with a smirk.

"Especially me," Rance responded without looking at her or acknowledging her satire.

Alyssa put her wrapper in the empty bag and rose to go to the bathroom.

"Where are you going?" Rance asked.

"Restroom," she answered.

"Use the one in the hall," he called after her.

She raised her hand and brushed the air while heading toward his bedroom.

Rance sat back and waited. He knew a lecture would follow.

Sure enough, Alyssa joined him with a stack of his girly mags in her hand. "I thought you quit this garbage."

Rance let out a big breath and shook his head. He took the magazines from her and stacked them in a corner. "It's not that easy, sis."

"Just quit buying them."

"I think I'm addicted." Rance rose from the table and threw their garbage away.

"Then get help."

Rance laughed. "I'm beyond help." He paused for a while, then took a deep breath and said something that surprised them both, "Unless I can find Jenny Gale."

5
Deployment

The prophets that have been before me and before thee of old prophesied both against many countries, and against great kingdoms, of war, and of evil, and of pestilence.

Jeremiah28:8

RANCE HUNG UP the phone and headed toward Alyssa's desk. "Mom just called. She wants us to cancel the party tomorrow and change it to a catered party. You and I have been assigned to pick up dinner at The Honey Tree."

"How come we're not having the going-away party there?"

"Dad's not feeling well."

Alyssa nodded her head and stared out the front window. "The injury?"

"Yeah," Rance muttered as he returned to his office.

Alyssa sighed and rested her chin in the palm of her hand. She was still a teen when Zay and Marcy married. She remembered her dad jumping from his chair and tackling Zay to the ground. The explanation given to the audience was the presence of a deadly snake about to bite Zay. Most of the wedding guests assumed it bit Buster instead. But as a member of the wedding party, Alyssa stood close enough to see there was no snake, and it didn't bite her daddy. After the tackle, she heard the groan of pain and his suit coat burned away, leaving a deep purple wound on his skin. It had been weird because none of the family seemed as shocked as she. Not even Jason, her brother. She knew there was more to the story. *Why won't they tell me what caused the wound?*

She sighed and picked up the phone book to call the Honey Tree and change the plans. At least the family would gather to spend a last night with Jason before he deployed to Korea. Alyssa watched the television in the waiting room blasting the war in Iraq all day, every day. *At least he's not going there.*

She watched another large group of the Iraqi army surrender. Jason told her the U.S. would prevail in the war because the military generals were planning it instead of the Washington politicians. Jason mocked the Iraqi leader, Saddam Hussein, saying his hot air was the most dangerous weapon the Iraqis possessed. Her dad had laughed at the statement and then said, "Never underestimate the enemy." He rubbed his shoulder as he said it.

Merilee, her mom, read her dad's cues and quickly rubbed his back with the ointment she made for him. His body would relax, and the wrinkles in his forehead would smooth out as she gently rubbed his shoulder. He would pat her hand and smile at her. An unspoken language linked the two of them that Alyssa wanted to understand. She wanted a man like her dad to love her as much as he loved her mom.

"Alyssa." Rance broke her reverie.

"Yes?"

He handed her a stack of papers, "I need you to go through these. See if there is anything unusual in them."

Alyssa nodded and took the papers and files and carried them to her desk.

"Be sure and get those boxes too." Rance pointed at three bank boxes stacked in front of his desk.

"What am I looking for?" Alyssa moaned.

"I'm not sure. Start with any reference to a company called Tender Expressions."

She nodded. Confused at the request, since all of these files contained contracts made by Rance and reviewed by Michael.

"Are you giving me busy work?"

Rance smiled at her question. "In a way, yes."

"Can you give me more details?" Alyssa asked.

He pursed his lips and shrugged his shoulders.

"Jennifer and Peggy?" She asked.

Rance nodded.

Alyssa scoured the files for the third time. She knew Rance felt they were missing a clue. This time she made a spreadsheet of her findings.

Patti, Cook, and Michelle sat quietly around a table, waiting for their last customers to leave. The clean-up from dinner service completed, they would be able to finish a few tables and mopping quickly. The three tired ladies trembled at a familiar odor.

Michelle broke the fearful silence as she softly wept, "I thought we left it behind in zee house, and now Jesus protect us."

Cook and Patti nodded. Cook lifted a finger. "Is it the same?"

"You smelled it; what do you think?"

"I smell sulfur and rotting flesh." Cook answered with a wrinkled nose.

"I'm new at trusting Jesus. I don't know how it works either." Patti put her arm around Michelle to comfort her.

"I don't want to go back." Michelle wailed.

"None of us do. Jesus is new to us. We know what's out there in the world, and it's vicious," Cook muttered to no one in particular.

"We need someone to teach us." Patti stared out the window at the office on the other side of the courthouse.

"Who?" Cook asked, following her gaze.

"Barbara Troye," Patti muttered in the present while viewing her past.

"Do you think she would consider teaching us?" Michelle asked.

"We are here sniffing the same evil that tried to possess her. Yeah, I think she'll help."

Michelle and Cook nodded.

Patti stared at the two women. She truly loved them, they had shared the horrors of perverted evil and survived them. Patti remembered the last time she saw

Barbara. The day when all Patti knew crumbled in destruction because of Barbara. She recalled Michael reaching out and asking her to come with them. Her heart hardened with rage and hate, she couldn't see the way of escape.

The other two women nodded. Patti rose from the table with the others following. They turned out the lights, locked the doors, and walked across the street to the only hotel in Church Creek Falls.

"Tomorrow, the Troye's plan to have a party here, we'll ask him then," Patti said.

"I almost forgot; Alyssa called and cancelled the party," Michelle blurted out.

"Why?" Patti moaned.

"They want to have it at their home because their father is sick."

"Did they ask us to cater?" Patti asked.

"No, they said to pack the food, and they'd pick it up."

"Call them back tomorrow morning and tell them we'll bring the food and serve at no charge," Patti instructed Michelle. "We need to see Barbara."

The other women agreed.

Patti whispered to herself, "And Michael."

Jason packed the last of his duffle bag. This would be his final deployment before his discharge. He'd signed up with the Air Force, planning to make it his career. Then Mr. Gerald Clement offered him a position and told him he'd be working alongside some of the greatest minds in the military. He wouldn't be active duty but would still be considered a part of the armed forces. The best part of the whole deal was Jason would be able to live and work right outside Church Creek Falls.

This deployment would be his last and possibly the most beneficial for his new assignment. Nonetheless, Jason needed to talk to his dad before he left. Buster Troye could give him information he could trust. Tonight, after the party, he'd talk to his dad. Michael and Sharon served as hosts at the party so the family could enjoy their guests and have plenty of time with Jason.

Zay and Macy arrived first with their son, Seth in tow. Being the youngest of the grandchildren, Seth ran to Merilee and squealed with delight to give his Mimi a big hug. Jason bent down and spread his arms wide inviting Seth to come in for a big uncle hug. Seth didn't disappoint. He jumped up on his Uncle Jason, squealing, "Swing me. Swing me." Jason complied.

Jason sat Seth down and helped his pregnant sister-in-law, Marcy into a straight chair. He sat beside her and chatted a minute before Merilee joined them. Even though Merilee saw them every day, each visit felt like a first. Marcy gave Merilee a big hug and said, "this baby may get here in time to tell Uncle Jason goodbye too."

Barbara and Daniel entered close behind with their teenagers. Hannah, the oldest ran to baby Seth, took him in her arms and swung him around in the air, much to his delight. The football playing Holloway twin boys, Ethan and Nathan kept an eye the food.

Ethan stared at Michelle as she prepared the feast for the family. He smiled in anticipation of the feast and a moment to flirt with her. "How's the prettiest French Girl in Church Creek Falls tonight?" He asked with a wink.

Michelle blushed and answered, "But, Mi sour, I am zee only French Girl in Church Creek Falls." They both giggled. Ethan took a cracker and nibbled it, while Michelle returned to the kitchen for more food. Nathan gave his grandmother an obligatory hug before walking over to his Uncle Jason. "You scared?"

"Always."

"What ya gonna be doin'?"

"Not sure exactly, but I'm a Master Sergeant now, so I get to bully some of the younger recruits." He smiled and patted Nathan on the back. "You ought to join and come with me."

"Why? So you can bully me?" Nathan answered.

"That's right."

"You've been doing that for a few years now, I don't need to join the army." Nathan winked at his uncle and gave him a slight fist bump on the arm.

Jason took on a more serious tone "South Korea is a funny place to go for someone like me who's already done two tours in Afghanistan and Iran."

"Why?"

"It's a guard job, taking inventory, trying to maintain sanity. Tell you the truth, I'm not looking forward to it."

Soon, the house bustled with friends and family and the caterers from The Honey Tree.

Patti noticed Barbara standing alone and approached her. "Hello, Barbara," she said in a soft voice.

Barbara looked up. "What do you want?" She scowled. "Do you have your next victim picked out?"

"I don't blame you, Ms. Barbara, but I'm not the same person."

"How do I know?" Barbara looked around the room.

"Jesus saved me."

Barbara's head made a swift rotation to stare into Patti's eyes. "For real?"

Patti smiled. "For real."

Barbara pulled Patti toward her and gave her a big hug. "Praise God, you got away from that horrible life."

"That's why I need to talk to you."

"What? I don't understand." Barbara let go of Patti and gave her full attention to her.

"I need help to study and understand the Bible."

Barbara gave her a big grin, took Patti's hand, and patted it, "You name the time and place, I'll be there."

Cook came behind Patti and reported, "The meal is ready."

"I'll tell Michael," she said. Then she turned to Barbara. "If it's okay with you, I'd like to tell him two things. The meal is ready, and I belong to Jesus."

Barbara gave Patti a huge smile. "Go for it!"

Jason sat in a corner sipping his coffee and watching his family. The evening proved to be delightful, even if it was his deployment party. Buster mingled with the guests, and Jason could tell he was at ease. A rare moment for him to enjoy his family. Once the last guest left, Buster retired to his chair. Merilee covered him and gave him some aspirin. Jason sat across from Buster.

"Is the pain getting any lighter?" Jason asked his father as he handed him a fresh glass of tea and a piece of his mother's famous chocolate cake.

Buster accepted the offering with a smile. "Thanks, son. This is one of the few pleasures of life left to me. The pain actually grows worse."

"What happened?"

"The dragons can inflict pain many ways; physical pain is an effective one. I read Job a lot these days. At least I still have my children." Buster took a big bite of cake and leaned back in his easy chair to savor the pleasure of the taste.

"Do you think Zay would have been wounded if you hadn't . . . you know?"

"Pushed him to the ground? I actually think the dragon had a more sinister plan for Zay." Buster took a sip of tea and watched his youngest child pace the room.

"Dad, do you know what happened to my parents?" Jason finally asked with his back toward Buster.

"We never found your dad, and your mother was protecting you and Alyssa from the blast. You were only a few months old and Alyssa was not yet two."

Jason sat near him. "Was it the dragon?"

"In that situation, the answer is yes and no. The dragon deceived and lured the townspeople into the worship of a man whose desire was to have a fat wallet to sit on. The pastor of the community church never confronted people in their walking away from God's heart, but instead he led them to believe their own hearts were true."

"I don't understand." Jason leaned forward to the coffee table and sat his empty plate and glass on it. Buster ate slowly. He sighed and put his half-eaten cake on the table. He intertwined his fingers and rested his chin on them.

"God destroyed Church Creek Falls."

"God?"

"We had become so wicked and corrupt in our dealings with each other, there was no chance of changing it, so God had to destroy the wickedness." Again Buster sighed and looked at the floor. "I fear we are coming back to that same state once again."

"Why do you think that?" Jason mused.

"There are more dragons around town now than there were twenty years ago when the bomb blast happened."

"Do you think God will destroy the town again?"

"No, I think He will let us live with them and let us suffer the consequences." Buster took a deep breath. "I'm sorry, son. I sense there's something else on your mind."

Jason nodded and proceeded to tell Buster about the government offer at the new plant outside town.

Buster smiled. "I like the idea of you being close. Do you know what they're doing at the new plant?"

"I think it's mostly research. In fact, the guy who hired me stated the reason they settled here was because of Zay and Marcy's lab."

"Do you think the job could be the reason they changed your deployment from Iraq to Korea?" Buster asked. He picked up his cake again and took a big bite.

"I think there's some connection. Don't know what it is yet."

Merilee entered the room and gave Buster a kiss on the forehead. "How are you feeling?" she asked.

He smiled at her and handed her his empty plate. "Better. Your chocolate cake is better than drugs."

Merilee retrieved Jason's dishes too. She looked at him and gave him warning, "Don't keep your dad too long. When he gets too tired, he has more pain."

Jason nodded. "I won't, Mom."

After Merilee left the room, Buster gazed at Jason. "Son, stay on your toes. Strange things happen in foreign lands."

"Details?"

"Have you ever seen a dragon?"

Jason ducked his head and shook it. He moaned, "Yesterday, over Rance."

Buster groaned and his eyes filled with mist. "No member of our family is immune, not even you and Alyssa."

"Dad, I don't think the dragon is after Rance."

Buster wiped the falling tear from his cheek and exclaimed, "What?"

"I think the dragon is using Rance as the tool, but I'm not sure he's the target."

"Why do you think this?" Buster leaned up with great effort to get closer to Jason.

"I was at The Honey Tree." Jason began his reasoning. Buster nodded, waiting for more. "I overheard the owner Patti talking to the French woman. They said they could smell it."

"I don't understand why that alarms you."

"It wasn't just their words, but the way they said it, and they looked fearful."

Buster leaned back in his chair and sighed. "I don't get the connection."

"I'm not sure, but there was something that told me they weren't strangers to evil. I don't know whether they knew it as victims or perpetrators or maybe both, but they were visible shaken."

"Keep your eyes open. There are many dragons in that land where you're going."

Jason nodded. "Dad, if the dragon is after Rance, how do you think it's going to use him?"

Buster gazed out the window, "Rance has always had a love for money, the dragon will put greed in his heart—so big, only the tragedy of losing Jennifer might cure it."

"That and his girly magazines," Jason huffed.

"Rance looks at the faces of those girls, hoping to find her and praying he doesn't," Buster said.

"Dad!" Jason groaned.

"I know, son. It's hard to imagine Jennifer that way, but I don't believe there is any girl who wants to have that kind of notoriety."

"What do you mean?"

"Girls and boys fall for the lies and deceptions of malicious people wanting to make money from their bodies. They promise them the moon and steal their souls."

"Do you think Rance is capable of selling people for profit?"

Buster steepled his fingers over his lips. He shook his head before he answered. "Son, no one is immune to the temptation of pleasure, even if it's at someone else's expense. Nonetheless, the Lord always provides a way of escape from that temptation."

"How do you know the Lord provides an escape?"

"Because He is faithful."

6

The Missing

Yet you turned and profaned My name, and each man took back his male servant and each man his female servant whom you had set free according to their desire, and you brought them into subjection to be your male servants and females servants. . . You have not obeyed Me.
Jeremiah 34:16-17a

RANCE DROVE TO the neighborhood of houses he recently purchased. Soon they would be turned into mortgages and investments. The cookie-cutter homes would sell quick to new owners creating a steady stream of fees for Rance and his investors, or rather investor. The income stream from the underbelly of life would be mixed with the happy first family home, and then would meld into rental property and retirement homes. It cleaned up the dirty money while making the bread and butter foundation for Church Creek Falls. He looked for the house number among the homes in various stages of decay. Rance pursed his lips with the memory of building these homes after the bomb hit Church Creek Falls.

The homes were built for survivors. He sighed when he realized how few houses remained on the far south side of town, a testimony to the small number of survivors. Most of the residents of this little neighborhood moved on or passed away within five years. Rance intended to modernize the neighborhood and make it a desirable place for new settlers to come. He drove the street at a slow pace, taking in the condition of every house. Suddenly, he stopped when a memory flooded him with emotion.

He stared at the home of Fred Strand and his family. His daughter Peggy had been Rance's first love. They even had a mock wedding ceremony on the playground when they were in second grade. They shared a childhood at the small school. He stopped and reminisced for a few moments. He helped most of these people move into their homes, including the Strands. Peggy taught Rance how to kiss at age twelve, and she taught him how to dance at age fourteen. She was comfortable in her own fiery personality and treated everyone as if they were her best friend. She wasn't the most beautiful girl in their class, but she was the most liked.

Then the world turned upside down for Rance the day Peggy's cousin Jennifer moved into town. Peggy introduced him to her, and he fell hard. It took a couple years to convince Jennifer to go out with him. Instead, Rance invited both Peggy and Jennifer to the dunes every Sunday afternoon. Peggy warned him to be careful. It was a warning he didn't take lightly from a five-foot seven-inch muscle-bound girl. Peggy could swipe a basketball and weave through the opposing team to make a basket before the crowd knew she had the ball. Those same skills made gentlemen of the male population in Church Creek Falls.

Petite Jennifer could hide behind Peggy, and Rance suspected she often did. He learned she lived her childhood as an army brat. Her dad was killed in Desert Storm. Her mother moved them in with Peggy's family while their house was being built. With a history of life in Church Creek Falls, Peggy knew everyone in town. Jennifer displayed a shyness unlike Rance had ever seen. She couldn't look anyone in the eye and often would only make a head gesture instead of answering a question. Her blonde hair and blue-eyes gave her a doll-like appearance. She was beautiful, beyond anything Rance had ever seen.

Rance pulled into the driveway. For some stupid reason, he wanted to go into Peggy's house. Maybe his trip through memory lane at Jennifer's house raised some kind of conscience in him. A conscience that died the day Jenny disappeared. Peggy disappeared the same day. Going inside, he noticed the bare greying wood of the once-white picket fence speckled with a few flecks of paint hanging on before taking their last breath and falling to the ground.

Rance saw the potential of growing a new community without the memories of a bomb. New people flocked into to Church Creek Falls on a daily basis to find a job and a new start. Housing served as a necessity which made it a money-maker. Along with the appreciation of the housing market, this community would be a gold mine. New businesses were opening every week, most of them solicited by Rance. He gave low-interest loans and helped with start-up costs. His plan didn't make much money in the initial phase of building the town. Bit it would pay off in the years to come, as each contract had a clause requiring investment in his hedge fund once they reached a certain level of prosperity. It would keep their business solvent and his fees flowing. He had the golden touch when it came to making money

Rance walked to the door and raised the key to open it. The loose-hinged door swung open with the small whoosh of air from his hand. He walked into the room lit only from the natural light streaming through the dirty windows.

He raised the lantern he brought with him at Alyssa's suggestion. She'd already visited the house and told Rance he needed to see for himself. Now he understood Alyssa's suggestion. Other than the wear of time, with a little cleaning, it would be inhabitable. A filigree lace tablecloth lay on the table with a bowl of plastic fruit sitting in the middle. Dishes were stacked neatly in the cabinet and canned goods filled the pantry. He looked at the refrigerator but didn't open it. As he walked through the house, he found family pictures, a television, and a telephone.

On a whim, he walked toward the dingy light switch clinging to the wall with all its fingerprints and smudges. With a flick of his wrist, the pale light flooded the room, revealing a Christmas tree awash in a water colored mist of light. Strains of Christmas music started, and he jumped. When he realized the turntable was the source of the sudden sound, his heart slowed from his recognition of the song as the tempo sped to a near-normal steady beat. He turned in a slow circle, taking in all the familiar scenes of the house.

"Just like Jenny's house."

Rance helped build the houses. Each of them had good bones. They were raised quickly by locals, volunteers, and groups of church youth from across the nation. There were two types of houses among the abandoned ones: those which were empty because the residents moved, and those left as they were that fateful Christmas of 1983. The gathered dust lay undisturbed and grew with time. He ran his finger across the stereo when he reached for the off button. "One could grow a healthy crop in this layer of dirt," he mused.

"I wonder what happened to the Strands?" he asked not expecting an answer.

But he did hear a voice of accusation, he swallowed and brushed the side of his face with his hand. That voice bubbled up more frequently in the last few months. The accusations now rambled around his head without any reason and in many cases, without any truth. They built upon themselves. When he dared to have a memory of those whom he loved and lost, it would soon be smashed by the accusation.

For the last few years, Rance had been imagining the day Jenny would come home to him or he would find her. He spent his time in the labyrinth of his mind embracing her. This stroll through the Strand house reminded him Jenny was not the only one. There were many disappearances and all at the same time with no explanation. Different people with no common thread, other than Jenny and Peggy, they were both in his circle of close relationships.

The reality of a lost future hung over his head like a cloud. As the cloud grew bigger, hope faded, while the other thing controlled his life. Even now, he wanted to escape in broad daylight to his fantasy world of forbidden fruit. He wanted to lust after the bodies of women he would never meet. If Jenny was lost, then she must be somewhere in that magazine with the other women. It started as a way to be with her, but now it was his comfort zone to deal with the anxiety.

Someone coughed behind him. He turned and saw Alyssa standing there. "What do you think?" She asked him as she looked around the house.

"Like you said, with a little cleanup and minor repair, Patti, Cook and Michelle could live here."

The plight of the women running The Honey Tree made Alyssa suggest this place. "While the three ladies keep the community fed, they spent their off hours in a musty hotel room. It's shameful how the community treats them."

Rance had to agree, so he would get the clean-up going soon. The work of rebuilding a community stole his escape into the imaginary future. It was a good thing. He feet touched reality again and he pursued the serious business in front of him to provide for living, breathing people. Still, in the back of his mind was the question raised by Alyssa's research into the files he gave her. *Where did these people go and why?* But the more frightening question raised in Rance's mind scared him. *Did he cause it?*

Two weeks later after the sale, Rance hired a housekeeper, a gardener, and a painter to get the house back into shape. He kept the furnishings for Patti, Cook, and Michelle. They'd be moving in tomorrow. Before he turned the house over to them, Rance took the time to look at the house in its complete state. Strolling through the familiar rooms he hoped to find a clue to the Strand's disappearance. He ran his hand over the bar where the teens would sit when he brought Peggy home from a Sunday afternoon at the dunes. The crowd of community teens met there for food, dune buggy rides, and fun. Small towns may not have all the things a city did, but kids of Church Creek Falls knew how to have a good time. They didn't have the water, but they had the sand.

Peggy didn't drive so Rance would most often bring her home from the dunes. He walked around. When he came to Peggy's room, he sat down on the bed and looked around her world.

"Where did you go?" he asked.

"With me." Came an answer from behind him. Rance didn't see anything except a green stuffed animal in the shape of a sweet dragon. He lifted the stuffed animal and looked at it. "I wonder if she liked dragons?"

Then the eyes of the stuffed animal shifted a bit to look directly into Rance's eyes. The eyes were staring at him, but they were only sewn-on buttons. He saw a book on the nightstand beside the bed. He picked it up and opened it. Her journal. He placed it inside his coat pocket then rummaged through her closet. He could remember seeing her in some of the clothes. Her suitcase sat on one side of the closet, along with a purse filled with personal belongings. Rance stuffed this under his arm. Before leaving Peggy's room, he took one last look. The stuffed dragon still stared at him. It was a strange sensation. *It took some talent to make those button eyes look so real.*

Mammon stared at Rance through the button eyes. All Rance could see was a stuffed animal.

7

Dragon's Breath

Nebuchadnezzar the king of Babylon hath devoured me, he hath crushed me, he hath made me an empty vessel, he hath swallowed me up like a dragon, he hath filled his belly with my delicates, he hath cast me out.

Jeremiah 51:34 (KJV)

RANCE SAT STRAIGHT up in bed, gasping for breath. A heavy weight pushed on his chest. He kept gasping. He slung his legs over the edge and sat up straight, still struggling for breath. *I must be having a heart attack.*

Mammon squeezed his chest harder with his clawed feet digging into Rance's flesh. A small stream of blood trickled onto Rance's chest. Rance stood. He attempted to take in a deep breath, but his lungs wouldn't open. He felt the blood. He raked some of it on his finger.

"Whaaa?" He didn't have enough breath to say anything more. He stumbled toward the wall. Just before he passed out, a vision of the stuffed dragon in Peggy's house appeared before him. The eyes stared at him with animation. They held buckets of hate. No sweetness could be found. He felt his body grow cold. And he fell into a pit of darkness.

When he came to, he saw his sister standing over him and his brother-in-law holding a foul-smelling bullet like thing in front of his face. He squinted and pushed it away.

"He's awake now." the man said.

Barbara leaned over him. "What happened?"

"I think I had a heart attack." Rance answered then grabbed her and held on to her. "Sis, something was here with me."

"What?" Barbara asked as she helped him back onto the bed.

"Awfulness, blackness, hate."

"Sounds like a dragon to me." Rance's brother-in-law, Dr. Daniel Holloway said. He took a stethoscope and listened to Rance's heart while examining his chest.

"What are you looking for?" Rance asked him.

"How about this." Daniel prodded the burn on Rance's chest.

"Yep, that's it." Rance yelped.

"What is it?" Zay asked and took a step back.

Barbara leaned over her husband's shoulder and answered the question, "A claw print!"

"You guys." Rance mocked them. "Are you trying to tell me I saw . . ." Rance gasped for breath as he tried to form the words.

"A dragon?" Zay finished the question while the four of them entered from the kitchen. Daniel and Zay helped Rance pull on a robe and slippers. The crew went to the kitchen where a delightful smell of bacon wafted. Daniel helped Rance sit in a kitchen chair. Barbara retrieved a glass of water.

While Rance gulped the water, Zay continued to make coffee.

"How'd ya know?" Rance gasped after he finished the water and held out the glass for Zay to refill.

"I don't know, maybe because I've seen the monster before." Zay mocked his brother.

"The dragons tried to marry me to a demon." Barbara groaned.

When Rance heard his sister's voice, he stood from his chair and put his arm around her small five-foot-one frame into his hulking six-foot three frame and squeezed her tightly. After several minutes, she pushed away.

"You saw him, didn't you?"

"No, I only saw his eyes, and . . ."

"And what?" Barbara prodded with raised voice.

"Darkness," Rance answered.

Zay nodded.

"I saw the illusion of a dragon, but those monsters still haunt my mind," Barbara mused.

"Whatever it was, I'm thankful you're both here."

Zay looked at his watch. "Only those who love you would be here at four in the morning."

"How'd you know to come?" Rance asked.

"I got a strange call. It was a husky voice breathing heavy and said your name." Barbara answered.

"Just my name? And you came?"

Barbara nodded and poured herself a cup of coffee, while Zay sat down with his and Rance's cups.

When Barbara sat down, she blew on the coffee and took a sip. She looked at Rance and simply said, "Tell us."

When Rance finished his short and frightening tale, he felt foolish. He ran his fingers through his hair. "It must've been a bad dream," he said sheepishly.

Barbara smiled and Zay chuckled. "It's your turn, bro. Just know this, you're not alone, and you can win a dragon battle."

"I don't understand." Rance took a gulp of the coffee and then rose, pulling a bottle of whiskey from his pantry. He poured a tablespoon of it into his coffee and offered it to Barbara and Zay. They both refused.

Zay started the explanation. "I considered the possibility I was gay."

Barbara continued. "I joined women's lib and went to witches' meetings. I was even part of a botched abortion."

Rance stared at his siblings. "What are you trying to tell me?"

"We've done our battle with dragons."

"Why do you think this is a battle?" Rance asked them, adding another spoonful of whiskey to his coffee.

"A dragon showed up and put his mark on you," Barbara mocked.

Rance shook his head. "I felt deep, burning hate, so deep it wanted to kill me."

"What do you think a dragon is?" Barbara quipped.

Rance smiled. "A hate-filled killer?"

"Yeah, and those yellow eyes look right through you," Zay said.

"Remember that first dragon on the farm that dad saw?" Zay asked as he rose and went to the pantry, "Do you have anything to eat?" he asked his brother.

Rance rose and pulled out a box of leftover pastries from The Honey Tree. Patti dropped them by on her way home from the restaurant. One of the girl's brought something most every night. Rance guessed it was their way of saying thank you for the house, or they were prolonging their rent free housing with gifts. Rance saw it as a fair trade. He refilled their coffee. None of them were going back to bed.

"Why are the dragons attacking our family?" Rance asked as he took a bite of a lemon fried pie.

"The better question is why do we see them? I think they attack everyone, but the Troye's see them." Barbara bit into a chocolate cream pie.

"Maybe it was the prayers of our grandfather, trying to protect us." Zay pulled out an apricot pie.

"It keeps us from following our own stupid imagination, that's for sure," Rance added. "But I still don't think all that religious stuff dad talks about is the answer."

"Then what are the dragons if they're not the evil dragons of the Bible?" Barbara asked.

"I don't know, but I do know there have been pictures of dragons around since forever. If there weren't dragons, then how did people know how to paint them, build them, so on and so on?" Rance questioned.

"Not sure I understand you?" Zay said.

"I'm saying dragons must be real because there are so many images of them; either that or the imagination of the artists have taught us what to see."

"I guess you would know imagination can look real," Zay said.

"What does that mean?" Rance put his hands on the table and straightened up to look Zay in the eye.

Zay took another bite of his pie and motioned to the stack of magazines next to Rance's recliner.

Rance followed his finger and nodded. "I know it's imagination." He lowered his voice.

"And airbrush. No woman looks like any of that smut." Barbara wrinkled up her nose at the stack.

Rance wanted to change the subject. "Do you think Alyssa and Jason will face a dragon?"

"They lost their parents because of that dragon our dad faced," Barbara said.

"Yeah, but they were so young. Jason was only six months old and Alyssa nearly two," Zay said. "Surely, they'll be spared."

"I pray they are, but I'm not so sure. After all, it says in the Bible the prophets speaking of their own imagination said, 'No calamity will come upon you, you will have peace.'" Barbara added.

"So, you mighty believers think tragedy is going to come to us all," Rance huffed.

"Not necessarily tragedy but there will be conflict." Zay smiled at Rance.

"Okay, bro, let's not start preaching. I was raised in the same church as you, and we both know Pastor Dan was a lazy fraud. Dad even said he saw the dragon telling him what to say from the pulpit."

The three siblings nodded at the memory of their childhood.

"Speaking of the younger adopted siblings, I got a letter from Jason yesterday," Barbara said.

"What news did he have from Fort Benning?" Zay asked.

"He's not there anymore; he's at Camp Casey in Korea," Barbara informed her brothers. "I think that's a safe place for now."

"As long as he doesn't get sent to Iraq again." Zay shook his head and groaned. "He's so young and innocent."

"At least the military leaders are fighting Desert Storm, instead of the politicians and movie stars." Rance said. The three of them nodded and chuckled. "We might even win this one—quick!" Rance added.

After an hour of conversation and coffee, Barbara gathered the dirty cups and empty pastry box. She read on the side, *The Honey Tree.*

"Rance I didn't know the Honey Tree had pastries."

"The French cook is quite the baker. You should go there . . . food's delicious."

"I will, the food they brought to Mom's for Jason's deployment party was delightful." Barbara said as she gathered her purse and coat and followed Zay out the door.

Rance showered and dressed. He arrived at his office early. The mail stack stood taller than usual. Rance sorted through it, discarding the junk and putting possible investments on one side, bills to pay in another, and the daily stats in another. He loved the job of creating wealth, or rather he used to love it. The appearance of the dragon bracelet came to mind.

Ten years ago, Rance took the bracelet to a jeweler. It appraised for 5.4 million. When he received that news, his little money-hungry brain started plotting his hedge fund. He possessed a degree in investment banking and could turn that million-dollar bracelet into a billion with the right products. He shared his plan with a couple of his college classmates who pooled their money with him.

By the time he opened his hedge fund, he'd accumulated a $60 million base. Tender Expressions entered the market as a legitimate player, and Rance was the hedge fund manager. All that money under his control. At the tender age of twenty-eight, Rance crossed over from farm-boy to billionaire. It was a heady feeling to have control of that much money. No one but himself and his investors knew. Not even his cousin Michael, the attorney who shared his modest office knew of his hedge fund and the shady investors.

Rance lived a frugal life while in Church Creek Falls, but his trips to Wall Street in New York looked like a fiction novel. He spent his nights making big deals in strip clubs and brothels. The girls working in these clubs knew him by name and treated him like royalty. The big bucks he paid them to entertain his future clients and the intoxicating caress of power consumed his good sense.

That was how he fell into a business deal with some of the vilest people he ever met. He wondered if they were really people or the dragons his siblings talked about. If he was dealing with a dragon, he didn't want to see the brute or confront it. He just wanted to be left alone to finish his life with as few problems as possible. But for some strange reason, he found his casual lifestyle and his secret habits being confronted and challenged. He didn't like it. He especially didn't like that his siblings told him it would happen.

He opened a strange envelope and found a prospectus from a previous contact and read over all the details. Once he finished, he rose and made coffee before Alyssa arrived. His younger sister and secretary didn't drink coffee, and when she tried to make it, he would toss it out with the rest of the garbage.

As he finished, Alyssa entered the office. Rance-felt an obligation to protect her from the world, so giving her a job, allowed her to explore her career possibilities and be safe under his watch. He didn't want her to ever know about his alternate life and its destruction on young women.

She walked over to Rance and gave him a peck on the cheek like she did every morning when she arrived. He patted her on the back of the head and their day would begin. He smiled at the ritual with a grateful heart for having her as his younger sister. The eleven years' difference in their ages made Rance feel like a father more than a big brother.

"What's on the agenda today?" he asked her as she opened her daily calendar.

"You have a meeting with Dale at ten; after that you have quiet."

"Sounds nice. Any idea what Dale needs?"

"No. He didn't say."

Well, whatever the mayor wanted, it must be important.

It felt like only a few minutes until the town mayor, Dale Meissen walked into Rance's office.

"Hey, Dale, you look worried."

"I am. Have you received the letter from that new company?"

"I was exploring it when you came in. I thought this might be your concern."

"Rance, we've done a lot for this community in the last twenty-five years since the bomb went off, and there is still a lot of work to be done. But my goal is to keep corrupted companies from coming into this town."

Rance nodded. "Do you think this is a corrupt scheme?"

"With a name like Dragon Wind. What do you think?" Dale sneered. "I also wonder why they want a worthless piece of property twenty miles outside of Church Creek Falls?"

"Did you notice the military will be leasing the property from Dragon Wind? Rance thumbed through the prospectus.

"More reason to question what they are doing out there." Rance handed Dale the prospectus and pointed to the paragraph stating the property would be used by the military.

"Have you been out there?" Rance asked as Dale read.

"No, just drive past it. It's nothing but sand dunes."

"Exactly, the perfect landscape to imitate Afghanistan."

Dale's mouth fell open and his eyes grew big, "You're right. Do you know what they want to build?"

"Not really, but it sounds like some kind of secret base . . . off the record."

"That's what I thought too." Dale intertwined his fingers and set his chin upon them.

"How can it be secret, when there's nothing out there to hide it?" Dale pondered.

"Underground." Rance answered as he turned the plans toward Dale and showed him the architect drawings.

"Why do they need us?" Dale asked, shaking his head.

"I don't think they do. If we don't sell them the land, they'll condemn it and take it by imminent domain laws."

"You think this is the dance they do?"

Rance nodded. "Yep! The real question is; do we take their money or just let them come in and take the land for free?"

Dale laughed. "You're the practical one. We might as well sell it to them."

"There's another problem."

"Oh?"

"We built our power plant out there only a mile from where they want to put their base."

"Why is that a problem?" Dale asked.

"Because they want us to provide them with power and look how much they want a month." Rance showed the mayor the prospectus.

"Geez! I don't know if that plant can produce that much power," Dale muttered.

"It can't produce that much and supply the city too. We'd have to build another plant."

"Can we say business is booming?"

"We can, but are we sure it's business?"

"Rance, I trust you to do what's best for the community. After all, you and I have practically rebuilt it from the ground up. But . . . I think this needs to remain just between us, at least for now."

Rance nodded and stood with Dale. They shook hands and parted.

After Dale left, Rance felt a blast of hot air blow on the back of his neck. He shuddered and rubbed his hand over his neck. "What was that?"

He heard a snort behind him.

8

Dragon's Lair

*Your wealth and your treasures I will give for booty without cost, Even
for all your sins and within all your borders. Then I will cause your
enemies to bring it into a land you do not know; For a fire has been
kindled in My anger, it will burn upon you.*

Jeremiah 15:13-14

A HOWLING WIND whistled through the cave where a sleeping dragon lay. The emerald-colored abomination rested his head upon the imaginary bones of his prey, Rance Troye. Destruction of the Troye family and all future generations stirred in the monster's belly of desires. The monster could taste the sweet flesh of the young ones, Alyssa and Jason, served up to the monster on a plate of evil planted in Rance's soul. A plot so deceptive in its construction, it caused a dragon named Mammon to smile with the idea of Rance Troyes' destruction.

The roar of man-made vehicles woke the sleeping giant from his delightful dreams. The creature sniffed the air and knew it was the little puppets arriving to begin work on the plant, conceived by Mammon and taught to the frail and easily manipulated humans. The plant designed to infect all mankind with an evil that would destroy existing families and prevent new ones. Mammon roared with delight. "I will be the one to destroy the Holy One's plan for family—me! Mammon, the mighty Mammon, the one humans cannot refuse." The big green hulk stood and danced in his arrogance and sang a little ditty,

> No man can refuse her
> women despise her
> No child can escape her lasciviousness
> She's the lecherous thief of innocence
> She corrodes the heart with lies
> and teaches it to the guys
> The destroyer of families and men
> Who worship at the altar of the profane
> Whose name is porneia, the passion of grief.

The whup whup of the helicopter blades caught Mammon ears. The brute raised a scaly head a bit to see the nuclear boring machine set down in front of him. The drilling would soon begin, and another deep underground military base, or D.U.M.B., would join the connecting tunnels to the more than one hundred bases already in existence in the U.S. Mammon blew a puff of fire in the air to celebrate this victory. *Dragon Wind Construction* set their roots down for the duration of building and maintaining a series of underground tunnels. Tunnels hidden from the prying eyes of curiosity seekers and oversight committees. Mammon instilled in the heart of his favorite servant a devious plan for transporting another kind of cargo.

The military men unhooked the nuclear boring machines from the Chinook helicopters. They gathered around the massive machines and made a preliminary check on the workings of the machine emblazoned with a star emblem set in a circle of blue with the words, U.S. Air Force clearly marked on the side. A group of fifteen men in hard hats shared amazement and plans. Some familiar with the machines, others seeing one for the first time. A machine that could bore through pure rock at a rate of five to six miles an hour. The machines may have been around since the 1950's but were seldom seen except by the chosen few. The machine could burrow through rock hundreds of feet below the surface, and the 'Subterrene', the name of the machine, heats whatever stone it encounters into molten rock or magma, which cools after the 'Subterrene' moves on. As a result, a smooth, glazed, lined tunnel is built which resembles black glass strong enough to support itself. Sand is the ideal element for building such a tunnel.

Mammon rose from his resting place and stood upon the sand dunes that would cover a dragon lair and evil plans. The scales on his green body shivered with the anticipation of the first death. It's too early to take a worker out now, but by the time the tunnel and the lair is built, it will be carpeted with the blood of these wily little bags of goo. Mammon roared the curse to the wind to be carried to the superior dragon, Nisroch.

How can the Almighty love them so much? The creature shuddered and took flight. The blood of the humans stank to the reptile until it was released, and the life of the human flowed and sank into the soil of the earth. Then it's perfume.

Three months later, Rance watched in amazement as the big machine unloaded. He held a clipboard with the documentation for purchase of the land. Michael was supposed to come with him to bring the paperwork, but he'd been held up with a new client.

"The less you see, the better," the construction engineer said when he noticed Rance watching the workmen with mouth agape.

"Huh?" Rance answered, still in an amazed stupor.

"Even the crews are changed every ten days so they don't know anything."

"Really? What's so secret about it?" Rance innocently asked.

The engineer gazed at him with a crooked smile and a shake of the head before he answered. "It's government compartmentalization."

"What's that?"

"You only have enough information to complete your task, and no one sees or knows everything."

"Are they hiding something?" Rance asked the foreman.

"Probably. I only know I deliver this, and I'm done." The construction foreman turned his back on Rance, waving good bye as he walked away.

Rance took the hint and headed back to his car and drove ten miles on the dusty hint of a road toward the highway. He looked in his rear view mirror and saw a glimpse of emerald-green. "Must be the sunlight filtering through all that sand." He stopped at the entrance, got out of his car, and unlocked the gate. He pushed the gate back to exit the property. *I wonder if they'll change the locks now.*

He stood at the gate and looked at the sky. He could hear something up there. The helicopters had been coming and going most of the day, but this wasn't helicopter sounds. The whooshing of wind whistled through the air with the eerie sound of a fierce sandstorm covering the land and all in it with a blast capable of pealing skin from a body. He gazed at the sky with his hand shielding his eyes. He felt relief at the sight of clear blue sky. Still the emptiness sent a chill through him causing his body to shiver in spite of the summer heat.

He shrugged and went back to his car. Once inside, he looked for on-coming traffic and snickered to himself. Little traffic came this route—only the people working at the electric plant and the few farmers who had land on the other side of the dunes.

On a weekend, scantily clad teens with illegally purchased beer roamed the dunes in their bare feet, singing and shouting. The broken beer bottles had presented a problem for some of the bare-footed teens when they ended up in the emergency room with gaping lacerations. Daniel, Rance's brother-in-law mentioned the increased frequency in cuts, sunburns, and bug bites. The curiosity of the surrounding teens increased the weekend party population.

"I hope they mark it off-limits soon before someone gets hurt bad," Daniel said to Rance the day before.

Rance took one last look at the dunes. He wouldn't be back, at least, not by invitation. It felt like a chapter closing on his life. His teen years saw many a Sunday afternoon playing in the sand. He and a few buddies purchased a dune buggy in the 80's and found the girls flocked to them for rides. Then the bikers found the dunes and the girls followed them. Rance smiled remembering the one girl that stayed with him in his dune-buggy, Peggy Strand.

With the memory of Peggy came the antics of growing up in a small town. Sometimes that memory led to other memories, some more sweet and some more painful. Peggy introduced her cousin Jenny Gale to Rance. The moment he laid eyes on Jenny, she swept his heart into her hands. Peggy winked at Rance when he saw Jenny Gale. She knew a match had been made.

Before getting back in his car, he took one last look, including the power plant across the street. The condensation from the stacks filled the sky with heavy billows of steam.

"Busy day." He said as he pulled away from the dunes.

"Hey Ran, what'ya doin'?" Alyssa asked her older brother when she walked into the office after lunch and found him setting at her desk.

"Lookin' for an old girlfriend," he answered while thumbing through the phone book. "She lived in the house we bought for Patti and her crew."

Alyssa put her purse in the drawer of her desk, rose, and looked out the window. She waved with a big smile.

"Who's that?" Rance asked.

"You're not the only one with a love life," she answered him and winked.

"No, but you are. Listen, I'm looking for this girl from my past. We spent a lot of time at the dunes when we were younger. Being out there brought back memories, and I wondered what happened to her."

"Maybe I can help. What's her name?" Alyssa sat on her desk looking at Rance sitting in her chair.

"Peggy Strand."

"Oh," Alyssa said and jumped off the desk, went to the coffee pot, and poured herself a cup.

"What's going on?" Rance stood and followed her.

"Nothing."

"Really, then when did you start drinking coffee?"

"Oh, this is for you." She turned and handed him the cold coffee without looking at him. She walked to her desk and sat down, busying herself. She opened a drawer to her desk and pulled out a thick file of newspaper clippings. She thumbed through the middle of it.

"Ah, here it is." She pulled out a clipping.

"Why do you keep all those clippings?"

"So we can build a history of our town. Here, look at this. Is this your girl?" Alyssa handed a newspaper ad to Rance. He read it silently, a startled expression on his face and the color draining from him.

"How did I miss this?" he asked, looking at the date of the clipping from four years earlier.

Alyssa didn't answer. She pushed the file toward him.

He opened it and began to scan the clippings.

"All of these people?"

"Yep, they have all gone missing over the last five years without a trace. I started out playing amateur sleuth, fantasizing that I would find them all in a well."

"What did you find?"

"Dead ends. I finally gave up and just collected the stories about them. I decided I would write a book about them so they wouldn't be forgotten."

"Good idea," Rance said while thumbing through the clippings and pulling out a few.

"What are those?"

"People I know." He pulled one out and held it up to his face. Alyssa saw the pained expression on his face. "I thought Jennifer was the only one. I never thought . . ." Rance stopped.

"I know, I thought something in one of these might help us find her. With her dad deceased and her mother gone, I felt like we were the only ones to keep looking for her."

Rance smiled at Alyssa, "I will never give up."

Mammon stood behind the two, unseen. He licked his lips with a split tongue and moaned with satisfaction. "Soon you'll know what happened to them. The harvest is coming."

Rance stopped looking and stared at the ceiling. "Did you hear something?"

Alyssa shook her head and kept reading. She picked one up and handed it to Rance. "Look at this . . . sounds strange."

Rance took the newspaper clipping and felt his stomach turn flip-flops. The heading of the story read, "The planting of seed is singular, but the harvest comes in multiples."

9
The Honey Tree

They have also cast lots for My people, they have traded a boy for a harlot and sold a girl for wine that they may drink.

Joel 3:3

THE TWO MEN found a table near the window and sat. Michelle approached them with menus. She welcomed them and asked what they would like to drink. The men removed their hats and sunglasses and set them in an empty chair. The driver looked up at Michelle with a toothy smile, "Hello, Mon Cherie."

Michelle dropped her pen and pad. She turned and ran into the kitchen.

"Ms. Patti, they're here!"

Patty looked out the one-way glass and saw the two men. "Ms. Patti, what do we do?"

Cook came over and saw them. "Oo wee!" She brushed her hand over her head. "What do we do?"

"I didn't think they would find us here."

"What do we do?" Michelle asked again.

"We serve them like any other customer. Don't show any recognition," Patti instructed Michelle.

"I think I already gave it away, I dropped my pen."

"Accidents happen. Calm down and treat them like any other customer."

Michelle nodded and approached the customers.

Standing in the kitchen and watching her, Cook asked, "Do you think they found that Christine woman?"

Patti shook her head. "If they had, they wouldn't be here."

"Think we can sneak out the back and get away?"

"Nope, we stand here and fight."

"But we're unarmed."

"Not completely. Remember, Barbara Troye and her cousin Michael live here."

Cook smiled. "Yeah. Do you think they'll take a stand with us?"

"I don't know, but they are our best hope."

By this time Michelle returned to the kitchen and handed the orders to Cook. She prepared them and Michelle served them. Patti stayed in the kitchen.

"If they don't see me, I don't think they'll bother you," she said.

"They asked for you, Patti," Michelle said.

"What did you tell them?"

"That you weren't here."

Patti smiled. "Look out the window. Do you see it?" she asked the two women.

They both nodded. "I've never seen a bright green dragon like that, though."

"Me neither, but you can bet it's what brought those men here."

Patti went into the office and picked up the phone. She dialed the familiar number. When the other party answered, she said, "When will I get my money for the house?"

She ducked her head and rubbed her forehead. "I need it now."

She looked up and sighed. "I can't do that again." Patti moaned.

After several minutes, she leaned back in her chair and said, "What are the specs?"

She nodded, groaned and hung up the phone.

Cook heard the conversation. "What is it, Ms. Patti?"

"He wants us to use our old skills."

"Oh no, please, not that!" Cook moaned. Michelle dropped onto a stool and started crying.

"I don't think I can," Michelle said through sobs. "We're different people now."

"What's our options?" Patti groaned.

"Why don't you meet with Ms. Troye?" Cook suggested.

"Her married name is Holloway, and I'm not about to take this to her. I don't think she would ever understand."

"She will be the only one to understand," Cook lectured Patti. "She's our only hope."

"I'm not ready to face her. Do you think she could forgive me for what I did to her?"

Cook nodded her head then asked, "What's the first order?"

"Domestic servant," Patti said.

"I think I can do that, there are a lot of migrant workers here for harvest." Cook stood up straighter, went to her kitchen, and started prep for the evening dinner crowd.

Patti looked at the notes she made from the telephone conversation. "They want a boy," she said without looking at Michelle.

"Okay, what age?"

"Twenties, strong," Patti answered without any expression.

Michelle nodded. "When?"

"Next week."

Mammon roared, "The harvest begins!"

10

Nightmare Hell

Woe to me, my mother, that you have borne me As a man of strife and a man of contention to all the land! I have not lent, nor have men lent money to me, Yet, everyone curses me. Surely I will set you free for good and cause the enemy to make supplication to you in a time of disaster and a time of distress.

Jeremiah 15:10-11

RANCE SAT IN the dark and listened to the knocking on his front door. Mammon rested beside Rance with a clawed foot wrapped around his arm. Although Rance couldn't see the dragon, he could smell it.

"I know you're here." Rance growled under his breath.

"I'm always here." The monster replied on a wave of hot air.

Rance steeled his muscles and yanked away from the beast before it had time to tighten its grip. "Leave me alone!" he yelled out at the top of his voice.

The front door opened at the same time.

Zay burst into the room where Rance stood dripping in sweat. He saw the monster gripping Rance's neck. "Get out!" Zay screamed at the monster. "You evil beast, you will be slain by the Lord, and no one will cry for you."

Rance fell to the floor unconscious. Zay formed tight fists in both hands, raised his shoulders, and marched toward the beast hovering over Rance. You will be nothing more than waste scattered on the ground. Mammon roared and blew a powerful blast of fire over Zay.

Zay laughed at the monster as he stood firm over his brother. "Get out!"

"You know you can't get rid of me," Mammon roared in his deep voice. The monster put a clawed foot on Rance's back and squeezed. Rance gasped for air.

Zay could feel his resolve to face this monster fading. He watched Rance struggle for air. "Get off him! you're killing him!" Zay screamed.

Mammon moved the foot from Rance's back. Zay knelt beside him and breathed air into his lungs. "Come on brother, don't give up."

After a few minutes, Rance coughed and took a deep breath. After a few more breaths, he looked at Zay. "I'm sorry." Was all he could say.

"Yeah, he's sorry," Mammon mocked him.

Zay ignored the beast.

Zay took his brother's hand and helped him to his feet. Mammon roared, and the dragon's breath of fire went around Zay. Zay pushed Rance back. "Stay behind me."

Zay raised his face toward the fire storm and shouted, "Do not listen to the words of this false prophet! He is leading you into a useless way that will destroy you and keep you from the Father."

Rance heard the words his brother shouted, but his heart didn't understand. Why was Zay standing in a burning building, shouting instead of getting out? Rance headed toward the front door and escaped his house. He ran into Marcy.

She was praying too. "Dear Lord, I don't understand your ways, but I trust You in all of them."

Rance grabbed her by the hand. "We gotta get outta here," he said.

She didn't move but stood still.

"Marcy, the house is on fire!" he shouted at her.

"No, brother. it's not." She turned toward the house. Rance looked and couldn't see any fire or feel any heat. He followed Marcy back into the house. She walked up to Zay and gave him a hug. "The dragon?" She asked him.

Zay nodded.

"You people are crazy," Rance said as he pulled a towel from the drawer and wiped his brow. "My house starts fire, and you think there's a dragon."

Zay took some ice out of the refrigerator and filled two glasses with water and ice. He handed one to Rance. "Sit down," he demanded of his brother.

Rance didn't argue. He followed his brother's instructions and gulped the cool water. Marcy refilled both glasses. "You want to go solo?" she asked Zay.

"Only in body. You keep praying," Zay answered his wife as she left the house and closed the door behind her.

"What's going on?" Rance asked his brother.

"Did you see the beast?"

"What? No. I saw you and flames all around you."

Zay took a deep gulp of his water, leaned back in his chair, and sighed. "Brother, there's a dragon living here with you, and it's consuming you."

Rance laughed. "And how is it doing that, brother?"

Zay rose from the table, put his glass in the dishwasher and turned toward his brother. "Look at you." Zay scorned. You stink of sweat and body odors. How long have you been in those clothes? How long since you washed?"

Rance looked down at his dirty pajamas. "I was getting ready to take a shower."

"Why at three in the afternoon?"

"I've been busy this morning," Rance muttered.

"I see." Zay looked at the computer screen with a sexual image flashing.

Rance walked over and turned off the screen. "In the midst of working, I take a little break now and then," he explained.

"You gotta quit that stuff; it's destroying you."

Rance looked at his brother with firm-set jaw. "No, my loneliness and memories of Jenny Gale is killing me. Did you know those things cause physical pain?"

"I'm sorry, but going into it deeper isn't going to relieve the pain."

"Yes, going into it deeper does relieve the pain. That's why I do it!" Rance yelled at his brother. "Go home to your sweet little wife and darling kids," Rance growled the sentence in harsh sarcasm. "I'm going to take a shower and go to work."

Zay turned from Rance and walked to the bathroom.

Jennifer and Peggy froze in the narrow corridor. There was nowhere to run and whatever was coming out the door at the end of the corridor would see them. The door swung wide open. The girls held their breath, waiting for whatever fate would overcome them. Jennifer closed her eyes tightly.

Peggy released her breath. "It's okay."

Jennifer opened one eye to peek. The door had swung open on its own, revealing a semi-empty room with only a small light bulb glowing in the center.

"What is it?" Jennifer asked as she waited for her eyes to adjust.

"Looks like an office. Come on." Peggy grabbed Jennifer's hand and pulled her toward the room.

Once they were inside, they discovered it was a small office. "If there's an office here, there's more . . .

maybe a way out," Peggy whispered to Jennifer, who nodded and surveyed the room.

"What if that's the only way in and out?" she asked Peggy.

"Then we go back out and find our way out of here."

"Where do you think *here* is?" Jennifer muttered with trembling voice.

"Not good." Just as Peggy answered, they heard a female scream.

"Sounds young," Jennifer said.

"Probably her first time." Peggy said in a low moan.

For a moment both girls stood still and quiet as they listened to the screams of pain. They finally turned into moans of grief.

"I wonder if men would buy that smut if they knew what the girls go through," Peggy scoffed.

Jennifer wept. "How many times—" She couldn't finish her question.

Peggy raised her head in thought. "I lived in that nightmare hell too many times to remember. What about you?"

"I haven't had to . . . you know . . . do the bad stuff that makes you scream," Jennifer whimpered as she felt the walls, searching for a crack that might be a hidden door.

"Really?"

"You protected me. Remember the times you would hide me," Jennifer said. Her fingers fell into a crack. "Here."

Peggy rushed over to help her swing the hidden panel, and when they did, the moans of pain became louder. Peggy gasped when she saw the face of the young girl being abused. The girl's tear-filled eyes saw Peggy. She mouthed the word *help*.

Peggy slammed the panel shut.

"What?" Jennifer asked.

Peggy pushed her back against the wall, breathing hard. "Do you remember that little girl they brought into our cell a few days before the fire?"

Jennifer nodded.

"That's her." Peggy pointed to the panel. "We've got to get her out of here."

"How are we going to do that without exposing ourselves?"

"I don't know. Look around for some kind of weapon. There's only the camera man, the one hurting her, and the other fiend."

The two girls scrambled around the room, opening drawers, looking under the sparse furniture . . . looking for anything to defend themselves.

Barbara felt a pinprick on the back of her neck. She recognized it as the needling of the dragon. The beast used Rance to work his evil on all the family. Barbara also knew this was a call for action. She scanned her charts, put sticky notes at her places, and closed them. She grabbed her purse and keys and walked to Daniel's office.

"We have an emergency," she said to her husband.

He followed his wife. By the time the couple reached their home, Barbara explained the prick on her neck to Daniel.

"I had a strange phone call," Daniel answered her.

"What was it?"

"It was the firefighters' association. They told me there was an emergency and to be ready."

"That's not unusual."

"No, but the speaker hung up, and when I called the fire station back and ask for more details, they said they didn't call me."

Daniel took Barbara's hand and kissed it, "So, who and what is our emergency?"

"I guess we have to ask the Lord because I have no clue."

The couple knelt in their little prayer room, which consisted of the small bedroom in their home. It had served as a nursery during that time of life and as an entertainment room for teens. Now as almost empty nesters with only Hannah still living at home, the boy's empty room became sacred in its purpose of a prayer and study room for Daniel and Barbara.

Daniel started their prayer, asking for clarification about the need for which they'd been called to pray.

Barbara gasped. "I think it has something to do with—" She stopped and waited a moment. "With the porn."

"Rance?" Daniel asked. "We pray for him every day."

"No, this is more, it's . . . it's for Peggy and Jennifer."

The couple began their prayer, "Lord for our missing loved ones we pray."

"I found something," Peggy called out to Jennifer as she pulled a gun out of one of the drawers in the desk.

Jennifer stopped and gazed toward Peggy. "Is it loaded?"

"I hope so."

"Do you know how to shoot?"

"No, but those bums ripping that poor girl open don't know that. Let's go. Keep your eyes on the guys, and here . . . take this." Peggy handed Jennifer a large, heavy sculpture of a dragon.

As always, Jennifer followed Peggy. They swung the panel open. The director sat with his back toward the two girls, they were somewhat hidden by a partial wall.

Jennifer felt a burst of power surge through her and a hatred for her captors. She raised the dragon high over her head and slammed into the head of the director. His head split open and blood spurted everywhere.

Jennifer shouted, "Now you know what it feels like!"

Peggy pointed the gun at the man over the young girl. "Get away from her!" He obeyed and reached for his pants. Peggy's pain and intensity sparked her reaction to his attempt to cover his naked body by pulling the trigger.

The gun fired directly into the man's groin. He fell to the ground.

Peggy smiled and sneered, "You'll never hurt us again." She helped the girl to her feet. She could barely stand much less walk.

"It hurts." She moaned. Peggy grabbed her by the waist. "I know, sweetheart; believe me, I know."

The camera man dropped the camera to the floor and ran out the door when Peggy shot the actor. He rolled on the floor in a pool of blood, crying like a little kid.

"Let's go this way." Peggy pointed to the door the camera man left open. She picked up the camera on their way out.

Barbara pulled herself up and sat in the chair over which she had been kneeling. "It's getting hard on these old bones." She smiled. "I think it's over."

Daniel sat beside her. "It's not over, but the emergency is past." Both of them sighed and leaned back, letting their heads rest against the wall.

"Not by might or by power, but by My Spirit says the Lord," Barbara said.

"Amen," Daniel answered.

Mammon huddled in a corner with his bulk reduced to the size of a small dog. He whimpered.

The man in the army fatigues waved his sword in his face. "Don't ever come back to this room again."

Mammon ran out as fast as his little puppy dog legs would carry him.

"She needs medical attention," Jennifer said to Peggy.

"We'll do the best we can," she answered and kept urging them along.

The young girl hung on to Jennifer and tried to run. The three girls were in an alley. The signs were all in English. "Look!" Jennifer pointed to a red cross sign.

Jennifer found a cardboard box. She put it on the ground and sat the young girl down on it. "Stay here. Help will be here soon," she said to the girl and then kissed on her forehead. "Jesus loves you," she whispered to the battered soul.

Once Jennifer was out of sight, Peggy banged on the door and rang the doorbell. Then she ran to hide behind the dumpster with Jennifer. They watched as they saw the door open, and two women helped their young friend inside.

"We stopped them," Jennifer said.

"Yeah, and we've got proof of their evil." Peggy help up the camera. "As well as something to sell."

Peggy pulled the video from the camcorder. They went into the camera store in front of them and sold the camera. Then they purchased some modest clothing from a discount store. "Now, all we need is shelter."

"I've got an idea." Peggy winked.

11

Desert Storm

They will burn your houses with fire and execute judgments on you in the sight of many women. Then I will stop you from playing the harlot and you will also no longer pay your lovers.

Ezekiel 16:41

JASON TROYE PULLED his ruck sack onto his back as he deplaned and entered his new home for the next eighteen months. This deployment to South Korea felt like a cake walk compared to his two tours in Iraq during Operation Desert Storm.

This tour had another challenge besides the desert heat of one-hundred-twenty-degree heat and a fifty-pound ruck sack. This time he wasn't a lowly grunt. He bore three stripes on his chest proving him an extra-special grunt. He chuckled to himself. Other than the pay raise, there wouldn't be much difference. He would still be doing the same job, but at least here no one would be shooting at him.

The one thing he wasn't prepared for was the terrible cold. He mentally went over the clothing he'd stowed in his duffle bag and hoped he put his insulates in there. After pulling all his clothes out, he knew a trip to the commissary loomed in his near future. He cupped his hands over his mouth and breathed into them. Then crossed his arms putting his hands in the crook.

Once he arrived at the commissary, he realized he wasn't the only one unprepared for the cold. They had no gloves left. He and three other soldiers stood bare-handed waiting for the clerk to check for more. There were none.

"Hey bud, you want a share a trip to town?" Jason called out at a nearby soldier. He nodded and the two of them were soon joined by a couple more bare-handed soldiers. The four men hopped the shuttle into town from the base for the hour-long trip to Seoul.

"Look at that?" one of the soldiers pointed out to the street. Saw several girls and young boys in a variance of seductive clothing stood on the sidewalk.

"They gotta be freezin'," another soldier said.

Rance stared out the window and said one word in bewilderment, "Why?"

"They's pimp makes 'em." Came the soft-spoken drawl of a young man.

The men nodded. "I bet they're glad to climb into a warm car with strangers in this cold."

"They get used to it," another leering soldier spoke up.

"No, they don't," Jason responded with disgust. He turned his head away, and in a quiet voice he said, "Lord Jesus surround them with the warmth of Your love."

The soldier in front of him heard the words and turned to Jason. "You a Bible-thumper?"

Jason smiled and nodded. "I guess you could say that. I read it more than I thump it, though."

"Learn much?"

"Every day." Jason responded and took another look at the girls. "Some of them look American."

The bus driver heard the conversation and added, "They come from every country. This is a pass-through for most of them."

Jason didn't know what he meant, but he knew it wasn't good. He didn't want to know. He turned his head and looked at the neon signs hovering above the street. He couldn't read them, but he understood the bright lights and blinking pictures covered the ugliness on the street with a promise of a good time. Those poor girls were the bait used to rob the soldier boys of their paycheck and their souls.

The men had an hour to waste before the shuttle returned to base. Jason purchased gloves, a scarf, a warmer toboggan and some thick socks. The guys went into a small café and found a table when another group rose to leave. They settled in and ordered some hot tea. Jason stared out the window at the strange sights, sounds, and smells. With a tour of Afghanistan under his belt and a year filled with battle, this assignment seemed surreal.

Being in a large city with every libation and sin known to man for the squandering of a paycheck had never been in his history. He remembered some of his dad's World War Two stories and smiled. He understood them better now.

She saw him looking at her from the bus window. He had a kind look in his eyes instead of the normal lustful look. On his way to board the bus, he handed her a woolen scarf. She dared to think, to dream, maybe he would rescue her. She rubbed her eyes with her cold hand. She didn't want to cry; it would freeze on her face. She watched him until the bus was out of sight, taking any hope of possible rescue with it.

The trip back to the base felt like two hours rather than the one. The heater on the bus did little to keep the guys warm. Most of them snuggled up in their clothing and ducked their head. At the back of the bus, one young man quietly sang a popular rock song while others moved to the beat. Others stared out the window into the blackness of the night, seeing nothing except the lost memories of home.

Jason Troye stared out the window, and the memories he saw in his mind kept pulling him to the girls he'd seen on the street only a few hours earlier. The streets of Seoul, Korea, had nothing in common with the streets of Church Creek Falls. Jason recalled the day he and his older brother, Rance, walked up and down the mangled streets of Church Creek Falls, checking on the residents who had rebuilt to make sure they had food and heat in the winter months. Even in the wind-swept Texas winter he never felt as cold as he felt now. The freezing air was almost a spiritual iciness that touched the soul with the emptiness of aloneness.

Then his memory came to the quaint little frame home of the Strand family. When they reached that house, Rance and he went inside. This was the only house in which they lingered. Rance drank some coffee which the daughter brought him, and he smiled at her.

"Oh, my goodness." Jason said aloud, "That could have been Peggy."

12

Days Without End

A clamor has come to the end of the earth, because the LORD has a controversy with the nations. He is entering into judgment with all flesh; As for the wicked he has given them to the sword,' declares the Lord.
Jeremiah 25:31

RANCE TURNED OFF the green bankers' light sitting on his desk. He rubbed his hands over his face and sighed. The days grew longer and longer. He felt grateful he didn't have a family, but also felt the loneliness of going home to an empty house.

He looked at the engagement ring on his pinkie. What would he do with it now? He couldn't bring himself to sell his last memory of Jenny Gale.

"Oh, my sweet angel, where did you go?" Rance asked the ceiling. He didn't expect an answer, but he received one.

"You should remember," came the growl of Mammon.

Rance jumped out of his seat. The sound reverberated in his ears with the sheer volume, but the words rattled his soul. He held his hands over his ears.

The voice softened, but the words cut like knives when it said, "She will soon be mine completely."

"No!" Rance screamed as he lowered his hands and looked around for the source of the voice.

Mammon's cruel laugh filled the room with anger. Rance balled his fist. "I'll—"

"What? You're a wimp and you know it."

"I'll find her; I'll get her back," Rance responded with fierce determination while fearing the dragon's words were truer than his own.

"She trusted and believed the Holy One would bring you to get her. She sure put her faith in the wrong guy." Mammon laughed, and when it did, Rance caught a glimpse of the green iridescent scales reflecting the light. He felt revulsion at the sight and fascination at its beauty. "After all, it's because of you she's my prisoner now."

Rance fell to his knees and wept. "No, no I didn't mean—"

"Yeah, I get that excuse a lot, you don't mean to trust in your own foolish ways. It's hardest on you guys who know the truth and still follow my lies." Mammon roared to a deaf heart.

Rance kept his face buried in the floor, chewing on the words Mammon kept slipping into his mind. There was both truth and clues in those words. He needed to get past his shame so he could hear the clues.

"And now, here comes the next dish you will hand over to me," Mammon roared. With a fading sound Rance could feel the evil leave the room as well as the stench of him and the awful sound of words. He looked at the window and saw Alyssa getting out of the car with that blasted boy she kept seeing.

She was coming into the office and bringing him with her. She didn't know Rance was still there. The lights were all turned off. He stood still and watched as Alyssa unlocked the door, and the two of them entered the office. Rance could feel the hot breath of the dragon breathing down his neck. He raised his shoulders and pulled his shirt color closer to his neck. He wasn't gone as he'd hoped.

"I'm pretty sure he keeps them in here," Alyssa said as she unlocked the filing cabinet.

Rance watched.

"I'm sorry, Matt, it's not here." She turned toward the young man.

"'I'll ask him tomorrow," she said, closing the filing cabinet and locking it again.

"No need, I'll ask him myself," Matt answered as he turned away from Alyssa and stared into Rance's office. "Let's go in there," he said and grabbed her hand and started pulling her toward the office.

"I can't go in there." Alyssa objected even though he was dragging her into the room.

"He'll never know." He grinned at Alyssa and stroked her face.

She smiled back but pushed him away. "No, I won't do it."

At that point, Matt grabbed Alyssa around the waist and pulled her close to him. "Yes, you will." He picked her up and carried her.

When he reached the door, Rance stepped out, towering over Matt. "What are you guys doing here?" he asked as he held his hat in his hand, hiding his pistol. With a dragon nearby, nothing good was going to come of this encounter. He could hear the dragon laughing at him, but he wouldn't go down without a fight.

Matt let Alyssa's feet touch the ground, but he didn't let go of her waist. She pushed herself away from him but still didn't break free of him.

"Rance," she said in a sing-song voice and inched herself toward him.

"Working late?" He grinned and winked.

"No, Matt just wanted to see the files on—"

"The unique filing system she has developed," Matt interrupted. "I thought I could use it in my business."

"What business is that?" Rance asked.

"Commodities," he answered quickly.

"Oh, what kind of commodities?" Rance took Alyssa by the hand and pulled her toward him and slightly behind him.

"Whatever," he answered.

"I think it's time you left," Rance said firmly.

"Come on, Alyssa," Matt said.

"I'll take Alyssa home. You go on." Rance lowered his voice and raised his head a little higher. Matt nodded and complied by leaving the office.

After he was gone, Alyssa let out a sigh and moaned, "Thank you."

"Shh." Rance put his fingers to his pursed lips.

Alyssa nodded.

Rance looked around the office. Then he took her by the hand, and the two of them left by the back door. Rance had left his car parked in the parking spaces behind the office. Once the two of them were in the car, Rance asked Alyssa, "What did he really want?"

"The files on the military work at the sand dunes."

"Did he say why?"

"Said he was interested in investing," Alyssa answered innocently.

Rance took her hand and kissed the back of it. "Sis, you know I love you more than life itself, and that's why you must listen to me carefully."

"Okay," she said, knowing he would do nothing to cause her harm.

"There is no investing in that work. He's up to something else, and I don't trust him. I would prefer you not see him anymore."

"I do like him, but his behavior tonight was pretty weird. I won't go out with him anymore," she answered with a smile.

When Rance and Alyssa arrived at the farmhouse, the lights were all on. He walked her up to the door and rang the bell. When their mother, Merilee, answered, Rance asked if his dad was still up.

"Yes, son, he is," she answered and opened the door. When Alyssa walked in, Merilee said, "I thought you had a date. It's kind of early, and why is your brother bringing you home?"

"I guess you could say he rescued me from an unscrupulous businessman."

Merilee looked at Rance and smiled, "Well, thank you, sir." She gave Rance a hug.

Rance joined his dad in the den. Merilee left them alone and shut the door.

Rance related the incident to Buster. "Dad, do you have any idea what's going on out there?"

Buster looked down at his lap. "I'm afraid I have some educated guesses, and none of them are good. Besides, we can't discuss it in front of your pet dragon."

"What?" Rance looked around.

"The beast is behind you. I suspect it's always there."

The dragon nodded and blew a puff of smoke. Rance swiped the air in front of his face. "What is that?"

"Your dragon, just agreed with me."

"Dad, how can you talk about a dragon so casually?"

"I've seen them attack every member of my family, and Jason's troop fought a giant."

"What?"

"You can ask him; he tells the story much better."

"He's in Korea for the next ten months."

"Okay, I'll tell you the story, but you be sure and ask him again when he gets back."

Rance smiled and nodded.

The dragon lay down beside Rance and rested his head on his claws. Buster looked at the dragon, "Scat!"

Rance's eyes grew large and his mouth opened.

"Not you, the dragon," Buster said.

Rance sat back down and asked, "Is it gone?"

Buster nodded. "I see them, but I don't let them stick around."

Rance chuckled. "I need to learn that trick if it's hanging around me all the time."

"It's found in the Bible," Buster said.

"I know you say it is, Dad, but the book doesn't do anything for me. I want to hear about Jason's experience with a giant."

"It was in Kandahar. Jason was one of fifteen men sent into the hills to search the caves for a unit that had lost contact with the base. They were several days out."

"What was their mission?"

"To locate the unit and discover the outcome. No one expected them to find survivors."

Rance shook his head in dismay. "It must be hard going out to look for bodies of those you've worked beside for months."

"Jason did have a hard time, and that's why he's finishing out his tour in South Korea."

"Did they find the unit?" Rance drew his dad back into the story.

"They found bones and U.S. communication equipment."

"How did they find them?"

"They followed the general direction of their last communication on a goat path. It was an easy climb but then they reached a sheer cliff. They could see a huge cave opening above them and movement inside the cave."

"What did they do?" Rance felt a bit like a kid getting a nighttime story from his dad. He smiled at the thought and the remembrance of his childhood nights when Dad told them stories.

"They went around a switchback and approached the mouth of the cave. At the entrance, they saw the bones piled together and mixed with American communication equipment."

Buster stopped and took a deep breath. He reached for his water glass and took a big drink then opened an aspirin bottle and took out four aspirins and swallowed them. He took a deep breath and adjusted himself in his chair.

"If you're hurting, Dad, we don't have to do this," Rance said, adjusting his father's back pillows. He pulled his dad's tee shirt up and looked at the wound on his back. It was deep and purple. "Is that thing going to heal? It's been more than six years since the incident."

"No, son. When Belial dropped the acid on me, the dragon spat a curse that it would not heal until my dying day." Buster found a comfortable position. He chuckled a bit sarcastically. "The ugly creature laughed at me when he said it. They're filled with hate for us humans, especially those of us who belong to the Father."

Rance ignored the last statement. "Do you want to continue?"

"Yeah, but I still want you to ask Jason when he gets back."

Rance nodded and plopped back into his seat on the couch opposite his dad's chair.

"The men saw something huge coming at them with superhuman speed, carrying something in his hand—a spear with a five-foot lance lashed onto it."

"Well, I don't think an animal would build a spear, and a big man couldn't weld that kind of weapon."

"You're right," Buster said. "But a fifteen-foot man could."

"Fifteen feet?"

"That's what Jason said. He said it came out in a second and speared one of their men through the gut and then carried him around on the end of that spear like a hamburger."

"What did the men do? Run?"

"No, they fired at it. The bullets bounced off the thick hide of that creature like raindrops in a lake. Jason said, he didn't know why, but all at once the entire troop of fourteen surviving men starting firing at the face of that creature. They shot him with M-4s, 308 and Barrett 50's, and eventually he fell."

"Then what?" Rance sat up and leaned toward his dad. He didn't really believe this tall tale, but it made for great story time.

"They called their base and asked for a helicopter to remove approximately eleven hundred pounds."

"Eleven hundred? It was that big?"

"It was an estimate, but the fourteen of them could barely lift it enough to get the netting dropped from the chinook around it."

Buster adjusted his pillow but kept talking. "Jason said the stench was the worst. It smelled like rotting corpses."

120

"But—"

"Probably because it ate the soldiers earlier." Buster moaned and ducked his head.

Rance stayed quiet while his dad processed the horror of the soldiers.

"Dad, you're telling this like it really happened."

Buster patted him on the knee. "It did, son, it did."

"How do you know?"

"The dragon told me." Buster wiped a tear from his eye. "Son, they are horrible creatures, and their goal in life is to destroy all human life, either by possession or death."

"You can't believe a dragon," Rance said with sarcasm.

"They live eternally either as a disembodied spirit wandering around a desert filled with waterless clouds, or they find an available body to possess, either human or animal, but they prefer human."

"That makes sense." Rance snorted. "So, does this mean the giant was a demon-possessed human?"

Buster buried his head in his heads and moaned.

"Dad?" Rance went to him to help relieve his pain.

"It's not the pain in my body."

"Then what?"

"The truth about the giant is more painful than any physical pain."

"What do you mean?" Rance felt startled at his dad's reaction to the tale about the giant.

"The giant—" Buster stopped and leaned his head back.

"What, Dad?"

"With a deep sigh, Buster finally said, "If it's true, then the giant must have been a demon."

13
Memories

"For you will no longer remember the oracle of the LORD, because every man's own word will become the oracle, and you have perverted the words of the living God, the LORD of hosts, our God.

Jeremiah 23:36

"DID YOU FEEL that?" Alyssa asked Rance.

"Yeah, what do you think it was?"

"Felt like an earthquake."

Rance smiled at his younger sister. "How do you know what an earthquake feels like?"

"I'm guessing. Okay?" She snarled at him with a wink.

"It's probably the work going on at the dunes."

"Really? That's over twenty-miles away."

"It's just a guess," Rance muttered as he looked down at a file he'd pulled. He went to his office and shut the door. Once inside, he opened the file.

Mammon whispered in his ear.

Rance didn't respond.

Mammon roared and spit a plume of flames.

Still Rance didn't respond.

Mammon wrapped his long tail around Rance's body. "Listen to me!" the monster roared in Rance's ear.

Rance stood and rubbed his ear. He walked toward Alyssa. "Do you hear something?"

"I told you I did."

"I hear it too." Rance shook his head. "It sounds like it's inside my head."

Alyssa wrinkled her brow, "I hear it out there." She pointed toward the window.

Mammon roared in Alyssa's face.

"Ow!" she screamed.

"What?" Rance ran toward her.

"It's in my head."

He still held the folder.

"What's that?" Alyssa pointed.

He sat down in the chair in front of her desk. "Alyssa, there's something strange going on, and I can't find it."

"Strange like how?" she asked.

Rance took a tissue and wiped his brow. He opened his mouth but didn't speak. Instead, he stared out the office window. From there, he could see most of the north side of the square and the new businesses he helped start. Like a wall of accomplishments. Most people in the town knew he was important to the economy, but only a few knew how. Each individual business owner knew his personal involvement in their endeavor, but nothing of his other endeavors. He was both a public spectacle and a deep secret. He enjoyed this little mystery surrounding him, but now this same mystery befuddled him.

"What took my Jenny?"

"Do you remember the day she disappeared?" Alyssa asked him.

"Like it was yesterday." Rance sighed.

"Tell me about it."

"It was Christmas morning." He paused.

"Go on," Alyssa prodded. She stopped work and leaned over her desk giving, him her full attention.

"I spent most of the week courting businesses to come to town and help us rebuild," Rance began his trip down a painful memory lane. "I couldn't wait to get home and ask Jenny to marry me. I stopped in Lubbock and bought the ring. I had them wrap it with their best paper." He smiled and stared at the ceiling. "I drove all day from Dallas so I would be here by Christmas morning to give her the ring. I arrived home around ten. I don't think I slept any that night." He chuckled.

Alyssa smiled in response. "What happened?"

"I called Jenny and asked her to breakfast. After all, I'd been gone a week and couldn't wait till evening to see her. We slipped out and had breakfast down at The Rambling Rose Café."

"Not the most elegant place."

"It was the only place in town to eat at that time. It served good coffee and horrible food. But we didn't notice. We had coffee and a sweet roll."

"Sounds like a good choice."

He nodded. "The only thing made by someone else."

"It started snowing while we were there. We decided we'd spend the day at her house. I told her I had to go home and get showered and cleaned up. I'd come over at lunch. I took her home, and we stood out in the cold letting the snowflakes cover our eyelashes and noses." Again, Rance drifted off in his memories and stopped talking.

Alyssa remained quiet as she waited for him to continue.

"That was the last time I kissed her. We were freezing but didn't know it because our love was keeping us warm," Rance said.

Alyssa laughed out loud. "That's so cheesy."

"Yeah, I know, but it was the truth. It was perhaps the most perfect moment of my entire life." He sighed. "When we went inside, I slipped the wrapped ring to her mother to put under the tree. I hadn't seen it again until a few months ago when Barbara and I cleaned the house."

Mammon listened to the sappy story and yawned. "Yeah, yeah, get to the good part."

"I went to my house quickly, got ready, and hurried back to the Gowan home. Once I arrived, the house smelled of Christmas trees, peppermint, warm fire, and turkey—the perfect Norman Rockwell picture of a family."

"Sounds great."

"It was. We ate until we couldn't move, but we still stuffed a piece of pumpkin pie down our throats." Rance rubbed his stomach.

With that action, Mammon raked an extended claw across his belly.

"Ouch!" Rance hollered and raised his shirt. A light trickle of blood inched down his stomach. He turned pale.

"What's wrong?" Alyssa stood and inspected the slight injury.

"That same thing happened that day."

"What?"

"Just like this, Jenny and I were making plans for our future when that happened. I went to the bathroom to wash the blood away, and when I came back, Jenny was gone."

"Gone where?"

"Wherever she is now, because none of us ever saw her again."

"Did she just get up and leave?"

"Her dad said someone came to the door and she left with them. They didn't see who it was and they didn't see a car."

"Why would she leave without telling anyone?"

"That's the mystery." Rance leaned back in the chair. A tear crept down the side of his face.

"Do you have any idea who it was?" Alyssa asked.

Rance shook his head. "I worry—" He stopped before he finished the sentence.

"About what?"

"If I caused it?"

Mammon sat nearby humming into Rance's ear, the justification for the deed. But in an agricultural environment, labor is short when needed and long when not needed. Buying hands for harvest and then moving them on would be a great advantage to the farmers. They wouldn't need to know all the gritty details. The deal would help him pay off the interest to investors.

"The farmers need help; the harvest is coming," Rance said in a trance like state.

"What does that mean?" Alyssa wrinkled up her nose at the odd statement. "Harvest is over. It's almost Christmas time again."

"You're right. Those were the same words I heard that fateful night."

Rance felt himself falling into depression. "It's money. It's always about money, and it was money that stole my Jenny!" Rance raged and left the office.

Alyssa watched Rance cross the street without looking. A car came near and stopped. Then he entered the courthouse.

Michael came out of his office. "Where's he going?"

"I don't know, but I think I know why."

"Why is that?"

"There may be a clue to Jenny Gale's disappearance."

Before long, Rance returned to the office without an explanation, and Alyssa didn't ask. She smiled and said hi.

He nodded in response and went straight to his office.

Alyssa rapped on his office door.

"Come in," he answered.

"Lunch time, I'm going home and probably won't come back unless you have something for me. Mom's cooking Christmas goodies today, and I'm going to help her."

"Just bring some back with you," Rance answered and waved Alyssa on her way.

Mammon kept blowing on Rance. Hoping he would be able to see him soon. His dad, Buster, saw the creature and told Rance. Stupid boy didn't believe. Mammon needed the human to see the beastly beauty in order to worship it. Mammon knew eventually Rance would believe and scream for relief, but for now, all Mammon could do was hang around and whisper in his ear. He would cave soon. Especially after his little sister became part of Matthew's product line for human slaves.

Mammon studied Rance. Sometimes his thoughts came through to Mammon, but not often. He had a secret that hid most of his thoughts from Mammon. But Mammon knew the greed in the man's heart would expose those secrets and make Rance a personal slave. He roared at Rance.

"I just came from the plant." Michael said as the two men entered Rance's office.

"What did you learn?"

"Just what you thought. They can't keep up."

"So, what are their plans?" Rance asked as he closed the files on his desk and put them back in the filing cabinet.

"Daniel, the plant manager, said the company building the tunnel sent out a crew to expand the plant."

"That sounds helpful."

"It does, except that crew is in town now."

"That should help business," Rance said, getting bored with the conversation.

"Did you look at the people at The Honey Tree's?" Michael asked.

"Not really, they look like workers," Rance commented.

Michael pulled the files from his briefcase and landed them on Rance's desk. "Look at this and see if you recognize any of them."

Rance opened the files, and the third picture he saw was the guy called Matt. The one wooing Alyssa. The picture was a mug shot. Every one of the men had been in prison. Some were released; others were escapees. All were working on building the new plant. "Whew, this isn't good."

"Not for this town, it was one of our own who set a bomb at the fertilizer plant. Just think what outside rebels can do with an electric plant."

"What do we do?" Rance asked Michael.

Michael slumped in the chair, and his tie was loosened. He ran his fingers over his chin. "I don't know. We have to pray."

Rance laughed at him. "That's your answer for everything."

Michael smiled and nodded. "It's the weapon of choice for our family. What's your weapon?"

"Money!" Rance answered.

Mammon roared.

14

A Breakfast Date

Behold the storm of the LORD has gone forth in wrath, even a whirling tempest; it will swirl down on the head of the wicked."
Jeremiah 23:19

WHEN MATT ENTERED the bustling Honey Tree with its bright lights, he groaned. Happy was not a good place for him, and smiling, laughing people inhabited this place. This could be both bad and good. The diners wouldn't see him nor what he planned to do. Or because his style didn't fit in here, everyone might remember him. There were no empty tables.

He turned toward his breakfast date, Alyssa Troye, "Do you want to wait for a table."

She didn't answer but walked toward an elderly couple Matt had noticed earlier. The woman rose to greet her with a smile and a hug.

Matt followed her, wary of the couple.

"Matt, this is my mom and dad," Alyssa said to him as she sat next to her daddy.

Matt gave a slight smile and nodded with a shy duck of the head. He slipped in beside Merilee.

"They aren't only my parents," Alyssa said, "they're like best friends."

Matt smiled at Alyssa then turned to speak to Merilee, "I'm sorry, my brain is like a static-filled radio. Who are you?"

"I'm her mother." Merilee pointed to Alyssa.

Matt had heard Alyssa introduce her parents, but he feigned the ignorance slump to gain some thinking time. This chance meeting threw his plans into disarray. He seriously considered waiting. However, that wasn't an option. The pressure to complete the plans weighed on him with the heaviness of a wet wool coat quickly shrinking around his neck.

Alyssa spoke up again. "She's actually more than a mother. She's like my doctor and my medicine. No matter what bothers me, Mother is always there to listen, to support and daddy's there to protect." Alyssa snuggled a little closer to her dad with a cautious move.

Matt could feel Buster's stare boring into his soul, searching for answers. He turned away from his gaze.

"When there's someone who cares, it's a fragment of heaven," Merilee said.

Matt groaned inside while forcing a pleasant smile on the outside.

Alyssa's dad leaned over and whispered in her ear. She smiled.

"The pastries are exceptional," Merilee said. She slipped something into Alyssa's hand.

Matt kept quiet, wanting this soirée to end. His work couldn't be completed until it did. Michelle brought Matt a menu.

"Coffee," Matt said to Michelle with a smile, but it wasn't returned.

Michelle's left cheek and eye were twitching. She chewed her bottom lip even though she held it in a tight grimace.

Buster looked at Matt. A twisted grin and bright sparkle in his eye held Michelle in a trance-like state.

"Michelle?" Buster called her name. She didn't answer. Instead she parted from their table as quickly as possible. Soon, another waitress came to serve Matt.

"Are you new?" Buster asked her. She looked at Buster and nodded, never completely raising her head.

Buster turned his attention toward Merilee, "I think we need to go."

Merilee agreed.

Once Buster and Merilee entered their car, Merilee sat behind the steering wheel, staring in the window of the restaurant. "Now I know why the Holy Spirit told us to eat breakfast out. "Matt sure had a strange effect on the waitresses."

Buster smiled and nodded.

"Did you give it to her?"

"I did, and you? Did you give her the message?"

"I did. She's in the Lord's hands now."

Merilee and Buster drove toward main street in silence and prayer.

After Michelle cleaned off the table, she gave Alyssa and Matt menus and a verbal list of specials.

Alyssa ordered the special while Matt stuck to pancakes and ham. "How dull, to come to a place with a French cook and order a West Texas staple," Alyssa mocked him.

He smiled at her and took her hands. "There's another West Texas staple I'm interested in besides pancakes and ham."

Alyssa couldn't help but blush a little. She ducked her head and let out a little giggle.

Mammon cooed into her ear.

Matt sighed. This won't take long. Then maybe I can get out of this dusty little town.

Patti delivered the food.

Alyssa thought it smelled wonderful.

Once she sat the plates down and ask if they needed anything else, she turned toward Alyssa and said, "I'm sorry to rush you, but your brother called. He needs you back in the office as soon as possible. Would you like for me to package your food?"

Alyssa smiled and thanked Patti. She rose from her seat to go pay. While she stood there, Patti whispered, "Be careful." She handed the receipt and packaged food to Alyssa. She glanced at Matt and could see him fuming. She thought she saw a little cloud of smoke floating in front of his face.

Once Alyssa arrived back at work, Michael called her into his office. She stood beside him waiting for a job assignment.

"Sit down," he said.

That was strange but she followed his orders. "Patti called when she saw you with that man."

"You mean Matt?"

"Yeah. Tell me how you ended up with him?"

"He came in and asked me to breakfast."

Michael leaned back in his chair and stared at her without speaking. Alyssa watched him and grew more uncomfortable with the quiet. She waited for an explanation for her presence in his office.

Before he said anything, Sharon came in. "Oh, thank goodness you're okay," she muttered and hugged her.

"You guys are making me nervous. What's going on? My dad instructs me to not get into the man's car, my mother hands me this newspaper article, and you two are acting . . . well weird."

"He works for *Dragon Wind Construction*," Sharon said.

"Yeah?" Alyssa swung her head back and forth between her two cousins, waiting for more details.

"He's dangerous," Sharon said.

"How do you know?" Alyssa heard her voice becoming hostile. "I think he's very nice. In fact, if you don't have anything more, I'm going back over there and finish my breakfast with my dining partner. You may not realize it, but I eat most of my meals alone. I take care of you two, but you seldom take care of me." She pointed to Michael and toward Rance's office.

She rose and headed back to *The Honey Tree*.

Mammon took his claw off her shoulder. His task succeeded. She jumped back into the game.

When she entered the restaurant, Matt sat there picking at his pancakes.

Alyssa slipped into the booth with him. He smiled and pushed a plate of pancakes toward her.

"Thank you. Sorry about the interruption," she huffed. "I don't know what's wrong with my family. They basically ignore me, and then when I find some company I enjoy, it seems they're all over me."

Matt didn't respond because his mind plotted her capture and sale. She would bring a pretty price for the monsters. Course she wouldn't see them as dragons, but he would. and he wanted to get his money and get out of town before any of her family missed her. While she continued to jabber about the mistreatment of her family, he plotted his next step.

"How would you like to take the day off and have a picnic? We could go motorcycle riding at the dunes."

"Do they let people do that anymore?" she asked.

"People who work there can."

"Oh, wow, I'd love to. I've heard my brother talk about how they use to play in the sand when he was a teen, but I never had the opportunity." She gave him a big, toothy grin.

"Well, now you do. We'll stop at the grocery store and pick up some beers."

"No, I don't want any, I'll just take some soda."

"And candy?"

"Well, of course. What good is a play date without candy?"

"Exactly." The word came out of Matt's mouth directed by Mammon.

When they arrived at the sand dunes in Matt's truck, Alyssa noticed there were no other people. "Are you sure we can run motorcycles out here?"

Matt gave her a slight nod and kept driving.

Alyssa turned and looked in the trailer Matt was pulling. She couldn't see anything in there. Wasn't there supposed to be a motorcycle in there? Her heart started beating a little faster. She felt a knot in her stomach. "Matt, did you bring a dune buggy?" she asked in a low voice.

He drove to the door of the tunnel. No one was guarding the door.

She put her hand on the door handle and attempted to open it. The door wouldn't open. She looked at Matt.

He flashed a big smile at her. "Don't worry sugar. There will be plenty people taking care of you."

With the statement, he stopped. She tried the door again, but it wouldn't open or unlock.

Matt got out and came to her side and opened the door. He extended his hand to her. She refused it. She sat in the truck. "I'll wait till you get the cycles out.

"Sugar bunch, there ain't no cycles, and this is not our playday, but you will be a plaything."

Alyssa felt sweat beading on her back and her throat closing down. *Why didn't I listen to my family?*

Mammon wrapped his tale around Alyssa. Matt grabbed her by the waist and carried her to the tunnel. A large red-haired man met them. Matt placed her on her feet. "How's this?" he growled at the man.

The man took Alyssa's hair in his meaty hand and used it to make her turn. She spat at him. He slapped her hard with his other hand, not letting go of her hair. He smiled at her and ran his finger over her lip where the trickle of blood seeped onto her chin. He took the finger with the blood to his mouth and licked it. "Humm, innocent blood, love it!"

Matt chuckled. "She's all yours. I'm outta here." He planted a hard kiss on Alyssa's mouth, and he too licked his own lips. "Yep, it's sweet all right." Matt returned to his truck. Before he left, he hollered at the big man, "Hey, Barley!"

The big man looked at Matt and groaned. He let his grip on Alyssa's head lighten. She felt the sting lesson. Without thinking, she yanked her head away from his hand, leaving a sizable chunk of her hair with him. She ran as hard as she could go. The big man yelled. Matt saw the commotion. He piled into his truck and took off at breakneck speed. The big man yelled at him and shook a fist in the air while he chased Alyssa.

Alyssa never ran so hard in her life. She didn't know where she was going or where she would hide. she only knew she had to get away. Rance had some awful pictures in his office, and her blood ran cold thinking about becoming one of the spectacles in those pictures. "Oh, God help me!" she kept saying.

A flash of light penetrated her eyes, causing her to close them. She kept running while waiting for the searing pain to leave. She heard the footsteps of the big man catching up to her. She smelled something, a strange smell. Then she heard a click and felt a movement under her foot. She kept running deeper and deeper into the tunnel and looked for a place to hide. Her lungs screamed in agony, begging for air and rest.

Then with the breath of a breeze, she found herself stepping into a bright, sunlit, forested landscape. With a pause in her running she twisted her head to look for the big red-haired man. Instead of the big man she saw the tunnel exit close and became part of the scenery. Still, she ran until she found a small cabin. She went inside and hid behind a bed.

Alyssa couldn't see or hear the big man. The only sound she could hear was her own body gasping for air. She took deep draws and willed her heart to stop racing. It took a while, but after a few minutes her breath came in normal rhythm. She didn't move for hours and fell asleep somewhere between overwhelming fear and total exhaustion.

When she awoke, the daylight gave way to encroaching darkness. She crawled up onto the bed. "Dear Lord, forgive me and help me." She prayed with great fervor before she fell into a deep restful sleep.

Mammon followed the runaway when she stepped into the speed zone. Her footprints revealed her direction, but now he stood in the middle of a forest looking at nothing. Even the footprints stopped. The beast shuddered. Soldiers from the Dragon Warrior's army must be nearby. He groaned and a blast of flames shot out of his nostrils. The breath fueled one of his largest blasts, but instead of burning the nearby forest, the flame fizzled within moments.

The monster slinked around, hoping to escape. The enemy held a powerful sword that would slash his scaly lithe body to shreds in a second. The dragon warriors had never spared a dragon since the day the dragons taunted the Warrior Himself as He hung on a cross. For three hours, they tortured the Christ, and when He died, they celebrated. The beast shuddered at the memory of the dragon warrior rising out of the tomb. Since that day, the dragons held no defense or protection from Him.

Mammon knew this little project called Alyssa Troye, belonged to a praying family, but the monster thought removing her would stop the prayers. A large bolt of lightning struck the ground near him. He had no choice. The prayers of her family continued and grew in strength. Several more bolts struck near him.

With each bolt, the dragon warrior soldiers came into view.

The powerful muscles in Mammon's long, slinky body rippled with fear. He lay his girth flat on the ground.

"Leave!" The Dragon Warrior Himself commanded.

Mammon had no choice but to obey.

15

The Depth of Depravity

They have gone deep in depravity as in the days of Gibeah: He will remember their iniquity; He will punish their sins.

Hosea 9:9

RANCE LIVED ALONE, which was both devastating and freeing. The new computer he installed in his bedroom met his needs—both in business and physical. He closed the spread sheet. Following Alyssa's instructions, he entered the world of cyberspace, where things were easy, assessable, private, and not real. He found a list of chat rooms and the titles of those that appealed to his primitive male drive. It didn't take long for someone with a funny—sounding but off-color name to invite him to a private chat. This time the title read, 'Scarlet Sugar.' He never knew who he was meeting, but he could easily leave if he didn't like this one.

After an hour of conversation with Scarlet Sugar, he felt a bit exhausted. This encounter proved to be unlike any other. Whoever was on the other side of this cyber date, knew how to tangle him into a hotbed of pleasure. Between her name and the words she typed on his screen, he could feel his own mind melding with hers. She had a way with words, and her descriptions of herself along with the things she liked to do, made Rance's body temperature rise into a heat of passion. He asked to meet with her again. She agreed. He turned off the computer, took a shower, and went to bed. However, sleep didn't come because he was thinking about Scarlet Sugar.

When sleep did come for a visit, he dreamed of this beautiful woman in her description. He couldn't see her full face, but it didn't matter, he felt comfortable in her dream presence. Her feminine presence drifted in the air with her shimmering robes flowing behind her naked body. He felt loved. She felt familiar both in his waking hours and in his sleeping hours.

The next morning, he took a shower. With the water running over his body, he wanted to stay there. The water washed away the guilt and shame for only a second. In that moment Rance promised himself he wouldn't do it again.

"Nice work, Mammon," Nisroch roared. "He's yours for sure."

Mammon released a small puff of smoke. "I do have one problem."

"What's that?" Nisroch asked.

"He can't see me."

Nisroch laughed at the green student. "Of course not. Can you not see the greatest scheme of devils in him?"

"What?" Mammon roared, losing his patience.

"He doesn't believe you really exist."

"He knows I do, he can hear me."

Nisroch swiped Mammon with his long tree-like tail. "You idiot!" Nisroch screamed.

Mammon kept quiet, but the smoke escaping his lips revealed his anger.

"The reason Rance even listens to you is because he doesn't think you exist."

Mammon calmed a bit before he asked his next question. "How does that work?"

"He doesn't believe in the spiritual realm where we live; he thinks his life is all there is."

"I don't understand?"

Nisroch roared with laughter. "That, young one, is the greatest trick of a dragon. Once you convince the wimpy human he is god over his own life, he will do whatever a dragon tells him."

"Because he thinks it's his idea." Mammon sat up on his haunches and roared. "Rance Troye is completely in my control."

Nisroch scowled, "Be careful. I'll keep him wallowing in arms of fantasy, and you'll control him. Do not underestimate the prayers of his family"

"Does the Holy One ignore their prayers? Otherwise, why would I still be around?"

"Excellent question."

"And the answer is? "

"Discover for yourself." Nisroch roared as he disappeared.

Mammon moaned. He didn't like this learn-as-you-go attitude, but he had no choice. He'd get that human under his control very soon.

16

The Hunt

Can a man hide himself in hiding places so I do not see him? Declares the Lord. "Do I not fill the heavens and the earth?" declares the Lord.

RANCE MUTTERED, "WHAT the heck are you up to, cuz?"

Michael rummaged through a shelf in the storage closet and pulled out a rifle.

"Are we going to war?" Rance asked with his brow furrowed.

"In a way . . . Alyssa's missing."

"What do you mean Alyssa's missing?" Rance puffed. His breath coming in short spurts. "I need more details." He reached into his desk drawer and pulled out a pistol.

"Never enter the enemy's territory unarmed. Here, you'll need this too." Michael handed Rance a pocket Bible.

Rance chuckled then sneered. "So, this is part of my armament?"

"You better believe it," Michael stated emphatically.

He was dead serious, so he took the Bible and dropped it into his pocket. He couldn't help making one more dig at his cousin.

"If we come across the enemy, are we going to whip out our Bibles and have a Bible study?"

Michael gently smiled at his younger and cocky cousin. "We might."

"What's the plan?" Rance fell into a more serious mode.

"We're going to the dunes. Most of the work goes on at night, and I want to see what's in those tunnels."

"Why? Do you think Alyssa is there? It's the government."

"Is it? We don't know anything about what's going on out there." Michael zipped up his duffle bag and slung it over his shoulder.

"What are you taking?" Rance. asked Michael staring into his empty bag.

"A change of clothes, food, water, flashlight . . . you know, all the usual emergency stuff." Michael pulled the door open. "You coming?"

Rance dropped his bag. He didn't have any of that stuff here.

"Bring it along," Michael said. "We'll stop at your house and let you pack."

He nodded and walked out the door. Once they were in the pickup, Rance opened the conversation. "I think you're falling for all the conspiracy talk going on around town."

"Maybe, but can you explain that stack of folders on your desk?" Michael referred to the files containing the pictures and details of missing residents of Church Creek Falls. "Maybe a conspiracy isn't so far off base."

Mammon slipped the diamond bracelet into Rance's bag. He stayed in the shadows between the human and dragon realms, so Michael wouldn't see. Mammon hated the trusting Christians. The Holy One would reveal their presence to them at times. Then other times, the Holy One would let the dragons play the human fools. Dragons simply couldn't understand The Holy One.

"You think we really need these guns?" Rance asked while packing his emergency bag.

"I pray we don't, but it's best to be armed when you think you're facing an enemy."

Rance took a deep breath, "Cuz, I hope you're wrong, Alyssa's not missing. She just wasn't at the office. She's an independent young lady who had something to do more important than work," Rance mused.

Michael smirked at the comment. "She was last seen with Matt."

Rance gulped. "That's why you are worried."

Michael nodded.

Rance turned and looked out the window. His chest hurt. He tried sitting up straighter. It helped some, but the pain in his chest came from the fear in his heart.

Michael pointed to the hospital parking lot. "We've got to pick up one more warrior."

Rance saw Barbara waiting, holding her own bag. He smiled at the sight of his older sister, five years his senior. She looked so . . . matronly. "Why is she going?" Rance felt relief to have her with them, but he also feared for her.

"She's our medical team."

"You must have been a Boy Scout because you're definitely prepared," Rance teased.

Michael smiled. "No, just a soldier. Once trained as a soldier, you always think like one."

Mammon watched the two armed men leave the hospital. He would get to the dunes before them and warn his servants. That is, if they would listen. Mammon hated being ignored, and these army dudes were good at ignoring, except for their leader. He was the only one benefiting from all this cloak and dagger stuff. He didn't know all the details, but he did know it made his bank account fat. The rest of the crew didn't seem to care about wealth; their thing was honor. That is a lot harder to manipulate. Honor knows truth and stands firm even in the face of extreme danger or extreme bribes. Mammon decided to watch this game play out instead of interfering.

Zay paced across the living room floor. Marcy sat on the couch with little Seth on her lap. She was reading him a story. Zay looked out the window and put a hand over his chest, which was tight from the inside.

Something, somewhere twisted out of place in the universe. Where could Alyssa be? Michael had called for prayer about 9:30 that morning. He said Alyssa wasn't at work, but her purse, keys, and sweater were all present.

"Have you talked to Rance today?" Zay asked Marcy.

She shook her head. "I spoke to Barbara and said she'd be out of her office all day."

"Where was she going?"

"Said she had to care for a patient."

Zay rubbed his chest.

The phone rang.

Zay answered, "Hello, Dad."

"Hi, son. Have you talked to Rance or Michael today?"

"No, what about you?"

"Something's going on, I just don't know what, nor do I know what to do," Buster said and groaned.

"You hurtin'?" Zay asked.

"Yeah, but not like normal. It's . . . it's a dragon hurt."

"I know, Dad, I feel it too. I'll go over to Rance's house. In the meantime, you call Sharon. Somehow, I think Michael may be with Rance."

"Hey guys, you goin' huntin?" Zay asked his brother and cousin when he drove up in front of their office.

Rance laughed, "And what brought you out at this late hour?"

"You did."

"You feel it?" Michael asked Zay.

"Yeah."

"What are you guys talking about?" Rance asked.

Michael and Zay looked at each other and then turned to Rance.

"Just trust us," Zay answered.

"Alyssa came to work, left, and we can't find her," Rance filled his brother in on their activities. "Michael seems to think she's at the tunnels."

At the mention of the tunnels, Zay raised his head with wide eyes. "You got another one of those rifles?" he asked Michael.

Rance, Zay, and Michael walked into the compound with no opposition.

Barbara followed a few steps behind, inspecting every inch of their pathway and marking a path with crumbs from the scones she'd brought. The chamber was huge with glistening glass-like walls. Several people in lab coats, carrying stacks of papers or small equipment were bustling about. They went from one door to another. Each time they opened a door, a series of beeps and whistles came from the room with a glimpse of flashing lights. Inside, they caught a glimpse of others dressed in jumpsuits or overalls.

The workers followed the tunnel track without ever going into a room. Except for one, who had a ring of keys hanging from his belt. He opened a door in the corridor.

Michael, Rance, and Zay crept closer and peered inside. Zay's heart jumped into his throat. Inside the room was a row of cells. The man opened one of the cells and removed a young woman. She was obviously sleepy or drugged. She was dressed in a similar jumpsuit, with her long hair tied back. Her eyes were blank, staring at nothing. The man in the jumpsuit brought her to the door near where Michael, Rance and Zay pasted themselves against a wall behind a narrow girder.

A uniformed and armed man stepped up and took the girl. He walked her to a golf cart type of car, and they took off into the tunnels. In a few seconds, the armed guard returned with an empty cart.

He spotted Michael. "I thought I told you guys to guard the Southern tunnel," he barked.

Michael nodded and the three men headed into the Southern tunnel. That is, they headed the direction the uniformed man pointed. Zay hoped it was south.

"Be careful and don't step into the forbidden zone," the guard called to them with his back to them.

"I thought this place would be heavily guarded," Michael said quietly. "I don't think they even know their own people."

"I just hope we recognize the forbidden zone," Zay said as he swerved his head from side to side.

With no one to stop them, the men plunged into the tunnel marked with a large SW.

"Here we go guys," Zay whispered with a trembling voice.

The opening of the tunnel took Zay's breath away.

"You could drive a 747 plane through here," Rance said.

"That may be the idea," Michael said, pointing to their right. "Look over there."

Zay followed Michael's line of sight and there sat three planes with room to drive cars around them.

"Now I know why they wanted to be out here," Michael added.

"Why?" Zay pondered.

"Space. We have plenty of it, and we are four-thousand feet above sea level. They can build a city down here, and no one would ever know it."

"I think they have . . . look more doors and corridors," Zay said as he approached a door with a window and peered inside. "It's a lab! If they have their own, why do they bring things to my lab?"

A noise came from behind them. They all froze and leaned against the glazed wall. The noise came from a couple older gentlemen talking.

Zay tried to understand what they said. He was the closest to them, but he could only pick up a few words: *soon, time*, and *money*. Out of context, the words held no meaning.

After a few minutes of inspection, the three decided to return. On the walk out of the tunnel, they came to the realization that they may have walked a couple miles.

"Did you notice the room with bunks in it?" Michael asked.

"Yeah," Rance answered. "But I figure since there isn't much housing in Church Creek Falls, they built their own housing for their staff. I bet they have a cafeteria too."

"Well, that explains why they need so much electricity," Zay said. "It's a small city."

The three men stepped out into the sunlight and gasped.

Zay was the last one out. As he raised his head he heard a slurping noise. He twisted his head toward the noise in time to see the exit of the tunnel close. "Guys!" he said to Rance and Michael.

"Yeah," Rance answered.

"Look." Zay pointed to the location where they'd emerged from the tunnels. The tunnel opening was gone. From this viewpoint there appeared to be an abandoned storage barn with rusty barrels scattered around. Tall grass and mesquite trees grew between the barrels as if they'd been there for years.

"Where are we?" Zay muttered, and the other two looked around at the hills and trees surrounding them.

"I don't know where we are, but I know where we aren't," Rance stammered.

"We're not in Kansas anymore." Michael mocked, referencing the movie line from *The Wizard of Oz*.

"We're not even in Church Creek Falls," Zay added with a more serious tone. He pointed to a street sign and exclaimed, "New Mexico!"

"Huh?" Rance said. "How'd we get here?"

"The bigger question is how do we get back? And where's Barbara? She was behind us." Michael started walking toward the highway. "I guess we'll now be added to that stack of missing persons." He beckoned to Zay and Michael. "Come on, guys, it may be a mirage, but it looks like a building in the distance. I think Barbara's on her own."

"Where did we lose it? I thought we were going in a straight line," Zay said, shivering.

"We were." Michael kept looking around. "Something must have curved so slightly we didn't notice, but hey, guys. we can get back. This still does not answer our questions about where the people went."

"What's going on here?" Rance asked.

Zay shook his head. This was looking more like a movie than real life.

Mammon howled at the situation. Their confusion delighted the monster.

Barbara stared into the small glass window of one of the rooms. When she looked up, the guys were well ahead of her. She ran toward them, still dropping her breadcrumbs. Suddenly, they disappeared into a fog. She stood there for a few minutes wondering what to do. A noise sounded behind her. Looking for a place to hide, she slipped inside the space of a larger steel girder and listened as a group of people approached. Five of them in lab coats, two in military-type dress.

"Have you ever done it?" One of the military men laughed.

"Yeah, it's a kick," the other responded.

The people passed Barbara, and before her eyes, they disappeared. There were no other people around.

Barbara looked for her breadcrumbs and followed them out of the tunnel. She rushed back to the hospital.

"Daniel, I've got to talk to you!" she said, striding up to him where he stood filling out a patient chart.

"I've got a pretty full schedule."

"Cancel it. I think my brothers and cousin just joined the list of missing people."

17

The Cabin in the Woods

*I will give them a heart to know Me, for I am the Lord, and they will be
My people, and I will be their God, for they will return to Me with their
whole heart.*

Jeremiah 24:7

AMAZING TO HAVE one's heart cut out and feel
no pain. Alyssa pulled her shirt up and looked at her
chest. "I'm a care bear!" she exclaimed while looking at
the clumsy bright-pink heart sewn into her chest. She
touched it with her finger. The heart was skin. She
looked for a mirror but couldn't find one. She could feel
herself floating upward and downward rather than
walking side to side.

The weightlessness caused her stomach to roil. She
swallowed, wishing her stomach to cooperate. It didn't.
A guttural reflux opened her mouth to let the contents
of her stomach out. Nonetheless, that didn't happen.
Instead, she woke up with sweat beads on her forehead.

Alyssa raised herself. Moonlight mopped the floor
and allowed her to see the wooden planks. Her gaze
followed them to the stacked log walls. "A log cabin?"

"Good observation," a strange voice spoke from behind her.

"Where I am?" she asked the voice while moving her head from side to side to find a body to belong to the voice.

The velvet words coming from the baritone voice both soothed and scared her.

"Who are you?" she asked.

"I'm called Davis," the voice spoke.

Then she saw the muscular form of a man dressed in army fatigues walking toward her. He pulled up a chair opposite her and sat down. "I'm your protector."

"From what?" she stammered, waiting for her eyes to adjust to the semi-darkness.

"Evil."

With that word, Alyssa's last memory came into focus and she startled and abruptly stood. "A man is chasing me." She ran to the window and looked out.

"You're safe here."

"Yeah? Where's *here?* And who are you, and how do I know I can trust you?"

"Faith," Davis answered her.

"Faith?" She wrinkled her brow and turned toward him. "In you?"

"No, in your Father. I am his messenger," Davis answered.

"Daddy? Where is he?" Hope filled her spirit like clear water on a hot day.

"Your other Father."

"I don't know him. He was never found after the bombing of my hometown," Alyssa stated, becoming a bit agitated.

"Still wrong Father."

"You talk in riddles." Alyssa stomped to the door and put her hand on the knob.

"I suggest you stay here with me. If you go out there, you will be out of the protection of your father."

Alyssa stopped. "I don't understand. Who are you talking about?"

"Your heavenly father," David said while letting his chin drop to his chest and crossing his hands in front of him.

"God? Is that who you are talking about?"

David nodded. "I do not speak of Him with such irreverence, but He is the Holy One."

Alyssa walked over toward Davis. She extended her hand and touched him. "No way. You're real."

"Of course, I'm real."

"What do you want from me?" Alyssa backed away from him.

Davis shrugged his shoulders. "I want or need nothing from you. I am here to protect you."

"From what?" Alyssa raised her arms in the air and screamed.

"Out there." Davis pointed beyond the door, "they are after you to destroy your family. I am sent here by your family's prayers, especially your daddy," he reported with a kind glow in his face.

"You know my daddy?" Alyssa calmed a bit.

"All his life. I have protected him."

"Then why does he suffer so much pain?" Alyssa accused Davis.

"This world is filled with pain of all kinds, but the worse pain is reserved for those children of the Holy One."

Alyssa didn't argue. Her daddy was a strong, faithful Christian, and she heard the stories of her grandfather all her life.

"Okay, I gather you're my guardian angel." Alyssa sat down on the sofa next to Davis.

He smiled at her and nodded. "For your family."

"How can I get back home?" she asked him

"For now, you are to stay here where you are safe. The Father is working with your brothers, sister, and cousin."

"Rance doesn't know the Holy One." Alyssa pleaded.

"I know, that is why you are to stay here, but you will have your own battles to fight."

Alyssa rose from her seat and opened the front door.

"Don't!" Davis yelled. It was too late.

Alyssa stood on the front porch of a cabin staring into the grisly face of Mammon. She screamed and ran back inside.

"What . . . the monster's out there."

"Yes, and that is why you must stay here in the safety of your father and in your family's prayers."

"I don't understand." Alyssa wanted an explanation.

"It's not yours to understand. It is yours to trust."

18
Running

I will make them a terror and an evil for all the kingdoms of the earth, as a reproach and a proverb, a taunt and a curse in all places where I will scatter them.
Jeremiah 24:9

JENNIFER FOLLOWED PEGGY. They strolled past bright neon lights in strange shapes. Men in dark vans with blackened windows drove by them slowly. Peggy looked up and saw a strange, double-sided barber shop pole.

A hunkered Korean man pulled up beside them and in broken English said, "Are you Russian?"

Peggy and Jennifer both said no at the same time.

He asked them three more times.

Finally, Peggy turned toward him and yelled, "No, we are Americans!"

"Where are we going?" Jennifer asked after the third block of strange sights and smells.

"I'm looking for shelter."

"I don't like it here." Jennifer moaned. "Look, those women in the windows are alive, but they look like dolls."

Peggy ducked her head, "We gotta get out of here."

"How?"

Peggy didn't answer Jennifer but took her hand and quickened their pace through the streets filled with lights and people. The street food smells awakened a new sensation in both of them—hunger. They watched the diners they passed for discarded, uneaten food and found a few tidbits along the way.

A quick grab from the trash can and back to their fast walk. Neither of them knew the language, the customs, or how to get out of this city. It seemed to go on forever. The crowded streets gave them cover, and their hats covered their round blue eyes and light European hair.

Jennifer stumbled and fell, scrapping her knee on the asphalt. "Ow!" she cried.

Peggy stopped and offered some momentary comfort before getting her back on her feet. "We can't dawdle."

"Do you know where we're going?"

"No, I'm looking. There!" Peggy pointed to a truck with a canvas cover on the back.

"It looks military."

"Yeah, the question is whether it's friendly."

Without discussing or answering their questions, the two girls climbed up into the truck. No furnishings were there except benches on either side of the truck bed.

"Look," Jennifer whispered loudly as she held up some wool blankets.

Peggy smiled.

Jennifer whispered a prayer of thanks.

Once the girls fashioned a makeshift cot, Peggy's stomach growled. She sat up and searched the truck.

"What are you doing?" Jennifer asked.

"If there are blankets, maybe there's some food."

Jennifer joined her in the search. A large box rested under the bench seat. She pulled the box out, opened it, and gasped.

Peggy came beside her. "Rations!"

The girls were awakened by the sweet sounds of American English. They listened.

"What's the assignment?" one man said outside the truck.

"We pick up the poor saps scalped by the juicy bars last night," another man answered.

The men climbed into the truck and started the engine.

"Do we stay?" Jennifer asked Peggy.

"Stay for now."

At the first stop, three weary young boys crawled into the back of the truck. Their heads in their chests, they didn't even see Jennifer and Peggy huddled under the wool blanket. The girls kept quiet and listened to them.

One man worked his hands while moaning, "What did I do?"

Another put his head between his knees and groaned in agony.

Yet, another held his head in his hand and wept.

In all, the truck picked up fifteen boys. None of them noticed the girls. All smelled of alcohol, cheap perfume, and shame.

The truck pulled into the gate of an American army base. Jennifer gazed at the gate from the back of the truck. The words across the top of the gate were backwards. Y E S A C.

"Yes sac?" she whispered to Peggy and pointed to the letters.

Peggy smirked at Jennifer. "We are behind the letters, they're backward."

"Casey."

"Sounds better than Yes ac, but still don't know where we are." Peggy squeezed Jennifer's hand, "Still it's better than where we've been."

19
Return

Turn now everyone from his evil way and from the evil of your deeds, and dwell on the land which the Lord has given to you and your forefathers forever and ever; and do not go after other gods to serve them and to worship them, and do not provoke Me to anger with the work of your h ands, and I will do you no harm."

Jeremiah 25: 5-6

MICHAEL PONDERED THE Santa Fe experience daily. The three men had rented a car and returned home the same day they stepped into a New Mexico forest. How was it that a simple thought could bring up long-buried emotions and stir what was thought to be settled? All the counseling and group meetings taught him to look forward and let the past alone.

How can I ignore this past when it's the way forward? The event wrapped him up in the same missions plotted out of an evil playbook—just like the lash and rip he experienced in Vietnam. He sighed and leaned his head back on his chair. He felt the familiar trickle down his cheek. Every time he recalled his experiences in Vietnam, the tears came involuntarily. How could an event settled long ago stir up emotions as if it just happened?

The Santa Fe experience with his cousins reminded him of the games played in the field of battle—games designed to dehumanize, destabilize, and antagonize.

As in Vietnam, the enemy appeared beguiling, bewitching, and peculiar. A dragon or a child, or an old hump-backed woman came to destroy. They appeared as genuine and convincing innocence. As they drew closer, whatever the image of the enemy, it would spread its treacherous wingspread over us with a vileness of heart intent upon shedding blood in great quantities. The deception began with the sound of breaking glass which shocked and paralyzed this huddle of young kids standing in unknown territory battling what they couldn't see but could only feel. The horror disturbed the mind and the emotions with a permanent wound and never-healing scar. The ambush, although expected, caused phenomenal devastation beyond repair or description.

How does one operate on a business level when the mind is bleeding with emotions that cannot be explained or healed? Michael signed the contract with the military to build the underground base near Church Creek Falls. As the legal representative of the city council, he fulfilled his duty by carrying out the paperwork of the counsel. In reality, Michael knew nothing about the activity taking place outside the city limits. He pulled out his copy of the contract.

Dragon Wind Contracting Company from Santa Fe New Mexico purchased the land. Once the company took the deed to the land, the city collected the check and relinquished any rights or input to the use of the land. *The Dragon Wind Contracting* Company dealt with the military or the purveyors of the underground city and its anomalies.

Michael bolted out of his chair and began pacing. A habit he picked up from Zay. Maybe the answers he wanted could be found in the contracting company. He needed to know about them. He needed to know how he and his cousins walked for thirty minutes and landed in Santa Fe? The city where the contracting company listed as home base. There had to be a connection.

Michael exited his office and stood in front of Rance. "Those tunnels hold the secret to Alyssa's location," he ranted. Do you have a phone number for *Dragon Wind Contracting* in New Mexico?"

"Of course." Rance sat at his computer and began typing. Michael took it as a hint he wanted to do some work and left.

After a few minutes, Rance found Michael at his desk and handed him a few sheets of paper. "Here's all I could find on Dragon Wind."

"Where did you get this?" Michael asked while perusing the papers.

"From the Internet." Rance paused at the sound of the copy machine whirring into action. "Here comes some more."

Michael didn't understand. "Any information about Alyssa on that thing?"

Rance nudged his shoulder with an open palm. "We'll find her."

Michael grabbed the first few pages as the printer spewed them out. His mouth fell open. When the printer finished, he took the pages to his office and shut the door. He stared at the words and pictures, having seen these pictures before. The passage of time didn't erase his memory.

He moaned as the picture in front of him came to life from that fateful night he and Paps were captured by the Vietcong. They shivered in the cold of the night, but the fear of approaching torture caused their bodies to shake uncontrollably. Then without any rhyme or reason, the Vietcong left them. He and Paps ran from a Vietcong ambush.

He sat back in his chair and said, "No way!" Then he looked up and said, "Lord, what's going on?

Michael knew God answered prayers in many ways, and the most prevalent way would be through the words of His book. Michael picked up his Bible and read. *"For thus says the LORD: Behold, I will make you a terror to yourself and to all your friends. They shall fall by the sword of their enemies while you look on. And I will give all Judah into the hand of the king of Babylon. He shall carry them captive to Babylon and shall strike them down with the sword."*

The passage from Jeremiah chapter twenty referred to the man named Pashur, who locked Jeremiah in stocks for a day. When Pashur released Jeremiah, he made that statement to him, and Michael thought about it. *A terror to yourself and all your friends.* Perhaps the message for Michael meant that Mr. Long Nguyen, the owner of Dragon Wind Construction, who had held him prisoner in Vietnam, would become a terror to the residents of Church Creek Falls. If so, what did the rest of the passage mean to his community? Fall by the sword of their enemies and give in to the hand of the king of Babylon as captives.

"Oh!" Michael held his head and groaned. "Lord, have I sold my neighbors into a horrible plight?" He raised his head and looked at the stack of folders on his credenza. The stack Alyssa pulled regarding the missing persons. He pulled one of the files from the stack and opened it. He stared at the words on the newspaper ad.

Three Teens Disappear. The bold headline pulled Michael into the story. Another involuntary groan escaped his lips when he looked at the date. He looked at the Dragon Wind contract. The teens disappeared the day after the signing. He looked at all twenty-three folders. All had disappeared within the month after signing, including Jennifer and Peggy.

"What's the connection, Lord? Help me. This puzzle makes no sense." Michael spoke out loud as he perused the files.

"Michael?" Rance asked with timidity as he entered Michael's office.

"Come on in. Tell me about how you obtained this information about Dragon Wind?"

"I got it from the Internet," he answered.

"What's that?" Michael asked. He attempted to explain Windows 3.1 and how to access information through it.

"That's going to be helpful," he said when Rance finished the lesson. "Thanks."

Rance pursed his lips and went back to his office. He tried all the things Alyssa had taught him about the Internet. He typed in words he pulled from his magazines. In an instant, a story flashed across his screen in all its erotic detail and pictures. Before he could sit back and take in the calming elixir of beautiful women, Michael burst through the door. He tried to sit up and hide the flush in his face and the screen on his desk. He couldn't operate the machine fast enough.

"Bounce your eyes," Michael said as he reached over and turned off the screen.

Rance knew the code for 'look away.' Michael had stopped addressing Rance's pornography addiction anymore.

Michael shuddered. "I hate those things."

"What things?" Rance asked as he regained some of his composure and harnessed his mental images.

"Dragons!"

"Where? I didn't see a dragon." Rance looked around the room.

"On the screen, there was a green dragon icon on the screen." Michael pointed to the small picture.

Rance searched for a dragon on the screen but didn't see it.

"Look at this." Michael handed the papers to Rance.

"Do you know this guy?" Rance asked, looking for an explanation for Michael's heavy breathing and pale expression.

"I did."

"Where?" Rance asked, thumbing through the information.

"Remember when I told you about Paps and me seeing Barbara in a vision?"

"Yeah, I remember . . . crazy."

"Crazier is that this is one of the guys who held us prisoner, ready to torture us to death. That is picture of their leader."

Rance looked at Michael with furrowed brow. "What do you think it means?"

"We just signed a multi-million-dollar contract with this guy, and I find out he—" Michael stopped when his throat grew tight and the words wouldn't come.

"It sounds like you think we signed a deal with the devil." Rance smiled at Michael.

Michael nodded and croaked out the words, "We did! And now the devil has Alyssa."

He pointed to the files of missing persons. "Look at the dates."

Rance's face turned paler with each of the files. When he reached Jennifer's file, he burst out, "No! No!"

"What are you going to do?" Rance asked as Michael stroked his chin and paced.

Michael looked at Rance with a blank expression, and then he spoke with authority. "I'm going back to Santa Fe, and you're coming with me."

"Why?"

"I think it has something to do with our missing neighbors."

20
Change

Moreover, I will take from them the voice of joy and the voice of gladness, the voice of the bridegroom and the voice of the bride, the sound of the millstones and the light of the lamp. This whole land will be a desolation and a horror, and these nations will serve the king of Babylon seventy years.

Jeremiah 25:10-11

JENNIFER APPRAISED HERSELF in the mirror. She looked like her former self. *If only my heart remained the same as my face.* Their host called herself "The Mom." She didn't know her very well and still remained cautious. Being fooled once makes a person cynical. Walking by large fish tank filled with strange looking fish, Jennifer moved closer to the opposite wall. She felt a slight touch on her shoulder and turned to see Peggy.

"Where are we?" she whispered.

Peggy shrugged her shoulders and put her index finger to her lips.

Jennifer nodded.

They continued down the bleak green prison walls toward the only opening they could see. They crossed a threshold from dark to bright, and it wasn't light. The room looked like an explosion in a paint factory. Splashes of color thrown onto a dark blue wall gave the room a psychedelic appearance.

Jennifer frantically attempted to take in air filled with incense.

They both turned to leave. A voice called to them. Neither of them stopped.

Jennifer had to escape the incense-filled room, and the need for pure air overcame her fear of disobedience.

She headed toward a heavy door with Peggy close behind. Once they reached the door, they slammed their bodies into the bar across the door, and it gave way into the bright sunlight. The girls scrunched their eyes at the light but kept going. They could hear footfalls behind them.

Their eyes adjusted to the sunlight. Jennifer wanted to stop and enjoy the warmth of the sun on her face. It had been . . . she didn't know how long since she'd seen sunlight and felt its warmth. Even if they were recaptured, this experience would be worth any beating that would follow.

Peggy stepped up beside her, grabbed her arm, and pulled her along into an alleyway. The footsteps behind them were gone. Peggy dared to take a peek from behind the building and saw nothing.

"I think they let us go?" she said with incredulity.

Jennifer slid down the wall and took in a big breath of fresh air. "What now?"

"I think we are still on the army base."

"What was all that about back there?" Jennifer pointed. "What about that Mom freak?"

Peggy laughed at her description of the middle-aged woman with the long stringy hair and housecoat-looking dress called a mu-mu. "I think she's on drugs."

"Seriously?" Jennifer asked.

"It's hard to say, but one thing I know for sure."

"What's that?"

"She's not American."

"Do you think she's Korean?" Jennifer asked.

"No, Philippino."

"Why?"

"I spoke to one of the other girls last night. She's Philippino. She said they are the juicy girls."

"What's that?"

"Girls that came here to find better jobs. A kind man offers to pay their passage, and they can work for him to pay for it. Once they get here, they work in the juicy bars, selling drinks to American soldiers."

"Sounds like the soldiers are the losers."

"Yeah, I think you're right."

"What happens to them after they get their passage paid?"

Peggy shook her head. "It sounded like they don't ever get it paid off. Like credit card interest."

"You think that's what we'll be doing?"

Once Jennifer settled into her clean, private room with a real bed, bathroom, chair, television, and desk, she didn't know what to do. She needed Peggy. She ran into the hall crying and shouting for her.

The door next to Jennifer's door opened, and Peggy came out and wrapped her arms around Jennifer. "Come in. You can stay with me." Peggy didn't ask what was wrong. She didn't have to; she was there the day Jennifer's innocence and her mind was stolen. As had been their custom, Jennifer curled up against Peggy like a child against her mother.

With a greater sense of safety, her breathing dropped into the steady rhythm of sleep. Peggy rose from the bed and covered her friend. She kissed her on the cheek. Then she went to the desk and sat in front of it. She sighed and whispered into the air, "I'm as damaged as she is. Her need for me keeps me going. What will I do without her?"

21

Attacked

They keep saying to those who despise Me, The Lord has said, "You will have peace." And as for everyone who walks in the stubbornness of his own heart, they say, 'calamity will not come upon you.
Jeremiah 23:17

THE DARKNESS SLINKED in front of Rance. He jumped before realizing a black cat sat on the hood of his truck, staring at him with super night vision. *This must be how a mouse feels.* Whap! The cat hit the windshield as it pounced without warning. The glass startled the cat as much as the cat startled Rance. The disappointed yowl rent the air with a more frightful sound than a shotgun. Rance took a deep breath and hissed back at the cat. It ran away.

This all-night stakeout produced nothing. The one tunnel opening found in the dunes remained as undisturbed in the twilight of morning as it had in the dusk of dawn. Rance yawned. His surveillance to discover what was going in and out of that tunnel entered its tenth hour. He wasn't sure he remained awake the full ten hours, but the one thing he did know, nothing was happening here. It wasn't even guarded. But then if Alyssa was in there—

He stopped his thought, not wanting to think about where it might lead.

Mammon hunched near the truck, feeding fear into Rance's mind. He started with the form of a cat. He knew the glass would stop him from attacking Rance, but it wouldn't stop the injection of fear into the grimy human's stupid brain. The monster could feel the rapid heart rate jump at the cat's attack, but its continuing racing tasted so delicious to Mammon. Rance's fear for Alyssa could be used to compound his lust for more of Mammon's girls. Mammon let the cat impression fade, hoping Rance would see his true form.

Rance watched the sun light up the entrance to the tunnel. The bright green door remained shut. "I wonder if I should try to go in," he asked himself.

Rance's mind remained blank as he stared at the door for the next ninety seconds. He shook his head, sat up in the seat, and drove off.

Mammon roared but noticed no increase in Rance's heart rate, neither did he display fear or any thoughts. "Stupid human!" Mammon growled.

After showering and shaving and getting dressed, Rance returned to the office. He pasted on a business face as he pushed the door open.

Mammon followed him, annoyed that the human still couldn't see him.

Michael saw the creature enter the office behind Rance.

Once Rance closed his door, Michael confronted the monster, "What do you want?"

"Get outta my way!" The monster growled and pushed Michael aside.

Michael regained his balance and headed for Rance's door. He stood there and looked straight into the smoky green hate-filled eyes of the grizzly monster and shouted, "The Lord will protect him from your evil!"

Mammon stopped at the words from Scripture. He released a curtain of smoke from his mouth as he huffed and countered Michael's sword thrust with, "In the mouth of the foolish is a rod for his back."

Michael smirked at the monster as he finished the verse from Proverbs. "But the lips of the wise will protect them."

Mammon opened his maw and roared. "You do know your precious Alyssa belongs to me now, don't you?"

The words tormented Michael, but he stood his ground. "She belongs to the Lord!" Michael retorted with fear creeping into his heart and using his own words. His sword the Spirit of God fell limp in his mouth.

Mammon grew stronger as Michael's sword blows lessened. The monster was slightly wounded, but it weakened Michael enough with the threat of capturing Alyssa, it was able to walk around Michael into Rance's office through the closed door.

It saw the rancid pictures flashing on the computer screen and the dullard look on Rance's face. The monster wrapped a long serpentine neck around Michael. "At least it didn't have any effect on him," The monster mocked.

Michael searches for Words from Scripture to slash the monster, but his mind couldn't grasp any of his stored Bible knowledge. *But you said, Lord, you would give me words when I needed them.*

"Wielding the sword of the spirit against a dragon has to be the work of the Spirit," the still small voice said inside him.

"Then help me," Michael whispered with fear creeping into his heart.

The voice answered, "Do you believe?"

"Yes," Michael answered. "But right now, I need help with my belief. The monster is too big. I can't fight it."

Silence hung over Michael's head, and his heart trembled with the thought of facing the monster with no weapon.

Then the still small voice quoted the Master from the book of Luke. "This kind of dragon only comes out with much prayer and fasting."

Michael fell to his knees. "Yes, my Lord," he whispered.

Mammon heard the words of obedience and turned to Michael, and with a hefty roar he bellowed, "That's more like it, you poor wretched creature. Bow to me!"

Michael opened his mouth to argue, but nothing came. "Don't argue with evil," the still small voice said.

Michael stood and walked out of Rance's office. Before he left, he turned and took one last look at Rance. The monster confidently wrapped his vile scaly body around Rance.

Rance smiled a lecherous smile as the picture of a female body slowly filled the screen. The chat line below it read, "Would you like to meet and have a real date?"

Rance jumped and turned the computer off.

Mammon fell to the ground. "What the heck happened?" he growled.

Rance stood and grabbed his coat. He was breathing hard. When he slammed his office door, Michael still sat in the waiting room. He saw Rance's red face.

"Rance, what's wrong?" H, stood and went toward him.

He stopped and looked at Michael. He put his head in the palms of his hands and ran them over his head. "I need help." Rance sat in a chair with his head ducked and tears streaming down his face.

"Rance," Michael said and sat beside him.

"I need help." Rance repeated.

"What kind of help?" Michael said.

"I've got to find her," Rance said through sobs.

Michael understood.

Mammon picked himself up off the floor and snorted.

"Not until I'm ready for you to find her, you big hunk of blubber," Mammon said.

Rance batted the air with his hand and looked around his head.

Michael saw the beast breathing his vile epitaphs on Rance.

When Michael heard Mammon's insult, he turned toward him and with a stern face and bolstered heart, he said, "This day the Lord will deliver you up into my hands, and I will strike you down and remove your head from you."

Mammon laughed at the words. "That was David talking to Goliath."

"The words of the Scripture remain true no matter what the circumstances. It may not be today, but you will be defeated."

Mammon appeared to shrink a little. But it would not be today. He roared and blew a flame over Rance's head.

"For the battle is the Lords, and He will give you into our hands." Michael saw the flame and shouted the words aloud in the foyer of the office. He heard a loud, pitiful roar and knew then his sword—the Word of God—had pierced the dragon, Mammon. In an instant Mammon stood in front of Michael's desk with a trickle of blood coming from the corner of his mouth.

"You horrid human!" The monster roared in Michael's face.

"No, I'm a redeemed human." Michael stood.

"You may be redeemed, but you are still weak flesh that can be devoured, and I think I shall start right now." Mammon grabbed Michael's throat with a clawed limb.

Michael gagged as the claws dug into his neck, and the grip of the claw strangled the air from his lungs. His tongue grew large inside his mouth, and he opened his mouth only to taste the copper stench of his own blood and the slaughterhouse smell of the monster breathing on him. Michael couldn't speak, but in his mind, he reminded himself, "The monster can't kill me."

The monster laughed and said, "You're right, but I can make you wish you were dead."

Michael could feel the grip of the clawed limb lifting his feet off the ground. "You've been nothing but trouble for us." The monster roared.

Michael could feel the hate scorching his body. "Lord, I could use some help." Michael thrashed his feet in the air, looking for a foothold.

At that moment Sharon came into the office and saw Michael dangling in the air, red-faced. She screamed.

The monster dropped Michael into a chair. He grabbed his throat.

"What happened?" Sharon ran toward Michael. She started undoing his tie and unbuttoning his shirt.

Michael gasped for air.

Sharon poured a cup of water then glanced at Rance. He was staring at the floor, oblivious to the drama playing out before him. He kept muttering, "I gotta find her."

When Sharon handed the water to Michael, he gulped it in big, deep swallows. Then he handed her his large mug and nodded. He still couldn't speak.

Rance finally heard the commotion from the other side of foyer. He saw Sharon fretting over Michael. "He okay?" He asked as he approached them. "Is he having a heart attack?"

"I don't know, but something is wrong."

Rance called the hospital and asked them to send an ambulance.

Michael could feel his body coming back to life. He looked at Rance and said one word, "Money!"

"What?"

Michael nodded, knowing his word didn't make sense, so he tried another word. "Destroy!" The word came out squeaky and with pain.

Rance didn't respond at first. "You want me to destroy our money?" He wrinkled up his brow at Michael.

Michael smiled and shook his head. "Money destroy us."

Rance chuckled. "Maybe, but what a way to go." Michael gave him a half smile in response and shook his head again. "You can't understand."

The ambulance arrived and loaded Michael into the back. Dr. Holloway met them at the Emergency Room. The whole team of ER nurses hovered over Michael, getting his physical vitals and financial details. Daniel did a cursory neurological exam. As the storm of people left and the room calmed, Daniel asked the question, "Again?"

Michael nodded. "It has Alyssa."

"How do you know?" Daniel asked him while examining the claw marks on his neck.

"It told me when it was dangling me in the air."

Daniel nodded at the comment. "I can see the claw print coming to the skin. I think you may want to invest in some good heavy makeup for the next few days." Then he quitted his voice. "How did you get away?"

"Same as always, but this time it attacked me with a choke hold." By this time Michael regained his strength and sat up on the gurney. "I'm okay." He brushed Daniel away.

"I know buddy. Get dressed and come to my office. We need to talk."

Michael responded with a nod.

Daniel shut the office door and sat in the chair next to Michael. "What do we do?"

"What can we do, besides pray over her?" Michael answered. "The biggest problem is Rance, I think the monster has Rance in a tight grip."

"Porn?" Daniel asked.

Michael nodded. "It keeps pulling him in. He seldom does any work, especially since Alyssa has gone missing. He's at his computer all the time."

"Do you think he's still looking for Jennifer?"

Michael shook his head. "I'm not sure he even remembers her; he is so wrapped up in the fantasy woman." Michael paused for a minute, rubbing his throat, "But there's one thing I know; the monster is filling him with guilt over her disappearance."

"Why?" Daniel asked as he handed Michael a glass of water and a pill.

"To keep Rance under control. Rance can't see the monster. It's around or near him constantly."

"That's strange. I thought all you Troyes could see those things; even me, an in-law." Daniel took the empty glass and leaned against the cabinet.

"All of us but Rance. Probably because he doesn't believe in anything spiritual."

"Really?" Daniel stood and took a step toward Michael. "Any better?"

Michael nodded. "Money is his god."

"That's what Barbara said. How do you stand up against that?"

"The problem with greed is the dishonest things it makes you do," Michael muttered through his hoarse voice.

"Yep!" Daniel agreed. "You know, of all the dragons this family has faced, this one is hardest to understand." Daniel groaned and rose to sit behind his desk. He pulled out his prescription pad and wrote on it. "I'm giving you some breathing treatments and mild pain medicine until your throat heals. It's pretty swollen."

Michael took the script. "What does this dragon want?" Michael pondered as he looked at the script and remembered the scaly claw wrapped around his neck.

"I think he has what he wants --- Rance!" Daniel answered.

"What can we do?" Michael responded and paused, looking at his hands. "My prayers don't seem to be helping, I think he grows worse."

"This little episode doesn't help either. That's the first time one of those beady-eyed snakes has attacked you."

"Barbara and I explored the tunnels yesterday looking for clues to Alyssa's disappearance."

"Did you find anything?"

"Yes, we did, and it scared us both."

"What? Did you see Alyssa?" Michael raised his head.

"No, we were walking along when Barbara disappeared. I followed her. I couldn't get close to her, and I couldn't catch up to her. It felt as though we were moving at twice the speed."

"Sounds like our experience that landed us in Santa Fe." Michael glanced at the calendar on the wall. "Ironic, but it was on this date I saw Barbara in Vietnam," he said.

Daniel smiled and nodded. "She's anxious to talk to you."

22

Back to Vietnam

*Should good be repaid with evil? For they have dug a pit for [fn]me.
Remember how I stood before You To speak good on their behalf, So as
to turn away Your wrath from them.*

Jeremiah 18:20

MICHAEL AND PAPS kept their heads down during the ambush. Bullets zinged over their heads. Michael could only describe it as feeling like icy drops of rain falling on already-cold skin. The muddy ground slowed them as they crawled away to find an advantage point from which to shoot that would provide shelter from the ambushers shooting at them.

Michael pulled one of his buddy's bodies over his and kept crawling. He felt the bullet pierce his buddy and protect Michael with each sting. The sideways attack pushed the body off him. Before he could find shelter from the rain of death, the shooting stopped.

The tatting sound of the Vietnamese language froze him in place with a rapidly beating heart. He prayed they would be friend and not foe. A second later, a hand pulled him onto his back. He blinked and rubbed the dirt from his eyes. He looked up into the dark eyes of about fifteen uniformed Vietnamese men. The white of their eyes pierced the mud-soaked faces like tiny flashlights. Most of them held machetes. A couple held old rifles, and another, a wooden rifle. The rest of them fingered American rifles they took from the many bodies.

Michael turned his head looking for Paps.

"Paps!" he hollered. Before he could make any more sound, one of the young men pulled a black bag over his head. He could hear Paps' muffled cries. Michael called out again, and when he did, one of the young men hit him in the head with something hard.

He remained quiet as the men raised him up. They tied his hands behind his back and pushed him. Michael stumbled and fell, unable to catch himself. Again, they pulled him to his feet and spoke at him in their language in angry snippets accented by pushing and shoving.

Michael stumbled several more times and fell twice. The second time he fell, the men yanked the bag off his head, and one a bit older, got in his face and spoke in broken English. "Ge good, GI Joe. I cut." He then slashed his thumb across his throat—a gesture everyone recognized, regardless of what one's nationality was.

The Texas Panhandle farm boy stared at the man with the dark angry eyes. The man spoke to the others in his native tongue with the sound of authority. The young men all approached Michael and raised their machetes toward him.

Michael whispered, "I think I'm coming home, Lord."

The North Vietnamese cut off his clothes, his shirt, pants, tee shirt, even his boots were removed and finally his socks.

He stood in the midst of the group in his undershorts with his pale white skin cooking under the sun in the clearing. In a few seconds, he heard feet shuffling and a groan. He looked and saw Paps hauled toward him, in the same state of undress. The men pushed Paps toward Michael. He stumbled and Michael reached out to catch him. They both tumbled to the ground. The men stood around them with hate-filled eyes, spitting on them and making obvious slurs of hate toward them.

"Think they're gonna' torture us?" Paps whispered to Michael.

Michael nodded. "The fact we're naked and sitting in full midday sun hints at it." Michael's voice quivered.

"It's okay, son. Think about that farm you worked on."

"It was hard work in the sun too." Michael smiled as the memory of hauling hay for cattle began to take life in his memory.

"I didn't know when I was a kid how poor we was, 'cause we never went hungry." Paps leaned up against Michael, providing him with a back rest.

"Yeah, we milked cows, separated cream, made butter and buttermilk, and fed the hogs scraps to fatten them up."

"Picked cotton pulling a one-hundred-pound bag behind our skinny one-hundred-pound bodies." Paps chuckled.

"I remember when I saw the first cotton shredder. I thought that was the most wonderful thing ever invented." Michael smiled.

"Did you have chickens?" Paps asked Michael.

"Yeah, I sold eggs to the grocery stores in town. Made a pretty good living for a fourteen-year-old boy."

"I didn't have chickens, I had turkeys. Dumb animals they were."

"Why turkeys?"

"We was too pour to buy chickens."

"But wouldn't turkeys eat more?"

"Yet, they were our insect and weed control."

"I sure wish we had a batch of turkeys here now," Michael said in a muffled voice as the group of young men approached them, and he shook uncontrollably.

Paps started singing, "Victory in Jesus, my Savior forever."

Michael joined him. "He sought me and bought me with his redeeming blood."

The two men let their voices raise with each note.

This must have angered the North Vietnamese soldiers and they raised their machetes and ran toward the two men.

"See you on the other side." Paps said.

"You bet."

They closed their eyes and lay their heads on their knees. Praying and preparing to meet their Savior.

"Are we dead yet?" Michael whispered.

The quiet became noticeable and eerie.

Michael dared to raise his head and peek around. Amazingly, his hands were untied. "Paps, look!" he said as he pointed to the sky. "The sun's setting. We must have been in prayer for hours."

Paps looked around.

"Whoa!" They both shouted.

"Hi Barbara," Paps said to the bright image in front of them.

"Paps," Michael said. "Meet my cousin Barbara Troye."

"I know; she told me." Paps smiled but didn't take his eyes off Barbara.

They stood and held their hands in front of their naked bodies.

"Fear not, for the battle is not yours but the Lord's," Barbara said with a smile. Then she started quoting from the Scriptures, "'For I know the plans that I have for you,' declares the Lord, 'plans for welfare and not for calamity to give you a future and a hope. Then you will call upon Me and come and pray to Me, and I will listen to you. You will seek Me and find Me when you search for Me with all your heart. I will be found by you,' declares the Lord, 'and I will restore your fortunes and will gather you from all the nations and from all the places where I have driven you,' declares the Lord, 'and I will bring you back to the place from where I sent you into exile.'"

Both men fell on their knees and gave thanks for the Word

Michael looked up and saw Paps talking to her. He nodded and motioned for Michael to join them. She kissed them both on the cheeks and gave them a message. Then she was gone. And so were the North Vietnamese.

23

Long Nguyen
(pronounced Long Wind)

The prophet who has a dream may relate his dream, but let him who has My word speak My word in truth. What does straw have in common with grain?" declares the Lord. "Is not My word like fire?" declares the Lord, "and like a hammer which shatters a rock?

Jeremiah 23: 23-29

MICHAEL RUBBED THE coin in his hand. Something he did to stop the anxiety from crawling up his spine. A trick Paps taught him in Vietnam. The tingling of apprehension reminded him that his journey to Santa Fe would bring him face-to-face with his worst nightmare. . . the Vietnamese leader of that torture squad that captured him and Paps all those years back. He stared out the window as the flat nothingness of the "enchanted land" passed. *It's been thirty years and it still makes my skin crawl with fear.*

"I wonder why they call New Mexico the land of enchantment?" he asked Rance, not really expecting an answer but feeling the need to pierce the quiet.

"I don't know. Maybe because of places like Red River?" Rance answered with a deadpan voice.

"This part looks like cow pasture."

"I think it is." Rance sighed and pointed to a deer or something like it in the distance. "There's some enchantment." Rance chuckled.

"Maybe they hide their enchantment like Oklahoma hides its culture in a museum."

"Funny." Rance smiled. "So, where does Texas hide its culture?"

"Right out in the open "cause there ain't any other like it," Michael drawled with as thick a Texas accent as he could muster.

"You okay?" Rance's voice turned serious.

Michael nodded. "It's a strange feeling. Walking into a man's office to do business when he once held you prisoner."

"I understand," Rance said.

"How can you understand?"

"Cousin, I am a prisoner . . . not a physical prisoner but worse."

"How so?"

"I'm in a prison of my own making, and I make no attempt to get out."

Michael nodded. "The pics?"

"It's strange . . . the guilt I feel after I spend hours looking at and reading all that stuff. I swear I'll never do it again, but then the guilt of it drives me to find relief for the guilt, and that relief is found in the act itself. It's a cycle."

"Thanks, you actually helped me."

Rance laughed. "My pain, your comfort? Is that what you're saying?"

"In a way. I'll face my capture today, and it'll be concluded. I'll either be able to do business with him or not."

"What if it turns out to be not?"

Michael took a moment to answer. "I guess there isn't a choice, is there?"

"Nope, we've already signed contracts and collected money."

Michael leaned his head back on the car seat. "Then my prison is more like yours than I thought. The difference is I have faith that my Lord will bring me through it. What about you?"

"My finding Jenny will be my salvation."

They found a parking space facing the front door of *Dragon Wind Construction*. The canopy over the entrance protected a well-kept and well-designed building. "Looks like a big deal to me."

Michael nodded. He reached for his briefcase and turned to Rance. "Are you ready to meet Mr. Long Nguyen?"

"I have no idea what I'm doing here; I didn't even know the guy's name."

"You're my supportive muscle. Just stand up and look mean. That shouldn't be hard with your six-feet four-inch, two-hundred-eighty-pound frame."

"I have you know I am only two-hundred-seventy pounds, and sadly, it's not all muscle."

"I know that, but they don't." Michael pointed to the front door and headed for it.

Rance followed.

Michael's apprehension showed in his legs quivering. He took a deep breath and steeled himself for a confrontation he felt would be adversarial. He stepped up to the front desk.

"I'm here to see Mr. Nguyen. Please let him know he has a visitor from Church Creek Falls, Texas." Michael handed her his card with his name followed by Esq. to denote his legal standing as an attorney.

The girl spoke into the intercom announcing Michael. She pointed to the chairs in the waiting area.

Michael's case of nerves and fake boldness bothered him. After facing enemies in war—both physically and spiritually—why was this so different? He prayed for a fresh dose of faith.

They didn't have to wait long. When the two men entered Mr. Nguyen's office, Michael cleared his throat and began his practiced speech, "Mr. Nguyen, I have the God-given right to protect those whom I love. But I will never stand up to protect your ideology based on well-chosen words and a greedy heart. My heart lives in a sense of liberty given to my community by the grace of God. I do not come here to battle your words or your goals, but you are now in my backyard, and I want you to know I will use whatever means necessary to protect my community and family from your greed."

Mr. Nguyen's eyed Michael with a squint of revulsion.

Rance rested a hand on his shoulder to help make the quivering less noticeable. Michael appreciated his comfort.

Mr. Nguyen leaned back in his chair behind a massive desk covered in carved dragons. He tipped his chin and widened his eyes at Michael before he spoke. "You escaped."

Michael knew then this was the same commander who held him and Paps prisoner. He slumped a little in his seat. Rance had never seen Michael in such a state of emotional wreckage.

"How?' I left orders for you and the old man to be killed."

"By the grace of my God," Michael whimpered.

Mr. Nguyen laughed. "No matter, you're still my prisoner."

Michael saw the dragon standing over Mr. Nguyen, and it wasn't a carving. He focused on the reptile flicking it's tongue over Mr. Nguyen.

"I understand your concerns. I remember you. But now we fight in courts not in Cuu Long River or in English, nine dragons, in the Mekong Delta."

Michael melted a bit at the words. "You do remember?"

Mr. Nguyen nodded, "Yes, I saw you in the Cuu Long River." He cupped his hands under his chin and nodded. "Do you know what Cuu Long means?"

Michael shook his head with his mouth agape. The memories of sloshing around in the murky waters of the Mekong Delta overcoming him.

"It means nine dragons." Mr. Nguyen snickered under his breath, put his hands down, and leaned over his desk. "How many have you defeated?"

Michael stared into Mr. Nguyens' face and winched.

Rance put both hands on Michael's shoulders and rubbed them.

"How many?" Mr. Nguyen almost shouted.

This time Michael answered, "Only one."

"No, you didn't defeat a dragon. The prayers of your people and the words of His book defeated him." Mr. Nguyen stood and leaned closer to Michael.

Then Michael saw Mr. Nguyen change into the image of a green dragon with the flat forehead of the dragon depictions he' seen in Vietnam. The voice of the man changed to the growl of the dragon. "My name is Long Nguyen, I am Dragon Wind, or the breath of a dragon. You will not defeat me!"

Rance thought Mr. Nguyen's complexion took on a green tint when he said the words. He could feel Michael's shoulder muscles that started out tense fade into jelly. His own legs quivered as he heard the man call himself a dragon. With sparks of light coming through the man's eyes on occasion, Rance would see the shape of a monster's head rather than a man's.

Mammon lost the human form in Michael's eyes and stood over him in full vile green dragon form, whipping his tale around both Michael and Rance but never touching them. "That silly fool can't see me." Mammon roared at Michael while displaying a four-clawed foot in front of Rance's face. "Why can't he see me?" Mammon's anger grew.

Michael stared, stunned at the transformation from man to horror. He could feel the water of the Mekong Delta seeping into his shoes. He shuffled his feet. They hurt. He patted his head. His helmet was missing. Where was his weapon? How could he face a monster without protection or weapon? He felt like a telephone pole in the midst of a kudzu patch. He couldn't get loose from the growing, green gruesomeness wrapping itself around him. He screamed.

Then he felt a hand on his back. "Paps?"

Rance answered Michael, "Yeah, it's me."

Michael relaxed. "How do we get rid of him?"

Before Rance could think of a response, the man walking around the two of them responded with a sharp order. "You don't!"

Rance repeated a phrase his father often used. "We pray."

Michael smiled. "Yes! Dear Jesus, only You can defeat a dragon."

Rance didn't understand why Michael kept calling the man a dragon, but he had to admit the man was as ugly as a dragon.

Then suddenly, the man screamed and threw his hands in the air.

Michael saw a slithering dragon that had filled the room with his scaly presence shrink, and the undulating tail became legs. He continued. "Father God, with your sword I slay this dragon." He stood and raised his right arm over his head and shouted Scripture verses at the top of his voice, "'But the Lord is with me as a dread warrior; therefore, my persecutors will stumble; they will not overcome me. They will be greatly shamed, for they will not succeed. Their eternal dishonor will never be forgotten.'

"O Lord of hosts, who tests the righteous, who sees the heart and the mind, let me see your vengeance upon them, for to you have I committed my cause.'"

Mammon, the dragon moaned and writhed in pain. Then Long Nguyen raised himself from the floor, shook his head and brushed his arms and legs. "I can see you have a formidable weapon. But can you fight the battle with endurance? The last time you fought one of my brothers was only for a short time. This battle is for many souls, including that idiot." Mr. Nguyen pointed to Rance. "This battle will be a long, long look into the evil one man can do to one another. Your pain will be immeasurable, and your silly words will give you no relief."

Michael shivered with the words. Rance put his shaking hand on Michael's shoulder. With a deep breath, Michael leaned over the desk and got in Mr. Nguyen's face. "I still need an answer."

"To what?" Mr. Nguyen growled.

"Why did you let us go instead of killing us in Vietnam?"

"I didn't; you disappeared. We all stood looking at you, and suddenly you were gone right before our eyes."

Michael didn't answer at first, but he let the words sink in. The vision of Barbara had clouded their view.

Before he could answer, Mr. Nguyen spoke again, "In fact it was that moment, I developed the idea for time travel through speed."

Mammon lay on the floor, licking his wound. It wasn't fatal, just painful. The monster harrumphed as he recalled giving Long Nguyen the idea. Later he gave the same man now called Harry Nguyen the engineering ability of such a feat.

"What?" Michael asked. "Wh. . . ?"

"I was chosen by the dragon god of my country to do this."

"Do what?"

"Destroy your community!"

"Why our community?" Michael raised one eyebrow with the question.

"Because Mr. Robert Troye and his offspring. I hate them."

"Don't you hate everybody?" Michael could feel his spiritual strength returning.

"Hate the Troye's more, they listen to the Holy One and obey. I have to destroy them before they take more of my prisoners and set them free in the name of the Holy One."

"You can't say His name, can you?" Michael smirked at Mr. Nguyen.

"Get out of my office and don't come back!" Mr. Nguyen shouted at Rance and Michael. "You will not escape from me so easily this time."

The road heading toward Church Creek Falls and home felt like a tortoise retracting into its shell. The troubles of *Dragon Wind Construction* behind Michael and Rance evaporated. To the world, Church Creek Falls looked like a typical community struggling through great tragedy and rebuilding. But the cousins felt as if they were headed toward a sanctuary.

Rance held the book, almost afraid to open it.

"Why do you think Long Nguyen gave us a book explaining the engineering?" Michael asked.

"To taunt us with enough knowledge we can't stop it. At least, that's what I think."

Michael kept his eyes on the road. "Have you read any of it? Remember the warning he gave us. *Don't use it unless it is absolutely necessary.*"

24

Don't Omit a Word

Thus says the Lord, 'Stand in the court of the Lord's house, and speak to all the cities of Judah who have come to worship in the Lord's house all the words that I have commanded you to speak to them. Do not omit a word!

Jeremiah 26:2

ALYSSA OPENED HER mouth to speak, but the words froze on her tongue. Even her sobs were swallowed in the stillness of loneliness and confusion. Davis provided some comfort but mostly warnings to stay in the cabin. No explanation, no instructions, no hope. She stood alone on the porch of the cabin staring out at the only other visible living thing around.

The horror of it kept her eyes glued to it, even though she felt as though she would vomit at the sight of the huge reptile draped in the tree, with the length of its body covering all the branches and its head wider than the truck of the old tree. The split tongue reached out toward her every time she stepped onto the porch and just before it reached striking distance, it would hit an invisible wall. Davis's strict warning not to leave the cabin wasn't hard to obey with that thing standing guard.

Although he told her the cabin protected her from the dragon, she wasn't sure about the burly man standing on the ground under the dragon's head, still holding the clump of her hair in his hand. His red face seethed with anger. He scared her more than the dragon.

She closed the door and looked out the window, scanning the outside yet not focusing on anything. The daydreaming served as a buffer between what she saw and what she knew she must do. The urge to run out and past the monster gatekeepers overwhelmed her like fear in a rabbit before it bolts in front of an on-coming car.

She turned on the radio and changed the volume to loud. Scanning the myriad of books lined perfectly on a ceiling to floor bookshelf covering all of one wall, Alyssa shifted her weight from her right foot to her left. Occasionally, she stroked the spine of a book but never pulled one from the shelf. The titles revealed a menagerie of genres—both fiction and non-fiction—along with a wide selection of Bible translations.

She pulled the New Living Bible from the shelf and let it fall open. Her frazzled mind couldn't comprehend a single verse or passage to study. Instinctively, she knew this would give her peace. She read, "'You have wearied the Lord with your words. 'How have we wearied Him?' you ask. You have wearied him saying that all who do evil are good in the Lord's sight, and he is pleased with them. You have wearied him by asking, 'Where is the God of justice?'"

Alyssa sat at the dining table dividing the eating area from the living area. She read the verse several times before she stated the last sentence out loud, "Where is the God of justice?" It wasn't a quoting of Scripture but had become a sincere question from her heart.

She's alone in a cabin somewhere in a forest far from home. She knows she's far from home because Church Creek Falls is flat farmland with no forest. One lone tree may stand wimpy in a field but never a forest.

She laid her head on the table and repeated the phrase adding, "What is my crime?" She rose from the chair and curled up in a fetal position on the bed. In the middle of the afternoon she fell into a deep sleep.

Alyssa felt herself floating above Church Creek Falls. Each store front and person scurried about their lives unaware of her watching them. When she awoke, she remembered the bland dream mocking the life of people running around and accomplishing nothing.

"Lord, what are you trying to tell me?" she shouted at the ceiling.

In response came the scrapping growl of the dragon and the shout of the man under the tree.

She buried her face in her hands. "Please, Lord, tell me something. I don't think I can continue in this prison without knowledge."

"My people perish because of lack of knowledge." A voice whispered to her. She raised her face and looked around. Then she heard it again, "By the foolishness of preaching, my people are saved." Alyssa recognized the words from the Old Testament prophets and the New Testament words from one of Paul's letters.

She set about the task of finding the words in the Bible. She found a reference to the first thought in Hosea 4:6, "My people are being destroyed because they don't know me. Since your priests refuse to know me, I refuse to recognize you as my priests. Since you have forgotten the laws of your God, I will forget to bless your children."

Alyssa pondered what she read. The children of Church Creek Falls are disappearing. Is there a connection? What laws of God are being broken?

"Humph, which law is not being broken? The town is more wicked now than when it was destroyed the first time," she said, and she rose and began to pace around the one-room cabin. She sat on the edge of the bed and read the Scriptures. After a while her back became tired so she moved to the table and read more Scriptures. Her legs began to tingle as they swung back and forth on the too tall chair. Walking toward the couch, she propped up her legs and read yet another passage. All of them speaking of lack of knowledge because of disobedience.

Finally, she closed the Bible leaving it on the couch, stood up in the middle of the room, threw her hands up in the air, and said, "I don't get it, Lord."

Scanning the refrigerator and cabinets, Alyssa realized there was enough food for one person for a couple weeks. "Well, I guess the grocery delivery won't be here for a while." She made herself a sandwich and sat at the table and looked around. "What am I going to do with all this time?"

Gain knowledge. It wasn't a whisper or even a thought but more of a natural response from her previous readings. She stared at the wall with all the books. "I guess I'll read." She started at the left-hand side of the top row and pulled the book out. "I'll read them in order and see how far I get." She smiled to herself and climbed down the bookshelf ladder and looked at the dust jacket of her chosen book—*How to Rebuild Civilization in the Aftermath of a Cataclysm*

She shook her head and sighed heavily. "I wonder if the world has been bombed, and I'm the only one left?"

Alyssa sat down and started reading. She fell asleep about page fifty.

A quiet shuffle woke Alyssa. She didn't move but scanned the room. A man dressed in military fatigues stood in front of the bookcase wall. He was thumbing through a book.

"Hello," she ventured.

He turned around. She smiled when she recognized Davis, her rescuer.

"When did you get here?" She tossed the afghan off her legs and raised her head.

"About twenty minutes ago," he answered and sat down opposite her.

She stretched and yawned. "I didn't get far in the first book," she stated as she closed the hardcover.

"That's okay, you didn't have the right one anyway."

"That's a relief. I thought maybe the rapture occurred, and I was left here with those . . . monsters," she muttered looking toward the window.

"Have you ever heard the expression that says to pray for a hedge of protection?"

"Yeah, I hear it in church all the time from people praying."

"Well, that is a hedge of protection." Davis pointed to the window. "There's no way they will ever penetrate that barrier, and yet they lurk there."

"Why?"

"Hoping you'll come out or your family will stop praying for you."

"You mean I could walk out there?"

David nodded. "But do you want to?"

"I wouldn't mind going home. Not sure I want to walk past that."

"Oh, you wouldn't get past them before they would have you captured."

"Okay, looks like I'm stuck here. What you got for me?" She leaned back on the couch. "You know . . . in the way of an explanation."

Davis grimaced and let out a slight chuckle.

"What are you laughing at?" Alyssa demanded.

"Usually, when this happens to people, they can't see the danger outside, and they spend lots of time begging to be let out or maybe even try to get out on their own," Davis answered.

"You mean this happens a lot?"

"Yep, every day with everybody."

Alyssa's jaw dropped and she tilted her head a bit. "No Way!"

"It's not always the same situation, but there's a gap between the physical and spiritual world," Davis explained. "You just happen to be able to see it with your physical eyes. That's rare."

"Still not getting it."

"You can see the prayer protection and the evil outside of that protection, so you don't have any reason to beg for release."

"No, but I don't really want to spend my life here in a one-room cabin alone. I'm worried about my family. They must be frantic wondering what happened to me."

"Yes, in a way, but the Father holds your earthly father in great compassion. The Father revealed your position in Him to Buster."

"My position in Him?" Alyssa wrinkled her nose.

Davis smiled and stroked her cheek. "My child, when you belong to the Father, He doesn't come to you, He takes you within Himself through the gift of Jesus Christ. You are *in Him*."

"Does this mean this cabin isn't real?"

"Oh, it's real all right, just not in the materialistic way you're programmed to think."

"You know I don't understand this, don't you?" Alyssa smirked.

"Good, because you have a task to complete; and the life and fate of your brother Rance may depend upon the work you do here."

Alyssa sat up on the edge of the couch and leaned toward Davis. She smiled and rubbed the palms of her hands together. "Good, a job. What is it?"

"You have been equipped to discover the meaning of the phrase your family keeps hearing, "The planting of seed is singular, but the harvest comes in multiples.""

"Hey, that's easy. You plant one seed, you get a plant that produces many seeds." Alyssa leaned back again.

"Yeah?"

Alyssa nodded. "It's an analogy of planting the Word of God, and it'll produce more Christians."

"Then why do the dragons keep using it?"

"I don't know," Alyssa said, pondering his question. He's right; it didn't make sense that the dragons would want more Christians running around.

"The answer to that question is your assignment. The answer will also be your armor when the battle arrives."

Alyssa gulped. Battle?

25
The Book

Then the Lord said to me, "What do you see, Jeremiah?" and I said, "Figs, the good figs, very good; and the bad figs, very bad, which cannot be eaten due to rottenness.

Jeremiah 24:3

THE GROUP OF siblings and cousins gathered at Barbara and Daniel's home for dinner. As they sat around the table discussing the book Long Nguyen gave them, they asked rhetorical questions. "How did we walk for twenty minutes and end up in Santa Fe? Mr. Nguyen's suggestion of a people-mover from Church Creek Falls to Los Alamos through a time tunnel proved to be even more fantastical than their imaginations. Yet, this little book contained the instructions to run that machine.

Rance shuttered at the way Long Nguyen made the announcement, more than the announcement itself. The explanation about their travel from Church Creek Falls to Santa Fe in his short speech convinced the men that Long Nguyen suffered from delusion. He explained the theory of time travel starting with Einstein's theory of relativity which said traveling at the speed of light would cause one to go forward in time and that time could bend. The theory proved correct, but the method of causing time travel hadn't been achieved . . . only studied. And it didn't allow for going back in time.

Long Nguyen explained the danger of going back in time. One could change the course of history. Or so the theory goes. The counter theory is that going back in time created another realm with another history running parallel to this one. The more Nguyen talked, the more the group felt they'd entered "crazy world."

However, the first type of travel caught Michael's attention. He remembered how Barbara was an older person when she approached him and Paps in the jungle of Vietnam. They assumed it was a supernatural vision, but now he wondered if they were actually talking to the older Barbara. But that would mean she traveled back in time. Michael made an involuntary sigh and muttered out loud, "She looked like she does now."

"What?" Barbara asked.

"Do you remember when Paps and I told you about seeing you in the jungle at Vietnam?"

Barbara nodded.

"You looked like you do now. You know, older. Have you been riding on that time machine?"

Barbara smiled a knowing smile and started to speak.

"What are we looking for?" Rance almost yelled at his twin brother Zay.

Zay tilted his head downward and looked Rance in the face. He waited for several minutes before he spoke. He needed his brother to calm. The anxiety attacks were coming more frequently now and lasting longer.

Zay glanced at Daniel, put his hand on top of Rance's, and spoke in a quiet calm voice. "Rance, we're looking at using the time machine in the tunnels to find Jennifer."

Rance's mouth fell open. "How?"

"I believe that somehow the contraption inside that tunnel is the key to the people's disappearance and the key to their rescue." Zay answered.

Rance sat back in his chair and sipped the soda Barbara handed him. He stared over the heads of his family. "I don't understand."

Zay sighed, "We don't either, but we're looking for options."

Rance smirked and leaned forward over the table resting on his elbows. The family all saw the monster wrapped around Rance. They listened as he spoke through Rance. "I'm surprised all you good Christians don't just have a prayer meeting. Isn't that the answer to all your problems? Pray about it, and she'll suddenly appear?"

The group all sipped their coffee and ate their dessert as if it was a normal day at a park picnic. They weren't going to talk to a dragon.

"Well?" Rance urged them to talk.

Zay took the lead. "You're out of your league," he whispered.

Rance looked at him and stood up in a huff, knocking his chair to the floor.

Mammon held on tightly but almost lost his grip.

The group saw it.

Marcy shouted, "Answer me when I call, O God of my righteousness! You have relieved me in my distress; Be gracious to me and hear my prayer"

She settled in beside Zay and set her cup on the coffee table then smirked at Mammon. "Take that, you big bad boy," she said mockingly.

Mammon grew bigger with rage but let go of Rance. When he did, Zay took the lead and pulled Rance out of the room.

Mammon turned to grab Rance, but then Michael shouted, "Hear a just cause, O Lord! Give heed to my cry; give ear to my prayer, which is not from deceitful lips."

Before Mammon could move, Barbara stood up and shouted, "O my God, my soul is in despair within me; Therefore, I remember You from the land of the Jordan and the peaks of Hermon, from Mount Mizar.

"Deep calls to deep at the sound of Your waterfalls; All Your breakers and Your waves have rolled over me. The Lord will command His lovingkindness in the daytime; And His song will be with me in the night, A prayer to the God of my life."

Barbara walked toward the monster as she shouted the words of the Psalm. She jabbed hard when she referenced the peaks of Hermon.

Mammon roared in pain and shrunk a bit.

Barbara got up in his ugly, sticky face and said one word, "Scat!"

He was gone.

Zay brought Rance out from the bedroom, and the rest of the crew settled around the table. Each took deep breaths.

Rance looked at them and chuckled. "You guys act like you just came from war."

The whole group hee-hawed at his statement.

Michael eased the tension when he said, "I've been to war, my friend, and what we just did makes war look like kindergarten."

"So, what did you guys do . . . fight a dragon?" Rance mocked them as he sat down at the table.

The group looked at him and smiled. They all nodded and licked their lips. Barbara reached over and kissed her brother on the cheek. "We just proved how much we love you."

"And how much is that?" Rance smirked.

"Enough to face a monster," Barbara replied.

Rance took her hand and rubbed it. "Thanks, sis."

"She proved herself a worthy adversary in my Vietnam battle today too," Michael added with a lilt.

"What?" Rance wrinkled his brow. "It's been more than thirty years since you were in Vietnam."

"Yep," Michael said as he winked at Barbara. "We experienced that time machine firsthand today."

Rance shook his head. "You guys are delusional."

"Maybe, but have you read the book?"

"No, I can't bring myself to open it." Rance moaned.

"I bet you can now that we got rid of your pet dragon," Marcy said.

Rance rolled his eyes at Marcy. He picked up the book and started reading. Those in the room remained silent as he read and scanned the few pages. When he finished a section, he looked at Barbara and Michael"

"Really?"

"Really. It happened yesterday," Barbara said.

"For her, it happened yesterday; for me it happened thirty years ago," Michael said.

"You guys, this is phenomenal." Rance grew animated and excited. They all smiled to see Rance as himself, even if it would only be temporary.

"Just think of the money we can make off this thing."

The smiles left the faces of the group, and a collective sigh went up.

Mammon slipped in through the wall, barely visible but present. Zay saw him first as a clawed foot appeared on Rance's shoulder. "How many times do we have to fight this beast?"

Michael answered while staring at the faint image of the beast coming into clearer view. "Until we trust in Him completely who can destroy the beast."

Barbara's eyes focused on the same scene. "Do you think we'll ever learn?"

Daniel brought the questioning to a close when he said, "It's not our unbelief."

The faces of the others turned toward him.

"It's Rance's unbelief."

"As long as the dragon breaths on him, Rance will not hear the truth," Barbara said.

Even though Rance was in the room, he couldn't understand the words being spoken by his family. "What are you guys talking about?" he muttered and wiggled in his chair rubbing his shoulder.

"You," Zay answered. "We won't find any answers as long as you—" Zay stopped.

"As long as I what?" Rance demanded.

"As long as you are involved in the pornography," Zay answered his brother.

Mammon gripped Rance's shoulder, leaned his ugly face into the midst of the group and growled, "He'll never let go of it. He's addicted." With an evil laugh, the dragon lit the room with a plume of fire. A fire with no heat or consuming power. Before his laugh was complete, another fire entered the room.

A powerful plume of fire enveloped Mammon's fire and consumed it before it reached Mammon with the sting of the burn. Mammon roared, "He's at it again!"

The group smiled because they all knew their dad had entered the battle. His body may be weak, but that warrior fought dragons with powerful prayer. The fire grew as the voice of truth spoke in the room. The voice came from Rance.

"When I kept silent about my sin, my body wasted away. Through my groaning all day long. For day and night Your hand was heavy upon me; My vitality was drained away as with the fever heat of summer."

Mammon growled, "That's my intention, dear boy." Mammon then released a horrific scream of pain from the burning fire and flew away from the family gathering.

Rance made eye contact with each member of family sitting around the dinner table. "You know, don't you?"

Barbara stood and walked behind Rance, rubbing ointment on the shoulder the beast had clawed. "My sweet brother, there's no good from pornography, and even you know it. The words you said come straight from the Bible."

"The Bible doesn't mention pornography." Rance raised his voice a bit.

"It doesn't use the word," Michael said, "but it speaks volumes about the activity."

"How so?" Rance pushed Barbara away. She went back to her seat and took Daniel's hand. She could tell Daniel remained deep in prayer. The battle the family fought would be long and hard.

"Paul related the five idols in our lives in Colossians 3:5. One of those is passion."

"So?" Rance sat up straight.

"The Greek word for Passion is 'pornia.' We get our word pornography from it."

"Coincidence!" Rance ranted.

Zay stood and walked outside. The sparkle of iridescence captured his eye. There on the roof sat Mammon and dozens of other dragons breathing lies into Rance. "Lord, how do we fight so great a temptation?"

The dragons danced on the roof, blowing plumes of fire and shouting.

Mammon lowered his head to face Zay. "Once, the lust of the mind takes over the body, there is no redemption. They cannot erase it."

The dragons roared in unison, "He belongs to us."

Zay walked back into the house and saw the redness on Rance's face. He was arguing with Michael and making ridiculous statements. Michael had stepped into a dragon trap of arguing about frivolous points. Zay knew he needed rescuing. The rest of the group were pulled into the argument too.

He walked up behind Rance and put his arm around him. "Brother, I love you," he said and turned his gaze to his family and put the palm of his hand in the air pushing it down. The family each took a deep breath and relaxed.

Michael rose and refilled his coffee cup.

It took longer for Rance to calm.

Zay took the lead. "How much do you weigh?"

Rance laughed. "Why? You gonna put me on a diet?"

"No, just how much do you weigh?"

Rance shrugged his shoulders. "Around two-fifty."

"I see where you're going with this," Daniel said. "Let's step over to my office and weigh you."

"Not unless the rest of you are going to do this," Rance said.

The women gasped but agreed. The dragons groaned. The family took Rance to a place occupied by the Holy One. A place where the dragons couldn't plant deceptive thoughts into Rance's mind because the Holy One guarded his mind.

Rance stepped on the scale when it came his turn. The scale kept going down. It landed on one-sixty. "That's a far cry from two-fifty." Zay said. "What's happening?"

"I don't know." Rance stepped off the scale and headed for a chair. He took a deep breath.

"Remember the verse you quoted, "My body is wasting away?" Zay reminded him.

"That's silly," Rance responded. "That book is ancient, and it has nothing to do with my weight problem."

"How about coming into my office tomorrow morning, and we do some test to rule out any physical problems?" Daniel asked.

"Okay."

Zay turned toward the group of dragons surrounding Rance. "No one is beyond redemption."

The dragons opened their mouth and spread their smelly breath over the room. The group stood mesmerized for a few moments.

Barbara broke the silence when she said, "Maybe it's not so bad. At least he's not hurting anyone else."

Mammon stood in front of Barbara then spoke to the other beasts around him. "See, even the strong ones are easy to control with a dragon's breath."

A large clap of thunder surrounded the dragons, and a bolt of lightning spread across the room. The beasts heard the voice of the Holy One. "I am their God and they are My people." The dragons spread their wings and swooped away as quickly as possible.

Buster lowered his aching body into his chair.

Merilee held him tight.

"They're gone," he said and leaned his head against the back of the chair and fell into a deep, restful sleep brought on by the comforting presence of the Holy One. Buster found rest from freedom of pain, and that only came when he clawed his way past the dragons to the throne room of his Lord. There, at the feet of Jesus, he offered his sacrifice of praise and his petitions for grace.

26

Korea

JENNIFER FINISHED HER breakfast and went to her bunk in a cold damp room with a variety of hopeless people. The cloud of darkness still hovered over her soul even though she was no longer in the concrete jail of a monster. Still, she knew they weren't free of the sex industry. They just didn't know where or what they would be doing in this camp. *Is there an honorable man anywhere?* The soldier who found them curled up in the back of the army truck hauled them in front of an important-looking military man.

He pointed to two chairs in front of a massive desk. "Sit," he commanded.

Jennifer ducked her head, but Peggy looked him straight in the eyes. "What are you going to do with us?" she asked him with determination.

He didn't answer. Instead, he stood, walked around the girls with his hands clasped behind his back. "How did you get into the truck?" he finally questioned Peggy.

"We crawled in."

He tossed his head back in exasperation and said, "I can figure that out, you idiot. I want to know where you crawled in and how you could do so without anyone seeing you?"

"That's a good question."

"Well," he said as he stopped pacing and stared Peggy in the eyes.

"I don't know."

"How can you not know?"

"Are you friend or foe?" Jennifer asked him, raising her head slightly.

"What do you mean?" he barked at her.

She didn't answer, placing her chin on her chest. He got in her face and repeated the question, spitting in her face and covering her with his coffee and nicotine breath.

Peggy stood up and squeezed between Jennifer and the military man. "Back off. She's not a soldier."

The man took a deep breath and sighed. "I don't know what to do with you," he lamented.

His watchful gaze from one girl to the other pierced the otherwise quiet with discomfort. Peggy stood behind Jennifer and put her hands on her shoulders. The man picked up a phone and waited a few minutes.

Then he spoke, "Can I pass some problem children to you?"

Jason set his rucksack in his closet and went to his kitchenette. The day had been long and tiresome. He pulled some leftovers from the fridge and stuck them in the microwave. While they heated, he hit the shower. The tepid water hit his hot body, sending a chill through him. As the water warmed, he leaned his head back and moaned. *I know too much and have no way to stop it.*

Once he dressed in his lounging pants, he pulled his dinner from the microwave and sat down in front of the television. There it was—the news report about his day; one dead, two seriously wounded. Jason and all the inhabitants of Camp Casey knew they were always ten minutes from death. Being so close to the enemy and pretending to live a normal life every day wore on his nerves and mental health. No wonder there were so many juicy bars around the base. Those bars consumed more of his energy than the military. Every day, he rescued his young soldiers from the devastation of poverty. The girls knew how to fleece a young man with exposure to their tight bodies with silky voices wooing them with empty promises of love and understanding.

He changed the channel to the music station, finished his dinner, and leaned back in his recliner. "God, what do I do?" With the statement, he remembered the letter he received that afternoon. He'd opened his mother's letter with a smile. It contained encouragement in the form of words and dollars.

My dear son, no matter the task or the difficulty, you will never be alone. Your Lord goes with you, and my prayers surround you every day.

Jason put the letter aside and looked up. "Does she know?" he asked the ceiling. Then he went back to the letter.

There will be times you will wonder about your decisions. That's one of the negative things about being a leader, but you've had the characteristics of a leader all your life. Even if you have to stand alone in the face of a dilemma, you will always have your Lord and your family standing with you.

"Thanks mom," he said quietly. Would she still say that if she saw the carnage of the men and the casket waiting to be shipped home? Sitting alone in his apartment at Camp Casey, Korea, he didn't feel alone for the exact reasons his mother stated. He knew his action was right, but this time he didn't know the danger. It might've changed his direction if he had known.

With a tear rolling down his face for his fallen friend, he said out loud, "I will find who did this to you."

Jason put the money in his drawer with the other money his mother sent him. If she knew what he planned to do with it, she would probably send more. He smiled, knowing in his heart she would approve of his plan. His thoughts were caught up in a sort of carousel. Every idea, notion, and the tragic event from the day replayed in his mind and demanded analysis. He wanted to go to sleep, but how could he when the carousel wouldn't stop. It slowed a bit, allowing his mind to meander freely with many random thoughts.

The last random thought riding the carousel before drifting off to sleep was of his brother Rance. He wondered if he would ever find his beloved Jenny Gale.

The phone rang, and he jumped, his reverie gone.

Peggy held Jennifer's hand as they were escorted down a drab hall. The silent woman opened a door and motioned for them to go inside. Peggy took a quick peek at the room. It contained two twin beds with a nightstand between them. A small table, refrigerator, and television. She turned to the matron holding the door, "Will we be locked inside?' she asked.

"No. If you want to leave, come to the end of the hall and tell me where you want to go, and I'll take you," the stiff matron answered.

"Can we go without you?"

"Whoever is at the desk will take you. It may be someone else. Do not leave without informing us."

Jennifer nodded her head and went into the room. She turned to the matron. "Can we get a shower and some clean clothes?"

For the first time the matron looked at them. "I'll get you some clothes, and here's the shower." She walked inside the door and pulled open another door, leading to a small but adequate bathroom.

Jennifer smiled. "Thank you." Never had a thank you been more heartfelt and sincere.

"Right now, I want to separate my body from my spirit and forget—" She stopped and looked to see if the matron still occupied the room as the door click closed behind her.

"I understand," Peggy said. "I want God to take me out for a walk and explain things to me."

"You think anyone ever will?"

"As long as we have a real bed and real food, I think I can be brave."

"I'm not brave. But I don't ever want to feel that cold concrete floor beneath me again." Jennifer moaned.

Peggy nodded. "I don't know if we'll get home."

"I don't want to go home," Jennifer interrupted, wringing her hands together.

"Why?"

Jennifer sniffled and opened her mouth to answer. Her throat tightened around the words. She squeaked out only a short intelligible sentence, "I don't want Rance to know." The words opened the flood gates, and her tears flowed freely.

The two girls sat on the bed, Peggy trying to console her while holding it together herself.

"We'll feel better in the morning; things have to get better. We're tired, a level of worn-out-ness that hurts."

The soft knock on the door startled both girls. They laughed at themselves as Peggy rose to answer. Before she reached the door, it opened, and the matron held clothing for girls. "Sorry, the choices are limited around here, but these will help you blend in with the rest of us."

She started to leave, and then she stopped and turned toward them. "You're not alone," she said in the cryptic tone of reluctantly delivering a message.

"What does that mean?" Jennifer shouted after her as she walked down the hall. She raised a hand in the air and waved. "Okay, either she didn't complete the message or God sent me a message." Jennifer walked to her bed, sat, and bowed her head. "God, if that was a message from you, I need it confirmed. I need You, if you still love me, please let me know. Please let Rance still love me."

A burly looking bearded man entered the room. His arms so thick they stood out almost perpendicular to his body. He didn't say anything but walked around the two girls, watching them with his gaze going up and down their bodies.

"I hear you two snuck in on a truck," he growled.

They both nodded.

"Tell me how you found the truck." He stood looking down at them with a steel gaze.

"It was parked on the street and empty, so we crawled in." Peggy kept her voice calm.

"How come no one saw you when the truck filled up?"

"I don't know. They were all pretty sad and wasted. No one looked at us."

The burly man smiled. "You'll be given instructions by the matron. If you follow them, you will be okay. This will be your room for now. The mess hall is down the hall. There is one rule here that is to be kept without exception." He stared at them a moment before he continued. "You do not ever under any circumstances approach or speak to any of the enlisted men. Do you understand?"

They both nodded, but Jennifer whimpered, "How do we know who they are?"

"Stupid girl, anyone in military gear," he answered.

"Are you enlisted?"

"What? No!"

"You're wearing military gear," Peggy pointed out, hoping to draw his attention away from Jennifer as his distain grew.

He shook his head and threw his palm in the air toward them, pushing them away. He opened the door and bellowed, "Margie, teach these idiots!"

A girl they hadn't seen before entered the room, presumably Margie. Hard features with no empathy expressed at all. She gave them a well-learned speech without pause.

"You will man the phones; you will be given a schedule. You will be trained to engage in conversation. You will receive calls from the lonely, the horney, and the suicidal. You will give them what they need through the tone of your voice. You will be expected to keep them on the line for as long as possible. Am I clear?"

Jennifer and Peggy nodded.

After she left, Jennifer grabbed Peggy's arm. "What are we into now?"

"I don't know, but it doesn't feel safe."

27
Money

Thus says the Lord, For three transgressions of Israel and for four, I will not revoke it punishment, because they sell the righteous for money and the needy for a pair of sandals.

Amos 2:6

RANCE DIDN'T GO to the office but instead sat in his recliner staring out the window. Wearing lounging pants and an open robe, he gazed at the tree outside his house. He no longer marked time by a clock but rather by season. The leaves crinkled on the edges and blushed a pale yellow. Soon, they'd fall in their embarrassment. Rance no longer added up the time Jenny had been gone. He marked his life by the approaching Christmas day. The day she disappeared. This Christmas would be five years. He marked his fading sanity by the slow demise of his community's coming financial crisis, which would have the same or maybe even a worse affect than the bomb.

He rested his chin on his fist. "And I caused it," he said out loud. These people have no idea what's going to happen.

Rance rose from his chair and with slow paced shuffles, he went to his bedroom and packed. His flight for New York was scheduled for nine in the evening. He scheduled it late so he could travel and arrive in the dark. The black of night covered him and hid his addiction. As the ground surface met the landing plane, Rance took a deep breath and whispered to himself, "Here I go again."

The profits from his dealing continued to pay off. But like most waves Rance knew it could come crashing down. However, the growth surge of the Internet kept fueling high returns on his investments. Ever since the Mosaic web browser hit the market and made the World Wide Web possible and accessible. The HTTP invention triggered the phenomenal growth of his portfolio.

In spite of the money that kept rolling into this community due to his financial engineering, he still couldn't find Jenny or Alyssa. Once he thought he saw Jenny on a porn website. He couldn't recognize her with the big hair and heavy makeup, and the come-hither demeanor didn't fit Jenny's personality at all. He didn't want to look anymore. What if he spotted her in one of those outfits? He felt his heart rate increasing. *I couldn't take it.*

His dad displayed a strange peace about Alyssa's whereabouts. He couldn't explain it, but Rance didn't care. His dad wouldn't say anything for the sole purpose of comforting him. When Buster Troye displayed peace, it was genuine. To Rance it meant his dear sister may already be dead. He gritted his teeth and made a fist. At that moment, the announcement came for the passengers to deplane.

Even at night, a New York airport displayed bustling life. Even though it was a much slower pace and not as crowded, the stores, restaurants, and kiosks stood ready to serve the deplaning passengers. Rance saw the magazine rack near the front of one of the kiosks with a couple of young men gazing at the seductive covers. With an indiscernible twist, he shook his head in sorrow. *If they only knew. . . the shame.* It didn't matter because in a few hours he would be hosting a group of those young men in a stripper club where the girls fawned over them while they bent over to pour watered down drinks. Rance would spend the major part of the evening with the young fools, all for a bit of information. He didn't know which he hated the most, the girls for working there or himself for being there.

Nonetheless, the wine, women, and song proved profitable for him. He was able to dump the bonds—the ones with potential poison in them called subprime bonds. Everything about this venture cost him sleep and dignity. His "Christian" family would scold him big time if they knew the things he did to keep Church Creek Falls and himself financially soluble.

The promises he made as a fourteen-year-old didn't seem so big at the time. That was a time of pain and loss. Every family in Church Creek Falls felt the loss of a loved one, and most of them felt the loss of property and jobs after the bomb. Rance's school friends lost their lives in the bomb; however, the financial plight of the people caused him to come up with the plan for rebuilding.

He convinced his mom to send out letters to churches, asking for prayer and donations of clothing or whatever. To their surprise, many churches sent youth groups to help rebuild houses. That was when Rance hatched the idea of buying a strip of land and using the free labor to build houses for those still left. The house frames were built by professional carpenters with the rest being little more than shoe boxes in the quality of work. It didn't matter, they sold quickly. Rance sold a house and bought a plot of land to build the next one. By the time he sold five houses, he raked in pure profit.

His dad served as the building advisor, and his brother helped with the sales. Barbara showed the houses, but Rance did all the financial work. It didn't take him long to realize real money could be made in real estate. He used his money to buy the devastated portions of town, and he paid for the clean-up and disposal. By the time Rance reached the ripe old age of twenty-two, he owned the majority of Church Creek Falls. Only the land under the courthouse and on the east side of the courthouse remained in a trust.

Rance had financed his hedge fund with the diamond bracelet Barbara gave him. She asked him to dispose of it, but he hadn't. He hadn't seen it until that day at . . . the day he entered Jenny's house for the first time since her disappearance. He shook his head, wondering how it could have been in the package Jenny wrapped for him. He sold it to an independent jeweler in

New York on one of his trips to his Hedge Fund Office, located on Wall Street, the one he called Pearl Investments. The one listed under the pseudonym of Kevin Hodge, the name of his friend he lost in the bombing.

Last year, Rance bought a thousand shares of a company no one had ever heard; a company called Books-A-Million. He bought one hundred shares of the company at three dollars a share on November 25, 1998, and by November 30 they were worth forty-seven dollars a share. He sold them December 1. Two weeks later they were only worth ten dollars. A return of forty-four thousand in five days.

It hooked him. With the Taxpayer's Relief Act of 1997 leading to high interest rates and lowering the top marginal capital gains tax in the United States, people became more willing to make more speculative investments. Rance hit the jackpot, and his wealth grew by the minute.

His staff of three rode the wave with him and never questioned him about his personal life. Rance liked that. During those times when he darkened the door of Pearl Investments, he felt the freest, especially from guilt. The whole of Wall street met in the strip clubs or the local brothels. Rance paid out two thousand a week to a local house, just to be available for clients. This was a different universe than his hometown and his family.

He kept this section of his life separate.

Tonight, as he watched the poor wretched girl strut around naked in high heels on the stage to the leering customers, all he could think about were Jenny and Alyssa.

One of the waitresses cozied up to him and offered to take his drink order. He turned his head toward her and looked into her eyes. Probably one of the few people who ever looked at her face. She was a hometown girl, made up to look like a big-city flirt.

"Where are you from?" he asked her.

She ducked her head and answered, "A small town you probably never heard of."

"It doesn't matter. Tell me about it," he prodded.

"I'm from a town in Kansas called Friend."

Rance smiled. "That's a nice name for a town."

She giggled a bit. "What can I get for you?"

"A coke."

She nodded. When she returned, Rance became more pensive and asked her another question, but whispered it in a guarded matter. "Are you here of your own free will or are you—"

She stopped him by putting her fingers over his lips. "Mister, I don't know what you're trying to do, but no one does this kind of work because they want to do it. And those kinds of questions can get me in trouble or killed," she said with a smile and a wink. She turned and swayed her hips a little more as she walked away.

Rance gulped. He didn't expect that. He looked at the girl on the stage—at her face. She was sad.

When she saw him looking at her, she flashed a smile and lowered her body toward him.

He looked away.

She walked away.

Rance took his coke back to a corner with his back up against a wall. He waited until his clients were ready to go, and from the look of them, they were like children in a candy store. This would be a long night.

During that time, Rance noticed all the sad faces of the girls.

An older woman came over to his table and sat down. "Mister, if you don't start buying something, I may have to ask you to leave," she stated with firm words framed by a fake smile.

"I've got buying clients over there. If I go, they go," Rance retorted with the same harsh voice.

"Sorry." She left.

He watched her leave. She managed the place, but he wondered who owned it.

Rance kept his Nokia cell phone near him, waiting for that phone call like the motionless wait of game hunting from a blind. He remembered last season with his brother in Southwestern Oklahoma. Starting before dark in the cold wind blowing around the canvas cover, waiting. Just waiting and hoping a good ten point or more buck would come. Neither came.

Instead, Rance fell asleep and fell ten feet to the floor of the woods. It knocked every wisp of air from his lungs and he struggled to breathe. He stared wide-eyed at his shocked brother climbing down the tree truck at the same moment a buck easily strolled by the tree truck. All this at once. He took a deep breath with the memory as if trying to fill his lungs on that past occasion. He could feel the tremble of fear and excitement meshed together and bouncing around his skull. In the same way the telephone ring stunned him with a greater fear and excitement when he answered it and heard,

"I've got her," came the growly voice of the caller.

"What do you want me to do?"

"Do you have the money?" The voice asked.

"Yes!" Rance screamed, wanting to know what to do. "Where is she?"

"Patience, old man, how do you know she still wants you?"

Rance opened his mouth to speak, but the words forming in his throat couldn't escape.

"What's the matter, old man?" the voice mocked.

Rance took three deep breaths to calm his heart. "Just tell me where we make the exchange."

"I'll let you know as soon as I confirm the money is in the bank."

The disembodied voice ended the conversation with a hang-up.

Rance held the phone as if his beloved would come through it for several minutes. His anxiety found release in a mournful, pitiful wail of a mortally wounded man.

Alyssa paced the room. She wanted to call and talk to some of her family, but her keeper had forbidden it. She must find the answer alone. She felt the craziness of imprisonment in this cabin. In spite of the room comfort and cute decoration, it still held her as prisoner.

The surrounding trees colored her view. The yellow and red leaves mixed with the needles of the evergreens.

She threw another log on the fire, her only source of heat. If she were on a retreat, this would be a perfect place to spend time with a romantic partner.

Matt came to mind. Her heart started racing. She put her hand on her chest and let out a long breath. The memory of his trickery caused fear to overtake her. *Calm down. You can get control. just do what you've been asked to do.*

Even with her self-governing pep talk, she felt like she rode in a car with the peddle stuck in high speed. With all that momentum, she couldn't think or reason. She wanted to run, scream, fight. She jumped up and down hoping to release or override the primitive part of her brain that sat on the edge of insanity in this cabin. She needed someone to help her. Strange that her first thought went to Matt, her abductor. Her fight or flight changed to anger—growing, seething anger.

She jumped and turned twice. The second time she saw the plume of smoke on the other side of the barrier that held the dragon back. It spoke to her emotional brain. "Rance is looking for you."

She ran out the door and stood on the covered porch. There were more dragons surrounding her now. All ugly and writhing as if trying to reach her. Her mouth opened as she looked at the repulsive reptiles.

She screamed at the top of lungs, "Help!"

As soon as she spoke, clouds gathered and hung in the sky. The dragons all belched fire toward her. It spread out and died when it hit the invisible barrier. The sky turned from a bright blue to a dark blue, all in shadow. The wind howled as if trying to scatter the clumps of clouds in the navy sky.

Drums resonated through the skies, occasionally piercing it with a loud crack of thunder, followed by the flash of lighting so bright, the plums of flames from the dragon's mouth could no longer be seen.

Then the first drop of rain fell and landed on her hand she'd extended beyond the porch roof. Another joined quickly, and she pulled the sweet-smelling water to her mouth and drank it in.

The power of hope filled her, and she stepped out into the pouring rain and raised her hands to the sky. "My God, you have the answer! Please, show me."

The rain fell in sheets. She went back inside and closed the door. But she noticed the dragons were gone. "Hmm, I guess they don't like the rain, especially if it's showers of blessings." She smirked. She didn't know if the rainstorm was from the Lord or the physics of earth, but either way it gave a precious commodity—hope.

Alyssa sat at the table covered in books and poured herself into the words. Soon, her mind rebelled against the mundane sentences. "There has to be an answer somewhere, but I'm just not seeing it."

She rose from the table, poured herself a glass of ice water, and leaned against the kitchen sink. From this angle she could observe the entire bookcase filled with material. "My keeper said, the answer is in that bookcase."

Alyssa took a deep drink and walked toward the bookcase. She plopped on the floor and read the spines of the books. At the end of the row of vertical books sat a neat stack of different versions of the Bible. The top one printed in large print attracted her tired eyes. She took the book to the table, sat down, and reached for the concordance. It gave her a starting point.

"Let's start with the parable of the sower." She opened the Bible to Matthew 13 and read, then turned to Luke 8. "The seed is the Word of God." Not an answer she was looking for. Using it as a springboard, she reasoned that if the seed was the Word of God for that parable, then the seed would bear more seed from gaining knowledge from the Word of God.

"Ok, we're onto something," Alyssa said.

However, the question remained why the phrase would be used by the dragon if the Word of God was the seed. After reading every verse containing the word 'seed', Alyssa came to Romans 9:8. "They which are the children of the flesh, these are not the children of God, but the children of the promise are counted for the seed."

She reasoned, "The Word of God is the seed and Jesus is the Word of God as noted in John 1:1. It states the beginning was the Word and the Word was God." Then the comment that the children of the flesh are not children of God. What does it mean the "children of the promise are counted for the seed?"

Alyssa sat back in the stiff kitchen chair to relieve the cramp in her back. "I need to discover more about the promise."

Long Nguyen stepped into the bank and asked the teller, "Can you check for a deposit in my account." He passed a slip of paper to her. She nodded and went back into an office. After a few minutes she returned and handed Mr. Nguyen an envelope. On the front it read, *Church Creek Falls*. He walked over to one of the private areas of the bank and opened the envelope. He pulled an eight by ten picture of a young girl. He smiled and nodded. Nice." When the picture was fully exposed, he read the name on the bottom, "Alyssa Troye."

His smile grew bigger, and with a twitch of his left eye, he said to himself, "The first of the harvest."

Marcy and Zay laughed with Patti at The Honey Tree. The crisp fall air demanded some coffee and delightful pastry. "I sure hope Michelle is baking today." Marcy said pulling her gloves and beret off.

"She is and some fresh pies just came out of the oven. What's your pleasure?" Patti asked them. Marcy didn't hesitate, "Lemon."

Zay nodded, "Same."

While Patti went behind the counter to cut the pie, a swish of wind swept the room as another customer entered. Or rather, another person. Christine walked in. Patti took the sauces of pie toward Marcy and Zay's table where Christine sat down with them. Patti took the other chair. This was not good.

"What are you doing here?" Marcy glared at Christine and asked through gritted teeth.

"Calm down, silly girl, I'm not here for you. Besides I've already had my fun with you." Christine snickered.

Marcy came up out of her seat, but Zay pushed her back down.

"Let's hear what she has to say," Zay whispered. "Then I'll hold her down while you do a little batting practice on her face."

Marcy smiled and ducked her head. She patted Zay on the hand.

He nodded and put his other hand on top of hers.

Marcy took a deep breath. "Ok, what do you want?"

Christine turned to Patti. "You want to tell them?"

Patti leaned forward and put her clasped hands on the table. "Christine bought my house," she announced.

Marcy looked at Patti with narrowed eyes and shook her head. With a wrinkled brow she said, "Oh, what does that have to do with us?"

Patti continued. "Her check didn't clear. She came here to say you owed her the money, and you would pay for my house back in Burlington Falls."

Zay gripped Marcy's hand at the announcement. Marcy felt her heart fall to her knees. "What?" She answered. "How do I owe you money, especially that much?"

With the smirk of the dragon directing Christine's actions and words, she answered Marcy, "Remember what you did to me?"

"Me did to you?" Marcy exclaimed. "You left me there in that hospital." Marcy stood, knocking her chair to the ground. This time Zay didn't stop her and stood too.

Marcy raised her voice and pointed her finger at Christine. "How dare you!"

"Look, if you don't want to pay me, it's okay; I've got a lien on your lab I'll cash in."

Zay picked up Marcy's chair and set it upright moments before she fell into it. He sat down beside her, and in a calm voice said, "We need more information."

"Whatever. Take your time. Each day—even each hour—that passes, I get compounded interest." Christine stood and waved at them as she walked out of the restaurant.

Marcy stared at Patti, "What the heck is going on here?"

"She's a dragon and . . . and . . ."

"And what?" Zay shouted at Patti as she ducked her head.

"And I don't think we can win. It's bad."

"How bad?" Zay calmed his anger.

"Rance has the details; he made the deals. I only know that horrible dragon dressed in Christine's image wants our souls."

"Whose soul?" Marcy asked.

"The whole town, and the sad thing is that the monster already owns us all."

Marcy and Zay huddled together on the couch of their home.

Marcy felt the tears rolling down her cheeks. "What will we do?"

"I don't know." Zay leaned his head over his wife's.

"She was the one that trapped me in that awful psychiatric hospital, and now she wants me to pay her? And how did she get a lien on our lab?" Marcy groaned.

"Like she said, we need to talk to Rance."

"I don't think that's possible." Marcy whimpered.

"Why not?" Zay asked.

"Haven't you noticed how he acts lately? He's in another world, at least another time zone." She smirked at the time comment.

"I know what you're saying. I've noticed him being aloof too."

"Barbara and I have called him Felix the cat because he's become so aloof. He smells too, not like he's dirty, but like his body chemistry is changing, and it's not for the better."

"You know, it's been five years this Christmas since Jennifer disappeared, and he's been getting her house ready for sale."

"Yeah, I know. But there's more to it than that."

"Do you still think about those months in the psychiatric hospital?" Zay changed the subject.

"Not much, but occasionally I have a nightmare about that awful dragon," Marcy answered while watching Zay. He turned back toward her and walked to his recliner. He sat down and rested his chin on his fist. He stared at the back yard through the glass door.

"Me too," he said in a simple manner as if he was asked if he wanted a cookie.

Marcy sat down on the couch opposite him on the edge. "What's going on in your mind?" She reached out and touched his knee.

"Those awful days I had to leave you there."

Marcy sighed and sat back. "It's wasn't so bad when you started coming to see me every day. Course, that was the time the old dragon quit coming." She smiled at the memory of his rescuing her from Christine's diabolical plot of trading places with her.

"You have to admit; it was pretty clever of her to trade places with you. Especially given the difference in your size and appearance." Zay still stared at the glass door.

"That was the biggest problem I had. Why couldn't anyone tell the difference?"

"They weren't looking," Zay answered quickly. Then he turned and looked at Marcy, "That's it!"

"What's it?"

"Nobody's looking."

"At what?" Marcy felt left out of the conversation going on in Zay's head.

"Nobody's looking at the financial records and deals Rance is doing."

28

A Long Look

Perhaps they will listen and everyone will turn from his evil way, that I may repent of the calamity which I am planning to do to them because of the evil of their deeds.

Jeremiah 26:3

SHARON, MICHAEL, AND Rance came out of a tunnel and examined the surroundings. "I don't know where we are, but it is isn't Santa Fe," Michael said.

"How do you know?" Rance asked looking at the ground.

Sharon pointed up in the air. "We're in Enid."

Michael followed her finger to see the word Enid written on a water tower. He started laughing.

"I think we got scammed," Rance said. "They don't need guards at that tunnel, they just send strangers to strange places."

"Well, Enid isn't that strange," Michael said. "There's an army base here, and rumor says there's an underground base where they keep aliens." He smirked and winked at them.

Sharon slapped him on the arm. "You silly. You know there are no creatures from outer space."

"Where do you think dragons come from?" Michael turned serious.

Sharon sighed and responded, "What does it say in Ephesians six? For our struggle is not against flesh and blood, but against the rulers, against the powers, against the world forces of this darkness, against the spiritual forces of wickedness in the heavenly places."

"Sounds more like dragons than little gray people." Michael laughed at their conversation.

"Why dragons?" Rance asked Sharon.

"Because that's the way the Bible describes them and the way we see them," she answered.

"I don't," Rance said. "Maybe you're watching too many sci-fi movies."

Michael took Sharon by the hand and squeezed it. This was not an argument they wanted to enter.

Sharon leaned toward Michael and barely whispered, "I see the outline form of Mammon standing over Rance."

"Me too," he whispered back.

"Maybe we need to find it and see for ourselves," Sharon proposed.

"Sure, we walk up to a military base and tell them we want to see their deep underground base. I'm sure they'd give us an escort," Michael mocked. He turned around and looked for the tunnel from which they emerged. "Look!" he pointed.

"It's gone." Sharon gulped.

Michael raised his eyebrows. *Here we go again.*

"Why do they need underground bases?" Sharon asked as she walked around looking for the opening.

"To hide things?" Rance smirked.

"Yep," Michael said without comment and started walking toward town. "I bet we can find someplace to eat. I'm starved."

"Then what?" Sharon took his hand again.

"Then we rent a car and go home. I'm thinking six to eight hours to get home," Michael said.

A flash of green caught the sunlight for a second. Rance noticed the sight without acknowledging it. Soon, the flash of color disappeared. He didn't mention it to his cousins, but instead, he searched their faces for any recognition of the strange sight.

Mammon walked beside the trio. They were so easy to pull into this wicked game of the master deceiver. Soon, he'd be getting the rewards of the master when he destroyed the Troye family. He couldn't help but puff a little smoke of pride when he thought about those before him who had tried: Nisroch, god of Agriculture, Jorkphat, his demon child, and Belial, the master and meanest of all dragons. They were too pushy, too forward, but Mammon wove the web and like a spider sat and waited for them to fall into an inescapable trap.

Today was a bright star day, for each member of the Troye family touched his web. What a delight it was going to be to see them squirm. The Holy One will not be able to rescue people from the trap Mammon sets because they are all consumed with greed. He even says so in His Holy Book when He sends His prophet Jeremiah to find an honest man. Mammon roared with delight because Jeremiah couldn't find an honest man then and there exist none now.

The drive back to Church Creek Falls remained quiet. Rance pondered what happened and how to put a stop to it and erase it. He couldn't have any of his family know what he was doing and what he had caused.

"Any news on the hunt for Alyssa?" he asked Sharon.

She shook her head. "We keep praying; Buster says she is not in harm's way."

"How does he know that?" Rance scowled.

"He says she's protected by a hedge of prayer."

"That's silly. Don't you think a dragon can step over a stupid hedge?" Rance raised his voice slightly.

Michael smiled. "It's an expression of how the dragons cannot reach anyone protected by prayer."

"Yeah? Barbara said that demon was about to possess her before you guys appeared," Rance recounted.

"The difference between Barbara and Alyssa is motive," Sharon added.

"Motive? What do you mean?"

"Barbara rebelled against her beliefs and went searching for the evil."

"Okay, you've lost me." Rance threw his arm up in the air.

"Barbara felt betrayed by her Christian beliefs, so she left the hedge of protection to see what was outside."

"And what did she find?"

"Dragons!" Michael stated. "Mean, ugly, despicable dragons."

Rance gave them a crooked smile. "And you think Alyssa is protected?"

"Yes. She will be obedient and not leave the hedge of protection."

"You guys probably believe there are aliens on earth too," Rance mocked.

"Evil comes in many forms, but it's still evil," Michael answered.

Rance smirked and dropped out of the conversation. He turned toward the car window and whispered, "God, if you are real, I hope they're right, and You are protecting that little girl."

Alyssa sat in the quiet, empty cabin surrounded by a myriad of books. Leaving them aside for a moment, she stepped into the kitchen and fixed a snack. She leaned against the cabinet and stared at the mess she created. *I need a computer to organize all this information.* She took a deep breath, stretched, and decided to go to bed. It was early, but she was tired. The statement was simple, but the answer to Davis' question about why a dragon is speaking it buffaloed her. There had to be a solution.

The blinds covered the windows, blocking the daylight from coming into the cabin. She took a deep breath and went to the kitchen window and opened the blinds. The sight outside was beautiful—no dragons. She opened another blind and beheld the beauty of the forest. *I may go out today.* First comes some work. Somehow, she knew the answer to the question would set her free from this place and return her back home.

She walked to the bookcase and studied the spines. Several small folders were squeezed between a few books. She pulled them out and read the titles on the front. They seem to be prospectus of different companies. The Honey Tree was one. After pouring herself a fresh cup of coffee, she curled up in the chair and opened the file.

Mammon watched the confused look on Alyssa's face from the perch outside the Holy One's protective hedge. He kept calling her name and attempting to lure her outside of the shielding circle. The angel the Holy One sent, known to Alyssa as Davis, guarded her fiercely. He served as her messenger from the Holy One. As long as she remained obedient. Mammon couldn't touch her or her mind. All he could do is sing a song to draw her away. Homer's Iliad called it the Siren's song. The only way his evil could operate would be in her curiosity.

The angel Davis tasked her to find the meaning behind the statement of dragons, *the planting of seed is singular, but the harvest comes in multiples.* Delight danced in the shiny green scales covering the hideous face of the heartless monster. This little girl would never find the truth Mammon hid. Heck, even scholars often overlooked it. So simple and yet so difficult for the human to see. *Pht! Stupid creatures. Why does the Holy One love them so much?*

The moment Alyssa entered the circle of the Holy One's protection, she left the monster's reach, but not his influence. Along with the other monsters in the realm of evil, the Troye family held a particular level of hatred among the dragons. "They must be destroyed!" Mammon roared.

The realm of dragons joined in the roar raised over the community of Church Creek Falls. It once again covered the place and the people with a thick cloud of anticipation of disgrace and calamity. This time the calamity wouldn't be so bold as to destroy the buildings in a blast, but it would destroy the hearts of the youth by making The Holy One's children worthless in each other's eyes.

If they could look at the abuse of one human to another in pornography, they would be able to injure another without feeling guilt. The pornographic images made some rich and violent, while terminating any sense of morality and obedience to the Holy One.

Rance didn't have the spirit of Christ with him. He belonged to the dragons, and they would destroy the family by destroying the son. In the same way, the dragons led the foolish humans to nail their only hope of life on a cross. Mammon's roar of pleasure soured with the memory of that dead man walking out of the grave.

Death is the weapon of the dragons—either the cause of it or by implanting the fear of it in the filthy humans.

The dragons could only torment the Troye's, but Rance still belonged to them. They would bring him and his Jenny Gale to their knees in a horrible death. It would be the first time Rance faced death, then he would feel the eternal sting of the second death. Mammon roared again.

Buster's prayer time continued throughout each moment of life. The pain in his shoulder throbbed with each heartbeat to remind him of the dragon's constant threat against his family. The wound didn't cause his body any distress of health. Instead, the nagging pain informed him of the state of his family members. The intensity of the pain relayed the current battle each one fought with a dragon.

When he fell to his knees and bowed his head to pray fervently for Alyssa, the pain stopped completely. This could only mean she had passed from this life and stood beside her Savior in heaven or she rested safely in His keeping on earth. Either way, Buster knew Alyssa was not in the grip of a dragon.

He turned his attention to pray for Rance. "Youch!" he yelped.

Merilee came running into his office. When she saw him on his knees she asked, "Which one?"

"Rance," Buster answered.

Merilee knelt beside him and the parents took their love for their son to the One who loved him more, and they pleaded for his soul to be rescued from the grip of the dragon.

In the midst of the petitions offered, Buster found complete relief.

Merilee and Buster prayed for all their children, but especially for Rance. They asked for Jason's physical safety and strength in leadership. They asked for Zay and Marcy to be strong in the face of tribulation. They asked for Michael and Sharon to endure. They prayed for Daniel and Barbara's wisdom. Then they prayed for each of their grandchildren and for their nieces and nephews. They gave thanks for each of them.

An angel dressed in army fatigues listened to their prayers and then carried it with care to the throne room of grace where the Holy Spirit delivered it to the altar in front of the throne of the One and only true God. The prayer burned, and its essence came to the Father as a sweet smell of worship.

The sound of Buster and Merilee's prayers touched Mammon's ears with the same intense pain Buster felt in his shoulder.

Patti, Cook, and Michelle closed The Honey Tree and went to their home. Rance provided them a furnished house in which to live. On nights like tonight, they expressed their gratitude to have a place of their own. With a busy night and tired feet, they each found their own seat of relaxation with a cup of hot tea.

"Do you think Marcy will come through?" Michelle asked Patti.

"I don't know what's going on." Patti answered as she rubbed her sore feet. "I'm going to find more comfortable shoes for working. These are killing my feet."

"The mean woman is killing my feet," Cook responded, referring to Christine.

"I don't think she'll leave us alone, even if Marcy does pay her. She isn't here for money." Patti groaned.

"Then what is she here for?" Michelle asked.

"Evil, pure evil."

"We know about that," Cook said, handing Patti and Michelle their cup of tea.

"Are we going to stop her?" Michelle asked.

"How?"

"Expose her!" Michele answered Patti.

"She won't care. Evil plots its own way, and it doesn't care who knows. Look what we did."

"I forget; we were once evil." Michelle took a sip of tea.

"I guess we still are. We brought Christine to this town. Do you think we need to leave?" Cook asked Patti.

"No, I think we need to stay and fight. After all, we know what happens when people disappear," Patti responded.

The three women dropped into a guilty silence. "We need to pray for those who we deceived and the ones who have disappeared," Patti said.

The Holy Spirit heard their prayers and He spoke words of truth to their minds. Words of hope. When he delivered the prayers to the throne of Grace, the Father smiled and said, "Go." It is time to set a plan of rescue into action.

Christine threw her coat over the bed and turned on the water in the bathtub. She gathered her bathing paraphernalia, settled into the warm water, and sighed as the water wrapped around her cold body. Her head fell back against the tub pillow, and the orchestral music played softly in the background from the radio.

"I think I may stay in this town. I smell opportunity."

Mammon spoke soothing but cruel words to Christine's mind. No one loved her, and no one ever loved her. She didn't even have a family.

As Christine pondered her worthless life, she heard a baby crying. She tuned into it. It was her own cry. She wanted to be held, to be loved, to belong to someone.

Over the noise of the crying, another voice whispered, "I love you."

"Who are you?" Christine demanded.

"I am Jesus, and I will never leave you. All you have to do is ask for Me."

Jesus? Yeah, that's a good one. It's a fairy tale.

Mammon gave her the words and once the monster grasped her thinking the ideas of worthlessness and being unlovable repeated in her mind. The baby crying became louder.

"Christine, you want to live. You need to live," came the soothing voice.

Mammon retreated.

Christine finished her bath and dressed. She sat on the edge of the bed and wept. When she opened the hotel nightstand drawer in search of tissues, she found a black book with the gold letters saying, 'Holy Bible.'

Taking the book in her hands she let her fingers trace the gold letters. There was comfort in the action. She had never read one of these books. She thumbed through it looking at the strange names. There were chapters and the sentences and sometimes paragraphs were numbered. *What do I do with this How do I find any answers?* She let the book fall open on its own. She read a few words of the place it opened. It was like trying to read a novel by letting it open to its own page. She sighed and turned to the table of contents. The book was divided into the Old Testament and the New Testament. She decided to go with the new. She started with Matthew 1:1, The *record of the genealogy of Jesus the Messiah, the son of David, the son of Abraham.*

Well, that's a good place to start with Jesus. She laughed at herself. The next verses read like a genealogy. It meant nothing to her. She closed the book and shouted in a loud whisper, "I need some answers to what just happened to me." She threw the book on the bed and made a pot of coffee. The voice she heard kept repeating itself to her, "you are loved." She took her coffee and retrieved the book again. This time nestling down into the recliner in her room. She read the first verse of every section with a heading. Mark 1:1 *"The beginning of the gospel of Jesus Christ, the son of God."*

"Matthew said He was the son of David. So what's going on?" she felt agitation. She moved on to Luke 1:1 *"we have undertaken to compile an account of the things accomplished by us."* This sounds a bit more promising. She turned to the next heading John 1:1, *"In the beginning was the Word and the Word was with God and the Word was God."*

Christine took a drink from her coffee and shook her head. "This is strange stuff; I'm going to have to read all the things in between to get this message." Intrigued by the pattern she continued to Acts 1:1 *The first account I composed, Theophilis, about all Jesus began to do and teach.* I don't know who Theophilis is but at least I'm getting into what Jesus did. She read the next words next to number 2, *until the day when He was taken up to heaven, after He had by the Holy Spirit given orders to the apostle whom He had chosen.*

"Sounds like the actions lasted his lifetime and they took him to heaven. Yep, that's what I want to know." Christine snickered and turned to Romans 1:1, *Paul, a bond-servant of Christ-Jesus called an an apostle, set apart for the gospel of God.*

This is the guy I want to hear. Sounds like he may have some answers. Christine found herself caught up in the book. She moved on to 1 and 2 Corinthians, Galatians and saw Paul started them all. She stopped at Ephesians 1:1. *Paul, an apostle of Christ Jesus by the will of*

God, To the saints who are at Ephesus and who are faithful in Christ Jesus.

"Okay, these are the characters, Jesus is the son of God who left a record of his teachings to his apostle which apparently is Paul. I think this is the guy with the answers." She turned the page. Before she could move on to Philippians, she noticed the words at the top of the next page, *Some of you were lost in your trespasses and sins.* She stopped turning, sat up in her chair, "Now you're talking to me." She put her coffee cup down and read the whole chapter and when she finished, she read it again. Tears began to stream down her face. "I want this love and this gift." She moaned.

Rance entered his big, fancy, empty, cold house. He turned on his computer, dropped his bag, and headed for the shower. After his shower, he slipped on a robe as the flicker of his computer screen alerted him that his mate for the evening had arrived. He went to the kitchen, made himself a sandwich and poured a glass of wine.

"Here I come sweetheart," he called to the computer.

After three hours at the computer talking to several girls in chat rooms—at least he hoped they were girls— he felt drained. He turned off the computer, gulped the last of the wine, and sat there staring at a black screen.

"Why, do I do it?" he asked the screen.

Mammon heard.

Rance saw the reflection of the ugly, giant, green serpent on his screen.

Mammon answered, "Because it takes away the pain of loneliness."

Rance buried his head in his hands and moaned. Those moans led to sobs. The sobs led to the medicine cabinet where he took two pills Daniel gave him for anxiety. Sleep came in a restless drugged state, which opened a doorway for Mammon to enter his mind and talk to Rance.

"It's time," Mammon said to Rance.

"Time for what?"

"The harvest. It's time to collect on your scheme," Mammon answered then roared.

Rance trembled. "What do you mean?"

"The planting of seed is singular, but the harvest comes in multiples."

29

Games

*Thus saith the Lord, the Godof Israel; Like these good figs, so will I
acknowledge them that are carried away captive of Judah, whom I have
sent out of this place into the land of the Chaldeans for their good.*
Jeremiah 24:5

MICHAEL RELUCTANTLY OPENED the book
Long Nguyen gave him in spite of the warning. Michael
could feel a little sweat bead tracking down the side of
his face. He wasn't warm enough to sweat, but the
anxiety of reading anything by Long Nguyen caused his
whole body to react.

The first chapter came as a surprise. It was like a
testimony of how Long Nguyen and Dragon Wind
Construction came into existence. Michael leaned back
in his off chair and read;

I came to hate the Americans when my village was
burned with their napalm. The fire that would not die. I
watched my brother's skin melt form his bones. When
the fire went out, I touched his foot and his skin came
off in my hands. I was young in 1950 when the French

came to set the land of Vietnam straight. They were defeated and followed by the Americans.

I found the American soldiers to be amusing in some ways. We watched them. All the time we watched them. Then we would surround them. The surprise of our sudden appearance from the tops of the trees and from the underground tunnels frightened them. Even though their firepower was much greater than ours, we could overtake them with fear. They were young boys in a foreign land, we were young men in our own land. I never felt sorry for them, even when we saved a few for entertainment.

Michael closed the book and shuddered. He could feel the eyes of Long Nguyen upon him. Especially the day he was captured. This book revealed that he and Paps were captured for their entertainment, otherwise they would both be dead. Michael released a long deep breath. Then Barbara showed up and saved our lives *How?*

Michael opened the book again. He flipped a few pages over and began to read again.

I knew the apparition was real. I heard the woman speaking. I understood her words even though they were strange to me. I walked toward her to hear more and ran into an invisible barrier. I could no longer hear the woman's voice, instead I heard a deep guttural voice say, 'look over there. I felt the voice in my head more than heard it with my ears. I examined the tunnel. I stepped inside. I looked around a few minutes. I drew diagrams and pictures of what I saw. I wrote it in my own blood on my shirt, for I had nothing else.

My men a ran away in fear of the old woman. I waited in the tunnel opening until she disappeared. I could see the captives startled. I listened to them talking and followed them to their unit. I hid until all were sleeping, then I took a uniform from a dead South Vietnamese soldier and took his place. No one ever suspected. I moved with stealth and boarded an American plane unseen.

My curiosity about Americans began as a means to injure them. Soon I was able to speak the language and move about in their world as easily as I had moved about in Vietnam. I earned an engineering degree and opened an engineering firm with my fake American citizenship. My first project in my new home with my new name of Harry Nguyen was copied from a bloody shirt.

Again, Michael closed the book. The next chapters explained how to work the machine and set it for different stations. Right now, he didn't need that information. He knew Long Nguyen meant Dragon Wind and Michael suspected the dragons revealed the plan for the speed machine to Long Nguyen.

Mammon flicked his tongue at Michael. "Think you're pretty smart don't you?" The monster mocked.

"I think you are pretty evil." Michael responded without flinching at the huge serpent tongue flicking around his face. He wouldn't give the lizard the satisfaction.

"Lizard. What an insult." Mammon roared.

"Good." Michael rose from his chair and threw the book on his desk.

Long Nguyen prepared to enter the speed machine and make a trip to Church Creek Falls.

Mammon stood beside his faithful servant. A man filled with hate. Mammon loved to plant the scenes of war in his fertile mind. The man would replay the scenes over and over and with each scene his heart would grow harder and more hate-filled. Just the type of man needed to take down the Troye family.

Mammon knew a heart filled with hate could understand the wisdom of his nefarious plan. A plan that would leave the soul of the Americans in more disarray than any physical torment would wound their bodies. Of course, Mammon hated Long Nguyen as much as he hated the Troye family, but Long Nguyen's cold hard hate made him useful as a tool for the coming harvest. Mammon's greatest anticipation of the entire harvest would be to watch the horror on Rance's face as the harvest of lost souls in Church Creek Falls began to pour into the augur leading to complete devastation of the community. Rance's plan to finance a community restoration would turn into a hellish nightmare for him and complete poverty of soul and body for the community. Mammon roared with delight at a plan that would even make Wall Street blush in its cruelty and corruption.

It would be like the message Jeremiah gave the people telling them their God would leave them and make them a curse because they didn't listen, so it would be with Church Creek Falls, only this second tragedy would destroy the town and the Troyes.

Mammon joined in the chorus of dragons as they roared, "Robert Troye all your descendants will die and fall into our trap!"

"That was the strangest lighting I've ever seen," Daniel said to Michael.

Michael stared at the sky. Dragons appeared to be carved into the clouds, until their dragonish ways awoke the terror of reptilian eyes glaring down at him, and their spiked teeth surrounding a split tongue crept into his soul with a fear that could freeze his blood.

A bur fire burned in the chests of the heartless monsters, and the scales burned with the cold of ice able to turn human skin into a sickly pallor. Their claws able to lacerate the strongest of human flesh into ribbons. They flicked their tongues to smell the fear of their victims.

The people attending to everyday chores of life had no sense of the hate-filled eyes watching their every move seeking an opportunity to deceive. Nor could they conceive of the total destruction from a knowledge unmatched by human intelligence, but the dragons were filled with a toxic greed for human blood.

Michael watched as the last dragon found his prey and satisfied his hunger, ungrateful for the sacrifice the humans made but rejoicing in the victory of demolishing another of the Holy One's children. His heart beat faster as he saw the ease with which the monsters were able to deceive and devour the unsuspecting humans.

A loud sound like thunder-on-thunder filled the air.

"I don't think it was lighting," Michael said.

"Then what?" Daniel followed Michael's gaze.

"The black-blood monsters are rejoicing." Michael trembled.

"You mean . . . dragons!" Daniel whispered. Daniel's face went pale. "Tonight—Rance?"

"Or Alyssa? Wherever she may be."

"We've got to rescue her. But how?" Daniel asked through gritted teeth.

"Same as always—with the sword of the Spirit and prayer," Michael answered.

"I don't think we have enough swords or prayer." Daniel gazed at the sky with open mouth.

"Can you see them?" Michael asked.

Daniel nodded. "Let's go get Zay, Marcy, Mom and Dad."

They quickly climbed into the car.

The money flowed into Silicon Valley, California, like a heavy rainstorm. No one cared if the companies were solid or not. Business plans were a waste of time, and anyone with a half-baked scheme could get thousands, or maybe millions, from venture capitalists. Now every venture capitalist and investor waited for the next big thing to appear, hoping it would be in their portfolio.

Rance studied his portfolio. His investments were huge, and his returns were head-spinning. He went underground to find his geeks—the ones creating the interaction between fantasy and reality. The ones selling sex—both real and imagined. The pornography industry didn't get on the public offerings except to legitimize their company names. Rance made his company, Tender Expressions public, and money from porn sites poured into it.

The plan conceived by himself and his little geek elves, produced a legitimate business and program. But for those willing to lay down a credit card number to buy a secret code the internet revealed more than a series of stuffed animals in all sizes and colors. With the right code, the stuffed animals opened a whole new world, and it didn't care who was looking or their age. It could be accessed by any search engine looking for the pot of gold at the end of the computer program. Quilting patterns, children's stories, and toys would make the search engine bring Rance's program to the top of the list. Once the victim took the hook, then the money had to be laid down in order to get inside.

Rance convinced his family he had a problem with pornography. He also convinced them he looked at the web sites looking for Jennifer. It wasn't easy keeping up the charade because his real eye candy was the millions of dollars coming into his account. The constant diet of fantasy girls diluted real girls to nothing more than objects. He even wondered how he would react if Jenny did return. His desire for a relationship with a woman had been replaced with this relationship. He leaned back in his chair, put his hands behind his head, and watched the numbers change by the second. In a few seconds he would sell everything, the balloon had reached its peak and would soon explode. While the rest of the world would moan about the loss, Church Creek Falls would be rolling in enough cash to build anything they wanted, even an airport. It's a fact in the money market business that for every win, there's an equal or greater loss.

The computer screen flickered with a greenish glow. For a second Rance saw a huge snake head strike at him from his computer screen. He jumped and yelled. "What the heck?"

The Dot.com bubble burst. Rance instantly became a billionaire.

Buster groaned constantly with punctuations of screams of pain.

Merilee rubbed salve on the throbbing wound.

Barbara and Sharon entered the tunnel at the sand dunes.

30

A Calling

For I will set mine eyes upon them for good, and I will bring them again to this land: and I will build them, and not pull them down; and I will plant them, and not pluck them up,.

Jeremiah 24:6

THEIR FOOTFALLS ECHOED in the quiet of the tunnel. Even the ground looked like glazed-rock flooring and sounded like shoes on tile. The light seemed dull as if there were too few bulbs for the space. The air flowed like a gentle breeze and smelled of a summer morning with dew on newly mown hay. Not an unpleasant atmosphere at all.

"Where do we go?" Sharon asked Barbara as they walked through the tunnels.

"I'm not sure. we need to find the invisible people-mover sections that take you to a different place or time."

"If they're invisible, how will we know?" Sharon chuckled.

"I guess when we end up in some far-off city or back in 1970," Barbara answered with a smile.

Sharon stumbled. "Sorry, I'm nervous . . . no, I'm scared."

Barbara took Sharon's hand. "Me too. I keep thinking about Alyssa. This was the last place she was seen, and that's why we're here looking for clues.

"It sounded like a good plan at our kitchen table."

"I don't think Alyssa's here," Barbara noted. "This serves as a pass-through, not a destination."

"What makes you think that?" Sharon asked looking from side to side.

"Matt."

"How so?"

"He came back to The Honey Tree after Alyssa left with him. According to Patti, he wasn't in a great mood and kept talking about that little . . . Well, he used words I wouldn't use."

"You think she slipped through his fingers?" Sharon asked. As long as they were talking, the creepy noises weren't as loud.

"She slipped through something."

"What do you think about Patti and her crew?" Sharon started another conversation.

"Their conversion to Christ is real."

"Why?"

"At Jason's deployment party," Barbara replied, "Patti asked me to lead them in some Bible studies."

"Have you?" Sharon stopped walking and looked at Barbara, who nodded.

At the same moment, Sharon saw the air waves move. "Look, there it is. How come we didn't see it before?"

"Strange, it's like someone turned a television on."

The two women stared at a vision in front of them of a rustic room with someone walking around in it. "What is that?"

"I don't know. Do you feel brave enough to enter?" Barbara squeezed Sharon's hand.

They heard a loud roar and a woosh behind them, then felt sudden heat.

They turned around to see the head of a huge green dragon with mouth agape, reaching out for them. Discussion was over, the two women ran into the blurry scene sitting atop a moving, almost invisible, ramp.

Michael poured over the files. They didn't make sense. Something was wrong, but he didn't understand the financial manipulations nor the terms. *No wonder they don't let just anyone trade. You have to speak their code language.*

The ringing phone startled him. He waited two more rings before he answered. It was Daniel, who sounded as though he may have run a marathon.

"You okay?" Michael asked.

"Have you seen Barbara and Sharon?"

"Not since I left the house this morning. Why?"

"I think something weird is going on," Daniel said between breaths. "I found a note from Barbara saying she and Sharon were going to the tunnels."

"Oh, yeah, Sharon did mention they were thinking of going out there and looking around. Thought they might find some clues about Alyssa."

"You know Buster told us she was safe."

"I remember," Michael said. "But Sharon's argument contended she was safe, so we didn't need to panic . . . just needed to look for her."

"Michael, I'm worried."

"So am I now. What do we do?"

"Meet you at the tunnel."

"On my way." Michael folded the file and put it in his locked desk drawer. This stuff was giving him a headache anyway.

They found Sharon's car parked on the side of the road near the gate into the sand dunes. The gate remained locked, but the smaller door for people stood wide open.

Michael and Daniel walked through the gate and entered the tunnels.

Marcy opened the envelope and pulled out one sheet of paper. She read, "Zay," and called to her husband. "Come look at this."

"That's strange," he said. "Who sent it?"

Marcy looked at the envelope. No postmark or return address. She shrugged.

Zay tossed the paper into the trash. "Doesn't mean anything," he said and went back to his lab. Before he continued working the samples into petri dishes, he poured a glass of ice water and downed it in a few seconds. He refilled the glass and again gulped all of the sixteen ounces of water. On the third refill, he stopped and turned his head, looking around the room. He went back into Marcy's section of their lab. "Is there a dragon in here?"

Marcy pointed to the trash can, where Zay had tossed the paper earlier. It was burning. "Could be."

Zay pulled the paper out and extinguished the flames. He examined the paper from all sides and then sat it on the table showing it, to Marcy. The flames revealed a hidden message. *Enter the tunnel!*

"What does that mean?" Marcy pondered as she stared at the words, waiting for more to become visible.

"If you're caught up with your work, we'll go to the tunnel and see, Zay answered.

When Zay and Marcy approached the entrance, they saw two cars sitting on the side of the road. "Looks like Michael, Sharon, Barbara and Daniel beat us here" Zay said pointing to their cars.

"I think we are a little old for a beach party," Marcy argued.

"Did you ever find anything else on that paper besides a demand to come here?" Zay asked her.

"The planting of seed is singular," Marcy said. "I tried to ignore it. I'm so tired of that phrase."

"Me too," Zay said and grasped Marcy's hand. "We're here. Now what?"

"Go see what's inside," Marcy answered, letting go of Zay's hand and entering the broad tunnel opening.

"Call Rance!" Buster called to Merilee as he held his shoulder and doubled over, falling out of his chair.

Rance made it to the farm in fifteen minutes.

"Dad?" he called when he burst through the back door of his childhood home.

"In here," Merilee called to him.

"What's wrong?" Rance pulled Buster into his chair. "What happened?"

"I heard him holler to call you, and when I came in here, I found him on the floor. I couldn't get him up."

Buster groaned and wriggled in his chair. Merilee rubbed the wound with the salve to calm it. The wound thumped with each heartbeat, growing larger, deeper, and more purple. Merilee winched at the sight.

"Dad, why is your wound growing? What's happening? Talk to me!" Rance shouted in Buster's face.

Buster struggled with his tongue, attempting to speak. A few garbled sounds came out of his mouth.

"Dad, I can't understand you." Rance held him by the shoulders to keep him from falling out of the chair again.

Buster bolted up, and with clear eyes he shouted at Rance, "Son, it's time!"

Rance raised his eyes to meet Merilee's. "What time?"

Merilee shrugged her shoulders.

"Time for what?" Rance put his face directly in front of his dad's face.

"Rescue Alyssa," Buster said.

31

In the Land of the Enemy

And I will deliver them to be removed into all the kingdoms of the earth for their hurt, to be a reproach and a proverb, a taunt and a c urse, in all places whither I shall drive them. And I will send the sword, the famine, and the pestilence, among them, till they be consumed from off the land that I gave unto them and to their fathers.

Jeremiah 24:9-10.

JASON KNEW WHO killed his men, and he knew why. He only needed proof and a plan. He suspected the military unit winked at the action taking place. He also knew the girls could be sympathetic and help a soldier through a rough patch when they're missing girlfriends, wives, and moms. They probably saved many soldiers from suicide. Still, they too were prisoners in the game of people as pawns of the powerful.

Jason often heard his Brother Zay tell about his battle with a dragon. His dad also shared stories, as well as his sister, Barbara. He once asked his dad why only their family battled the dragons. He answered that all people battle them, some people see the evil in the world while others are captured by it. He warned Jason, there would be evil in the military machine, but the military served a good purpose, there would be some bad people, not a bad military.

Jason liked listening to his dad talk about World War II and his cousin Michael tell about the Vietnam. The two wars were so different from each other and the present war. Jason served the military in a different type of war. Desert Storm lasted two years. The scuttlebutt around camps in Iraq claimed the politicians let the military fight the war to win. But there was more. He'd been in combat and had taken one of those mass surrenders of the Iraqi military into custody. They weren't fighting a battle. The Iraqis were undertrained and under armed to fight any battle. He also knew the United States had supported Saddam Hussein through the war with Iran. He didn't know the politics of war, but he knew loyalties shuffled faster than a deck of cards.

Now as an NCO in Korea, he saw the two sides of military might. One cared for the soldier; the other cared for the power of strength. Jason Troye felt torn between. But today, the message was clear. His military was using captured and enslaved human beings as resources. Preston Bush, father to President Bush #1, used enslaved Jews for free labor during World War II and came out quite wealthy in the end. It wasn't a new idea to mankind nor to the military.

The deed disgusted Jason. He wanted to release those poor girls, but he didn't have the means, the money, or the influence. He had nothing except a heart of sorrow for both his men and the women used by the wicked men using the military as cover for their abuses.

Jason finished his breakfast and his mental exercise in justice. He washed his plate, fork, and coffee cup and placed them in their place on the small shelf of his mini-kitchen. After dressing, he checked himself in the mirror and departed for his office, where he would complete letters to the family of the dead and insurance claims for the wounded. It would be a hard day.

Peggy entered the bedroom she and Jennifer now shared. Their jail keepers kept them apart for the first two weeks they were here. Peggy knew what happened to her during that two weeks. She wondered if Jennifer experienced the same. She wouldn't ask because they both knew the room had ears. They dared not talk of their treatment for it would become worse. Sometimes, after bedtime, they'd write notes when the power brokers assumed they slept. But with the long days they worked, they seldom lasted more than a note or two.

Still, Jennifer passed a note to Peggy about the caller. He said his name was Jason.

After the girls were served a skimpy breakfast of one small yogurt and a mini-muffin, they started their ten-hour workday of taking sex calls. Sometimes people talked about their routine lives, and other times they had to use sultry voices with suggestive ideas.

Jennifer hated those calls. She was getting less of them because she had a hard time acting enthused, and the caller paid a high price for them. However, she received a call today that caused the hair to stand on the back of her neck. She recognized the voice. It had to be Rance. He didn't talk long. She prayed he would call back.

Taking a bathroom break, she counted her points. She almost had enough for an afternoon off. The phone started ringing before she could get back to it. If it rang more than three times, the burly jail keeper would come in and "teach her a lesson," which could be a beating, withholding a meal, or a walk on the street. She ran to the phone with her pants around her ankles and answered before the third ring.

"Hello," she said while struggling to gather her clothing. She took a deep breath, realizing she wasn't listening. She didn't know how to answer her caller. She tried to recover. "Tell me about your day," she cooed.

Silence met her. *Oh, Lord, please don't let him hang up.* That would be the worse. The jail keeper made his money on the time spent on the call. They didn't like short calls, and a hang-up called for drastic measures.

For a phone girl, the bruises didn't matter. Jennifer had already lost two teeth in the beatings.

Finally, he spoke in a soft tone of voice, "Hello, I need to talk."

Jennifer started her timer, she learned to keep her own records because the dragon lady cheated on their time so they would work longer. She listened to the soldier for a few minutes before determining the persona she would take with this one. Turned out, he really just wanted to talk.

She didn't have to do anything except say, "Uh huh" occasionally.

His sad mood made it hard not to make promises she would never be able to keep. He spoke of his job as an NCO at Casey. His unit suffered a loss—a needless loss. He mourned over his men. She wondered if anyone mourned for her. Did Rance still grieve?

The escape and recapture stole her hope. She struggled every day to pray. During the physical abuse, prayer kept her going—that and Peggy's protection. But now was different. The prayers felt empty and meaningless. Why would they be able to escape one cruel taskmaster to end up in the tight fist of a crueler taskmaster? The first wouldn't beat them. They would be starved or overworked, but bruises didn't work well for glamour photos. This batch of taskmasters felt no remorse at leaving one black and blue. Jennifer fingered the yellowed bruises she received with the last beating. She found it difficult to keep listening to the soldier. No doubt his plight wasn't good, but it was nothing compared to her life. Then he made mention of something that caused Jennifer's heart to race. She asked him to repeat it.

"My hometown of Church Creek Falls . . ."

She didn't hear anything after that. She pondered ways to make him mention his name. He probably told her at the beginning of the conversation. Nonetheless, she didn't remember.

"Did you grow up in Church Creek Falls?" she ventured to ask, knowing the matron and the bully would be listening.

"Yeah, my parents were killed in the bomb that hit the area back in the sixty's. I was adopted when I was a few months old by the man that found me under my mother's body."

Jennifer sighed, it had to be Jason. She resumed a caring tone of voice but kept it distant. She smiled to herself. Peace flooded her with the realization she experienced an answer to one of her prayers, a contact with someone from home.

Mammon listened to the call with a fire building in his belly. Margie, the matron, felt the heat from his anger growing inside her heart. She gritted her teeth and pushed buttons to listen to conversations. All of them made her mad, but the one coming from Jennifer's room infuriated her.

Mammon purred with satisfaction as the cruel hatred crew in Margie's heart. The hotter the flame, the more damage she would inflict, and this woman could make a serial killer look like a gentle grandfather. Mammon directed her anger at Peggy because a beating on Peggy would hurt Jennifer more.

The beast needed to create some chaos for that stupid Jason Troye. Instead, the beast decided to stay . . . at least for some of the beating. It gave the brute such pleasure to see the girls squirm in agony. The beating raised Mammon to new heights. Jennifer screamed and tried to stand in front of Peggy, but the matron pushed her aside. The matron started the session with a slap across the face. A hard, loud slap that brought Jennifer into the room.

Peggy's lip was bleeding. She looked at the Matron and asked? "What was that for?" She scowled ready to meet the woman's attack with one of her own. The horse whip in the Matron's hand found its mark on Peggy's chest, leaving a bleeding slash across her neck and throat.

The bully stepped in at the crack of the whip. With a big, pasty smile, he said, "Need some help?"

At that moment Peggy ripped the horse whip out of the Matron's hand, followed by slapping the Matron across the upper arm with the handle of the bull whip. The Matron answered the Bully, "Yeah, I think so."

Jennifer jumped in front of Peggy, "Stop it!"

Peggy pushed her aside and said, "Get out! This is my fight, and I'm not standing for this abuse anymore!"

Jennifer pleaded with Peggy to submit and for the Matron to stop. Both ignored her, and if she got in the way, they pushed her away. The blows came hard and the bully man watched with laughter and a camera.

"Stop, Please Stop! Jennifer yelled. She jumped in front of Peggy and took an especially hard blow. It knocked her out.

Mammon pushed Peggy closer to the Matron and whispered suggestions in her ear. "Hit her on the shin with your battering ram." She did.

Peggy crumbled to the floor with the loud crack that broke her shin bone. The blood-curdling cry of pain aroused Jennifer. The Matron came down on Peggy's other leg. Again, a cracking sound of broken bone met her ears.

The matron laughed. "We're just getting started." She beat Peggy with the baton again and again.

Jennifer pulled herself over Peggy, taking a few of the blows, but Peggy pushed her off.

"Get out of here, now! And don't argue with me." Peggy said. "If you love me, leave."

Jennifer crawled toward the door, when she reached the opening, the bully and the matron focused on Peggy and the continual blows with fists, baton, and horse whip. Peggy muffled her screams, but with two broken legs, all she could do was pull herself away as much as possible. Standing was impossible.

Jennifer looked at her again with the desire to help.

Peggy wrinkled her brow and shouted between groans, "Go!"

Jennifer found the back door unlocked. She ran out of it and headed toward the infirmary. Peggy needed help. She ran as fast as her short legs would carry her. Boom! She plowed into something hard and stationary. She looked up into the face a soldier, but it wasn't just any soldier. She caught a glimpse of his name plate.

Troye.

32

Hope Renewed, Hope Restored

And seek the peace of the city whither I have caused you to be carried away captives, and pray unto the Lord for it: for in the peace therof shall ye have peace.

Jeremiah 29:7

THE ROAR OF the beast startled Rance. He held the phone receiver in his hand and looked around his darkened office. He saw the reflection of the green monster in his computer screen.

"What do you want?" he mustered, still holding the phone.

"Hang up!" the beast bellowed, the heated wind scorching the back of Rance's neck.

"No!" Rance's legs quivered. He felt grateful he was sitting in a chair for he would surely collapse if he stood.

"You Troyes." The monster growled out between spiked gritted teeth. "We will destroy you soon for the planting of seed is singular, but the harvest comes in multiples. We'll get every last one of you."

Rance didn't answer for a few minutes. Instead, he did something he hadn't done in years—he prayed. Because he had no other defense against the beast. He felt his heart calming and his body getting stronger. He swirled his chair around to see the ugly behemoth in full view. He gasped at the sight and gagged at the stench of it.

Then he heard the voice on the phone calling to him. "Rance?"

"Jenny Gale!" He screamed into the air, still holding the receiver in his hand in a death grip.

The monster snarled at him. "Hang up. She's mine."

"Dear Jesus, give me the words," Rance yelled. But the only words that came to mind were, "Don't omit a single word."

The phrase repeated itself over and over. The beast roared loudly, but the gentle words came into his mind loud and clear. He put the receiver to his ear, "Jenny Gale, I'm coming after you." He spoke confidently without any quiver in his voice. He could hear her crying.

The monster seemed to shrink but didn't lose its ugliness or stench. "Don't fight with me; you'll lose."

"Not against this sword," Rance pulled out the dusty Bible his mother placed on his desk several years ago. He'd never opened it, but the sight of it caused the monster to fade. Rance noticed the smell in the room changed to the pleasant scent of his beloved. He picked up his phone and called a familiar number, although he seldom dialed it.

"Hello?" The weak voice of Buster Troye answered.

"Dad, I need to see you. Do you feel like talking to me?"

"Of course, anytime. I always feel like talking to you."

The twenty-minute journey to his childhood home filled his head with questions and thoughts. They traveled the range from humble too scary to anger. At least twice, he pulled over to the side of the road, debating with himself about talking to his dad.

Merilee answered the door and gave Rance a big mother hug. "So good to see you." She hooked her hand into this arm. Rance smiled at the warm welcome he received from his mother. It both delighted him and filled him with guilt. He patted her on the hand and smiled at her, noticing how small she seemed.

Buster sat in his recliner, his body wracked with agony from the dragon's wound. In spite of the pain, Buster's spirit still shone with a smile.

Rance sat down across from him. "Do you feel like talking dragons?" Rance ventured to ask.

Buster shook his head. "Never, but always." He smiled knowing Rance would understand.

"Dad, do you remember when I was taken to jail for attempting to kill Zay?"

Buster nodded. "We had to speak in code because you were fighting the dragon—not aiming at your brother."

"Yeah, well it's happening again, and I don't know what to do or how to handle it." Rance ducked his head after he spoke, and he made a soft swipe at his pant legs with his hand.

"How?"

"I made contact with Jenny today, but the dragon . . ." Rance choked up and couldn't complete the sentence.

"Showed up?" Buster finished the sentence for him.

Rance nodded as he struggled to keep the tears at bay.

"How do I rescue her?" he moaned between sobs.

Buster reached over and patted his son on the leg. "We pray."

"But what can I do? I've got to get her back home."

"We pray!" Buster added emphasis.

"But—"Rance wiped his eyes with his shirt sleeve.

"But nothing," his dad interrupted. "The dragon fears nothing or no one except Jesus Christ, and if we don't bring Jesus, the one and only Dragon Warrior into this battle, we will *not* win."

"Daddy, look at you. You didn't win. That stinking dragon at Zay and Marcy's wedding has wounded you for life."

"But I am still alive and here to irritate the beast and all his minions."

"I don't agree but tell me what you plan to rescue Jenny Gale."

"First off, recognize she's not alone. She had a deep faith in the Lord. He will not desert her."

"Seems to me, He already has."

"No, son. If you use the trials of the Israelites from the book of Jeremiah, you'll notice in chapter twenty-six where God told the people to go and live in the land of the pagan. He told them to build lives there."

"But dad, I found her on a pornographic site, how can that be living? I shudder at the horrors she must be experiencing." Rance stood and yelled at his dad.

"Listen son, whatever she is going through, she will endure. Her fate is not a surprise to God. I promise you; He's watching over her. He's allowing you to connect with her. The dragon is attempting to stop that connection, but the beast will not prevail."

"How can you be so sure?"

"I've been battling dragons since you were a young pup. I know they're smarter and stronger than we are, but they are subject to the will of our Father."

Rance sat back down and chuckled. "Want to hear something funny strange?"

"Sure?"

"When the dragon's face appeared in my computer screen, I picked up that Bible you and Mom gave me last Christmas."

"What happened?" Buster smiled with his hands over his mouth.

"The dragon faded."

Buster put his hands down and said, "Uh huh. Just think what could happen if you read it and follow it."

"Where do I start? The only thing I know about the Bible is the things you've told me."

"Start with the book of Jeremiah. In fact, start with Jeremiah twenty-three."

Rance took a deep breath. "Ok, Dad, I trust you."

He enjoyed being with his parents as he ate lunch with them. A calm and a peace came upon him like nothing he'd ever experienced before. But in the middle of the meal, he heard a blood-curdling scream. "What was that?" he shouted.

"It's okay," Merilee said without missing a bite of food. "It's the mask in the incinerator and that bracelet you brought out here is joining it."

"Does that happen often?" Rance asked.

"It happens when you kids are here. It doesn't bother Buster and I so much. We're immune to its screams."

"What is it?" Rance turned toward the scream.

"It's their cry from the abyss they can't escape from. They really are in great pain."

"I don't understand." Rance put his fork down and walked toward the back window facing the incinerator.

"Jesus taught in the synagogue saying a wicked generation seeks a sign, but there shall be no other sign than Jonas in the belly of fish, so shall the Son of man be in the heart of the earth. He says the men of Nineveh will rise in judgement from this generation. You know that Nisroch was the god of agriculture in Nineveh, don't you?"

"What?" Rance wrinkled his brow and sat at the table with his parents. He took a big bite of potatoes and pondered the statement as his dad explained.

"The dragon we first saw on the farm . . . that's the same dragon Jonah faced at Nineveh."

"Dad, aren't you getting a little too deep into the Bible fairy tales?" Rance teased.

"You saw the monster. I didn't see a fairy tale; I saw a pagan god."

Rance could feel his stomach collapsing, even filled with his mother's delicious food. "Are you saying that stupid dragon in our field is the same one from the story of Jonah?"

"Beware, son. That dragon is anything but stupid, and yes, same one."

"How do you know?"

"The beast told me. In fact, it gave me an interesting point of view of the story. If I hadn't known the true story from Scripture, I would've felt some sympathy for the beast. That's why it hates me so bad, I study the Scripture, and it can't deceive me."

"Okay, dad." Rance looked at his mother with a raised eyebrow.

"It's true, son, Jesus told the people in the synagogue that one greater than Jonah was in the temple. I don't think they understood," Merilee said as she refilled their tea glasses.

"I don't get the connection." Rance said and took a deep draw on the fresh tea.

"It's pretty simple, really. The people were asking Jesus for a sign. He told them the signs had already come and that He was a greater sign than the things they'd already seen. But the biggest mystery was yet to come." Buster winked at Rance.

"Okay, I'll bite, what is that?"

"It's the reason the idols in the incinerator scream. You see, of all the signs already given in the Old Testament accounts, Jesus told the people the greatest sign stood among them."

"Himself?" Rance asked.

Buster nodded. "Then Jesus talked about the dragon."

"Come on, He didn't?" Rance mocked his dad.

"He called the dragon an unclean spirit. It's in Matthew twelve."

"After what I've seen, I would agree with that description," Rance concluded.

"Jesus told them when an unclean spirit leaves a man, he goes through dry places seeking rest, but doesn't find any. But if he returns to that man's house and finds it swept, clean, and empty, then that dragon goes and takes seven more dragons more wicked than himself, and they return to dwell there, and this generation is more wicked than any."

"Oh, my goodness, Dad! Are you saying Nisroch brought more of those vile creatures into our life?"

Buster pursed his lips and nodded.

"Seven?"

"Our battles are only beginning; we've only battled three. But number four showed up on your computer screen."

Rance shook his head with his mouth agape. "What do I do"

"Sharpen your sword!"

Once back in his office, Rance picked up the Bible still laid it in front of his computer screen. This time he opened it. He turned to Jeremiah and stopped at chapter 25 verse 15. The words caught his attention as he read, "Take this cup of wrath and cause all the nations to whom I send you to drink, and they will be drunk because of the sword I send among them."

Rance stopped reading and leaned back in his chair remembering his dad's words, 'sharpen your sword.' The first sentence in this said, *Thus said the Lord.*

"I guess the Bible is the Word of God, which is the sword." Rance chuckled at the lessons his dad had taught them. He didn't remember the verse, but he remembered the context. "For the Word of God is active and is sharper than a two-edged sword."

The only thing Rance knew for sure about his Jenny Gale was that she was not in the US. She was somewhere overseas, and this passage seemed to speak to other nations. Of course, he knew this meant other nations besides Israel, but the thought occurred to him that this could be God giving him instructions about rescuing Jenny.

He continued to read. He eyes fell on verse thirty. "The Lord will roar from on high and utter His voice from His holy habitation; He will roar mightily and against this fold, He will shout like those who tread the grapes, against all the inhabitants of the earth. A clamor has come to the end of the earth, because the Lord has a controversy with the nations, He is entering into judgment with all flesh; as for the wicked, He has given them to the sword."

The wicked held his Jenny Gale. Rance set the Bible on his desk and leaned back in his chair. "But I'm as wicked as they." Standing behind him stood Mammon whispering words of guilt into Rance's ears. "I've been looking and lusting at the word pictures, at the mental images of people in the chat room, and at pictures of girls and making money from those images. Girls in the same dilemma as Jenny Gale. How can I rescue one when I contribute to the abuse of others?"

Mammon spit a small plume of fire at Rance attempting to erase the last thought. He replaced it with the wicked version. "You needed to find Jenny Gale. So, what if a little pleasure came with it?" Mammon whispered to Rance, but it fell on deaf ears because Rance was reading that blasted holy book.

"Stand in the Lord's house and speak, do not omit a word, and perhaps the wicked men holding Jenny Gale will turn from their evil way." Rance said out loud as a personal interpretation.

Mammon roared and Rance heard it. He turned and saw Mammon hovering over him with smoke coming from the side of his scaly mouth and baring his large teeth. "Don't provoke me," the beast roared.

Rance stared at the monster with mouth agape and trembling. This monster twinkled with green sparks flashing from his scales. He looked at the pretty color and attempted to ignore the horrendous huge serpent head over him flicking a huge tongue around him.

"You're afraid," the monster whispered into Rance's mind. "Good, you need to be afraid. Do not try to fight me."

The memory of Nisroch came back to him with those words. The family stood against the beast on the farm. The difference between then and now could be found in the numbers of warriors. A family of five with a prayer warrior fought Nisroch, but today the battlefield consisted of a small room and one forgotten, lonely, weary, beaten wimp. There were no warriors to face this monster.

"That's right!" Mammon pulled back away from Rance and let himself shrink to a normal human size.

He took on a human form. Rance sat up in his chair and said, "You?"

"Surprised?" The human form sat in the chair opposite Rance. Even though he now looked into the face of a man, he could see the yellow eyes and the green cast of his skin.

"How?" Rance knew it was a stupid question, but his brain had shifted into stupid gear and was stuck.

"Remember the day your beloved Jenny Gale disappeared?" Mammon said.

Rance nodded but didn't speak, neither did he take his eyes form the creature.

"I watched that romance blossom and grow. You truly loved her." The man Rance knew as Long Nguyen said. This was the man whom Michael and Rance signed a contract for Dragon Wind to build an underground military base outside of town. This was the man whom Michael faced in Vietnam.

"Did you . . . "Rance started to ask his question but knew the answer before he finished.

Long Nguyen looked over his glasses into Rance's eyes. "I plotted the whole thing, starting with the offer to lease the city land."

"To what end?" Rance asked, not pursuing the kidnapping of Jenny any further. He knew his heart would burst with pain if he heard any more from the monster.

"Business," came the one-word answer from Long Nguyen.

"What kind of business?" Rance trembled at the sound of his own voice.

"The marketing of sexual immorality and the trading in human flesh," Nguyen said with a calmness and a smile that hid the evil of his remark. "And you were the perfect target and subject. Your heart spoke only of greed.

"But, I loved her and—"

"Remember who I am, and I think you know what I am capable of doing. After all, I think my brother Nisroch put you in prison for a few days."

"True, but they didn't keep me, because—"

"We know, but now the soldier is mortally wounded and can't help you this time."

Rance wrinkled his brow.

Mammon saw his confusion and answered his puzzlement, "Your father, you imbecile."

With those words the façade of a man faded, and the scales of a reptilian monster reappeared.

33

A Revelation

Then shall ye call upon me, and ye shall go and pray unto me, and I will hearken unto you. And ye shall seek me, and find me, when ye shall search for me with all your heart. I will be found of you and I will turn away your captivity,

Jeremiah 29:12-14a

ALYSSA HUMMED A tune with a big smile on her face. "I don't know why I'm cooking this huge roast," she said as she peeled potatoes and carrots. Using her mother's technique, Alyssa prepared a meal for a crowd, and this was a crowd of one. She didn't care. The time of celebration arrived. She had the answer to the riddle.

Her joy broke out into full song. "Praise the Lord. He can work through those who praise Him." She belted out the rest of the song by the Imperials, and when she reached the chorus, she stopped her task, raised her hands, and with tears flowing down her face, she sang out to the empty cabin, "Those shackles that bind you, serve only to remind you, that they are powerless when you Praise Him."

She heard the roars and screams of the myriad of dragons outside the cabin. She ignored them. The pain of the horrible beasts delighted her. Those monsters were the shackles that were falling from her. She didn't know how this scene would end, and she didn't care. If she stayed in this cabin the rest of life, she'd soak up knowledge and be content.

Again, she sang it out. "Praise the Lord!" Her heart felt light, and her body floated in the kitchen. In between belts, she heard a strange noise. Alyssa stopped and listened. She heard a knocking on the cabin door. She froze. Surely the beasts couldn't reach the door now.

Then she heard a voice call out. "Hello!"

It sounded like Barbara. Alyssa exchanged the potato peeler for the butcher knife on the cabinet. She tip-toed toward the front door and peeked out the side window. Barbara and Sharon were standing on the porch. She swung the door open and squealed with the delight of a girl scream.

Barbara and Sharon also squealed and the three of them hugged.

"How? Where?" Barbara sputtered without being able to form a complete sentence.

"I don't know, I ran from a huge, ugly, mean man, and ended up here. I've been here ever since." Alyssa tried to explain the whole ordeal in one sentence.

"Smells good." Sharon said, sniffing the air.

Alyssa laughed, and then the laughter turned to crying and garbled words. "You're the reason," she finally was able to blurt out.

"The reason for what?"

Alyssa's words became trapped in her sobs. She pointed toward the kitchen and make a circle motion with her hands.

"Whoa!" Barbara said as she stepped away from the big butcher knife in Alyssa's hands.

The tears turned back to laughter. Alyssa sat the knife down and hugged her sister and cousin. While they were still hugging, another knock on the door interrupted them.

Sharon answered the door. "Michael, Daniel! How did you get here?"

"We followed you two," Michael answered. Then saw Alyssa standing by Barbara.

Alyssa attempted an explanation again. This time a little bit more information revealed itself.

The family rejoiced with tears, laughter, and in between a few words of explanation for about five minutes when another knock startled them all.

"This must be Zay and Marcy." Sharon winked and opened the door.

"What's going on?" Marcy asked.

Alyssa regained a bit of her composure and said, "Let me finish my kitchen duties, and we'll get to the bottom of this." Before she left the crew to put the roast in the oven, she put her hand on the open door and peered outside. The air smelled sweet, and the blue sky filtered through dancing leaves of trees with beauty unseen since Alyssa arrived. She smiled and closed the door. Facing her friends, she announced, "It's safe to leave now; there are no dragons.

Rance curled up in a ball on the couch in his office.

Mammon sat on top of him. "You'll find her when I'm ready." A lightning bolt hit Mammon. "Would you shut that idiot up so I can do my work?" Mammon roared.

"Who are you talking to?" a gruff voice reached Mammon's ears.

"Any dragon that can hogtie Buster Troye and his praying to the Holy One."

Mammon heard only silence. Maybe the dragons succeeded in silencing Buster Troye.

Jennifer mumbled to the soldier, "Help her, please, they're going to kill her!" She pointed to the barracks behind her.

Jason whistled at his men. "Come on." He motioned for them to follow him.

"We can't go into that barracks," one of the enlisted men proclaimed.

"We're not supposed to go in there, but we can. There's a life and death situation now," Jason calmly retorted.

"You aren't obligated to go with me, but I would like it if you did," Jason continued to calm the young man.

The band of fifteen young soldiers would follow their leader, Jason Troye into hell if necessary. There was no more hesitation.

Once Jennifer opened the door, Jason heard the pounding of flesh and the screams after each blow.

"Hurry!" Jennifer begged.

Barbara helped Alyssa serve the dinner she made. The family gathered around the small table and sorted out the details of their recent adventures.

"I wish Rance were here," Alyssa said as she picked up used plates and refilled glasses.

The group nodded.

"There must be a reason why we're all here," Zay said.

"To rescue me, of course," Alyssa answered with a toothy smile.

"Looks like you rescued us." Daniel rubbed his full tummy. "Why do you keep looking outside?" he asked Alyssa as she stopped by the window and stared out.

"Their gone."

"Who?" Barbara asked.

"The dragons. Ever since I've been here, one or a dozen dragons remained outside that perimeter."

"What have you been doing here?"

"Looking for answers and boy, did I find them." Alyssa whistled. "First, I had to discover why the dragons kept using the phrase, 'The planting of seed and so . . .'"

"I'd like to know the answer to that too," Barbara smirked.

Alyssa didn't acknowledge Barbara but continued setting folders on the table in front of her family. "I found these in the bookshelf."

"I've seen this before," Michael said, thumbing through the sheaves of paper.

"What is it? Zay asked.

"It's the details of Rance's dealing with Dragon Wind Construction and Tender Expressions."

The group fell quiet as they studied the papers. Alyssa proceeded to clean the table and the dishes while they read.

"What do we do now?" Zay pondered, his face pale. The group shook their heads and pursed their lips.

"We help him out of this mess," Alyssa said.

"Alyssa, there's no way we can come up with billions of dollars," Barbara argued.

"We don't have to. We expose the hedge fund and close it."

"Sounds simple. Can that work, Michael?" Daniel asked the family attorney.

"I think so, but Rance has to be the one to close it. He pays off his investors and walks away."

"It would be easier to come up with a billion dollars," Barbara moaned. "We thought he was into pornography. Well, I guess he was, but on the production side, not on the consumer side and we . . ." Barbara gasped.

Sharon picked up on the thought at the same moment and met eyes with each of her relatives then she expressed their cumulative thought. "Did he sell Jennifer?"

Rance sat on the couch with head bent. He groaned. He stood and strolled over to The Honey Tree and ordered a cup of coffee. His shaking hand caused him to spill some of it on the floor. He took a napkin and bent over to clean up the drops, when he heard a familiar voice.

"I knew you would bow to me."

Rance stood quickly and looked into the face of Long Nguyen and about twenty men standing with him. They all stared at Rance with yellow eyes. Rance gulped but didn't speak. He searched for Michael. No one else occupied the restaurant. He sat up in the booth and stirred his spoon around his coffee cup, searching for a way out of this jam.

He never knew a Long Nguyen or any of the men surrounding him who slid into the booth opposite him. He knew they were not men. Before this moment, they were pictures in a movie, doing horrible things to other humans, mostly young girls. He kept his eyes down. He couldn't stand to look at the scaly faces.

Long Nguyen grabbed Rance's shoulder, "I can give you a wound twice the size of your dear old daddy." He smirked.

Rance remained still even though his heart beat like a sledgehammer inside his chest.

"What do you think you're going to do?" Long Nguyen taunted Rance with an evil laugh.

Rance searched for a way of escape.

"There is no escape from us. We own this world of yours." Smith howled with laughter so loud Rance felt someone would come running. He spun his neck to find his rescuers. The streets were empty. The courthouse across the street loomed over his office, ominous and dark.

Smith and his horde reverted back to their reptilian state.

Rance screamed with terror, "Help me!"

The reptiles gathered around him, closing in closer. Like a ball of snakes, they surrounded him and wrapped the scaly lithe bodies around Rance's body.

He could feel the rapid beat of his heart, knowing it would soon burst from his chest. In the reptile roll of the dragons, Rance caught a glimpse of light on the other side of the courthouse.

His office. He saw people there—his family. Once again, he screamed.

The bodies of the dragons squeezed him tighter until there was no breath in him and no expansion left in his body to take in another breath. He was being smothered by a ball of giant reptiles, and no one seemed to notice.

With his last breath before death overcame him, he screamed one more time, "Jesus, help me."

With the words he felt a rush of air into his lungs. He gasped.

The dragons maintained their grip on his body while they spewed vile stench of yellow phlegm over him. The phlegm covered his face, again cutting off his air.

Mammon put his face in front of Rance and roared, "You will not win, you belong to me!"

Rance again searched for a way of escape.

"I won't kill you now," Mammon continued, "because I have a surprise for you."

With those words, the front door opened. Mammon and the ball of dragons turned Rance toward the door where he saw Jason walk in holding the arm of another person dressed in sweatpants and a hoodie over their face.

"Guess who?" Mammon roared.

Alyssa put the folders in her bag along with a few other items and the Bible where she found her answers. She spent the last hours sharing her findings with her family. They came to a consensus among them.

"Now, it's time to fight for our brother," Zay said.

She walked onto the porch and took in a deep breath of air. "It smells nice here without the dragons." She smiled and led the way toward the forest.

"Where are we going?" Sharon asked her.

"Where the Holy Spirit leads us," she answered and moved forward, bursting out in song, "Praise the Lord."

The others joined in.

Buster and Merilee sat on the couch side by side. "It's time," Buster announced.

"It sure is hard not to fight our children's battles," Merilee said and sighed.

Buster nodded. "We fight with them."

"I pray this will be the last time," Merilee said but the screams from the incinerator drowned out her voice. She put her hands over her ears.

"It's beginning." Buster took her hand, and the two of them fell on their knees in front of the couch.

Hovering over them unseen were warrior angels with flashing swords drawn. "We are being dispatched," the leader, Davis, said. With a flash, the army disappeared to engage in their mission.

Patti entered the dining room in response to Rance's groans. She saw the ball of serpents fell away from him.

He looked around at the empty room. "Am I going crazy?"

Patti sat next to him, "No, you're being attacked by t dragons."

Rance shook his head. "I'm dreaming. There's no such thing."

The phone rang. Patti picked it up and handed it to him.

"Rance?" The familiar voice said with urgency.

"This is Jason. I need help."

"Jason, where are you?"

"I'm in Korea, so listen closely."

"What do you need?"

"Money!"

"How much?"

"All you can gather."

"Brother, I have a lot of money; tell me how much you need?"

"All of it?"

"What for?"

"To bring your Jenny Gale home."

Rance dropped the phone receiver for a second and swallowed the lump in his throat. Then he spoke again. "Give me the account number, and I'll transfer it now."

"He fell for it, didn't he?" The burly man growled at Jason.

Jason nodded. "Now let the girls go."

"As soon as I have the money."

Jennifer held on to Jason's arm. The fifty other American girls stood in a huddle, surrounded by fifteen young soldiers. The Philippine girls jabbered to each other in their language.

One of the soldiers stepped up to them and spoke in their native language. They calmed. He looked at Jason. "I had to explain what's happening."

"Hot Dog; the money's there!" Burly man said. "The girls are yours, I'm retiring to a tropical island."

The young soldier speaking to the Philippine girls asked the obvious question, "Now What?"

34

Overcoming

For I know the plans that I have for your, declares the Lord, plans for welfare and not for calamity to give you a future and a hope.

Jeremiah 29:11

THE QUESTION WOKE Jason to the logistics behind their problem. How do you get fifty people returned to their families? He surveyed the scene of broken people standing before him in different styles of dress, however, each one wore tattered clothing.

"Kelly, can you do something about their clothing?" He asked one of the women in his unit. She looked them over. "Yes sir, I can."

"Shaun, call the logistics office and schedule these girls on planes nearest their homes."

Shaun nodded and headed toward the office.

"Timothy?"

"Yes sir," said a young man who stepped up to face Jason.

"Don't you speak Korean?"

"Some."

"See if you can find someone to help the other girls find their families."

Timothy nodded and went to work on his task. Jason stood looking at his troops, standing at attention, ready to help in any way they could.

"Ernie, did the MP's get the scumbags holding these people?

"Yes sir."

"See if you can get the money transfer aborted or returned."

With the major difficulties in the hands of capable people, Jason dared to ask a question of the group of former prisoners. "How many of you are from Church Creek Falls?"

Twelve people raised their hands. Jason formed a tight smile with a mist forming in the eyes.

Only twelve? He focused on the faces as he tried to remember their names. "Craig?" he asked one of the young men with his head resting on his chest.

He nodded.

"Do you remember me?" Jason asked him.

"Yes, you're Jason Troye."

"Can you tell me what happened and how you got here . . . how all these people got here?"

"I can't tell about all of them, and I don't know much about myself. I was at the grocery store with my mom. I remember something coming in front of my face. I pass out and when I woke up, I was in the back of a cattle truck with the other people from Church Creek Falls.

Jason groaned. "We've been looking for you."

With that announcement, the young man's face lit up with a big smile.

Jason realized Jennifer was not among them any longer. "Where's Jennifer?" he asked the soldier closest to him.

"She went to the hospital with her friend, Peggy," he answered.

Without another word, he checked out a jeep and headed for city. He arrived at the hospital in fifteen minutes. He found Jennifer sitting in the hallway, staring into space. He sat beside her.

"You okay?" he asked and took her hand.

She shook her head. "Peggy. . ." She shook her head and moaned. "She took my beating. Why?" Jennifer looked into Jason's eyes as tears streaked down her face.

"They listen, you know," Jennifer whispered.

"Who?"

"I'm not sure, but if they don't like what we say, the beating starts in less than five minutes."

"Is it always this bad?"

Jennifer shook her head and worked one hand over the other.

"Why this time?"

Jennifer shrugged her shoulders. "I don't know."

The doctor came out and called Peggy's name. Jennifer stood and ran toward him, "How is she?"

The doctor motioned for her to sit.

Jennifer knew it was bad and prayed she would recover.

"The bones in both legs were shattered. There is some cranial damage; we had to relieve the swelling of the brain. There may be some kidney damage . . . not sure yet. Can you tell me what happened?"

Jennifer took a deep breath and spoke ever so softly, "If I do, I'll get the same." She shivered.

Jason took her hand. "No one will ever do that to any of you girls again."

"How can you be sure?"

"Because we're taking you all home."

Jennifer's posture straightened with those words, and she spoke one word as her cracked lips spread in a cautious smile, "Rance!"

35

When Angels Sing

Thus says the Lord, the God of Israel, "Write all the words which I have spoken to you in a book.

Jeremiah 30:2

EVERY FEW STEPS, Alyssa stopped to drink in the beauty of the outdoors. She'd hold her nose in the air, close her eyes, and take a deep breath. "How long was I a prisoner in that cabin?' she asked her sister, Barbara.

"Several months."

"Did you guys look for me?" Alyssa wrinkled her brow.

"We went crazy looking for you, until Daddy said you were safe."

Alyssa smiled at the thought of her Daddy knowing she resided in the strong tower of Christ, a perfect refuge.

"Look!" Sharon exclaimed. "The tunnel opening!"

"Well, I'll be, first opening we've seen. I wonder why?" Barbara said.

Davis stepped into visibility with the group and answered Barbara's question, "Because you were looking with your physical sight, now you see with eyes of faith."

"Has it always been there?" Sharon probed Davis.

"Yes. However, it's not a desirable path."

"I don't understand," Daniel broke in.

"A dragon constructed this path. It is wicked counsel to follow a dragon anywhere anytime."

"Well, that's how we got here," Zay argued.

"Yes, the dragons delight in deception."

"Wouldn't that make the dragons stronger than God?" Marcy gasped.

"It would appear so, but no. Have you ever read Job forty and forty-one when God gives Job His attention?"

"I don't remember it if I have," Marcy answered.

"He asked Job where he was when God created the earth and where was Job when He put a hook in the nose of Leviathan or conquered the Behemoth."

"I don't understand what you're saying." Marcy wrinkled her nose.

The others listened.

"The Leviathan and Behemoth are dragons. God is saying, He created them, and He controls them, but that doesn't mean they don't rebel."

"Kinda like us?" Barbara whimpered.

Davis nodded, "Yah, just like you and all humans. God makes a way, and when the dragons pervert it, God overcomes it."

"What does this have to do with the tunnel opening?" Michael pondered.

Davis smiled. "You came here on the dragon's plan, but you're returning in God's will. I think you'll see the difference."

With that statement, the crew stepped into the opening to the tunnel one at a time.

Whoosh! Daniel arrived first, followed in a split second by Barbara and Alyssa, and then the others all appeared in a twinkling of an eye. Next to their cars.

"God will put you where He wants you, either by obedience or by providence. You all arrived in His protective cabin by His providence, but you returned by your obedience. You don't have to walk the dragon's path when you're obedient," Davis said in greeting the crew.

"Where are we going?" Daniel asked as they climbed into their cars.

Davis smiled and whispered to Zay who answered Daniel's question.

"Mom and Dad's," Zay answered. "I'll meet you there after I find Rance."

Rance stood facing the door, holding a baseball bat over his head and drops of sweat dripping from his face. His breathing came hard with expectation of his vision becoming reality. He feared the anger of Jason and the unknown person. Rance knew his deeds were about to be exposed. Could he harm Jason to protect himself?

The door opened. "Whoa!" Zay exclaimed. "What are you doing?"

Rance dropped to his knees. "Brother!" he moaned.

Zay helped him up to the couch and handed him a paper cup of water from the water fountain. "You okay?"

Rance shook his head. "I'm sick, crazy, mean . . ."

Zay stopped Rance's litany of self-deprecating terms. "We're going to Mom and Dad's." his brother pulled Rance's coat from the coat rack and held it for him to put on.

Rance gave him an empty stare. "There's no hope. I sold the town to the devil."

"I know, come on." Zay urged Rance to stand.

"How?"

"The Holy Spirit showed us."

"Us? Who else knows?"

"The whole family."

"Then I can't go there. They hate me knowing what I did."

Zay pulled Rance's coat over his shoulders and led him out the door. "They'll never hate you."

"But . . . you don't know . . . awful things I did."

"It's not as bad as you think." Zay smiled at his brother and closed the car door.

Rance let out a painful moan and the words, "Jenny Gale, I didn't mean to, I didn't know. I would never—" He broke into unrelenting deep sobs of sorrow, regret and self-hatred.

Zay patted him on the knee. "It's going to be okay now, brother."

As the Troye family expected, Mama Merilee had laid out a homemade feast. She didn't say much with words, but she gave long speeches with a table full of food. After their experience that day, the gang spoke exclamations of gratefulness for the food. The smell increased the hunger pangs roaring in their stomachs. Each person sat in their place.

Except for Rance. He stood near the coat tree, holding his coat in the air but not moving to put it on the rack. Buster walked over to him and took the coat. He placed it on the peg and took him by the arm. He led him to his chair and sat him down. The gang watched the father's love for a wayward son. They continued their banter about the food and the forest.

Rance sat next to his dad. He raised his head and met his dad's eyes. "I'm sorry," he mouthed so only his dad could see.

Buster pursed his lips and nodded. "Enjoy the meal your mother has prepared for your homecoming," Buster said.

"I haven't been anywhere," Rance said, puzzled by what his dad had said.

Barbara laughed out loud. "Not physically."

"What do you mean?" Rance turned toward his sister, and for the first time saw Alyssa sitting next to her.

"Oh my!" he gasped.

Alyssa smiled at him. "Hello, brother. It's good to see you," she said in a soft tone.

The dishes stopped clattering and the people quit eating as the smiling faces watched their brother take it all in.

"I don't understand," he managed to say with broken words.

Alyssa explained the events to him. "I was given the task of exploring the meaning of the phrase, 'the planting of seed is singular."

The rest of the table joined her in the last part of the phrase, "But the harvest comes in multiples." They said in unison and laughter.

"What's so funny?" Rance queried in seriousness.

Zay answered, "She found the answer."

"Is anyone going to tell me?" Rance asked.

"Finish your meal, then we'll retire to the living room, and Alyssa will give us some eye-opening insight."

36

What It Means

We have peace with God through Jesus Christ whom also we have obtained our introduction by faith into this grace in which we stand; and we exult in hope of the glory of God. And not only this but we also exult in our tribulations, knowing that tribulation brings about perseverance, and perseverance, proven character; and proven character, hope; and hope does not disappoint, because the love of God has been poured out within our hearts through the Holy Spirit who was given to us.

Romans 5: 2--5

"I FEEL THE CURSE of a bewildered heart," Rance moaned to his family. "There is no hope."

The family sat around their brother, cousin, and son. A sound of slurping hot coffee would penetrate the overall silence. The crunch of ice from iced tea answered.

Rance took in the face of each of his family members. "I got deep into pornography," he stated, mostly for shock value. The slurp and the crunch responded without alarm.

"Not the way you think." He spoke in short sentences with long pauses between them. Only the slurp and the crunch filled the pauses. "I helped produce it." He moaned. "It . . ." He paused, unable to go on for a moment. "When the Internet reached into every school, office, and home, it presented fertile ground for making money. I didn't realize the high cost in human dignity and lives. All I saw was money."

Merilee hugged her son. "You rebuilt our community," she offered as comfort.

"At what price? How many families lost loved ones? Including me?"

There was no answer to the question that would offer comfort.

Alyssa offered the number, "Fifteen."

"What?" Rance looked at her.

"Remember the files?" Alyssa answered. "There were fifteen."

"Oh, but that's not the worse I did. Those business trips I took were—"

"We know what you did in New York," Buster interrupted and offered the empathy of a father to make his confession easier.

"How?"

A few in the group snickered.

"Sin is deceitful, especially to the one doing the sinning," Michael said.

"But—"

"You left breadcrumbs everywhere, hoping we would come rescue you," Alyssa added.

"Then why didn't you rescue me?" Rance raised his head indignation.

"You didn't want to be rescued; you wanted to justify," Merilee interjected in her soft voice. "Besides Long Nguyen scared me."

Rance smirked, "Yeah, he did. I remember your shaking when you faced him."

"Did you know him then?" Michael asked.

"Only on paper. That was the first time I saw him. I think he recognized me, and that was why he gave us the book explaining the operation of the tunnel system. His greed exceeded my own."

Michael nodded.

Rance hung his head and shook it. "So, what's going on now?"

The group yielded the floor to Alyssa. "It's time," she said.

The group nodded in approval.

"My dear brother," she began while moving from her chair to the empty space next to Rance. "Did you know there was a time there was no sin?"

"Sure, before the serpent tempted the woman." he said. "I may not believe all that Bible stuff, but I've been taught it. Been drilled into me since childhood," Rance stated with anger rising in him.

Alyssa patted him on the knee. "No, there was another time there was no sin."

Rance yanked his head up to look into her eyes. "What?"

"From Adam to Moses, there was no sin." Alyssa let a tender smile cross her face as she laid the groundwork for the explanation of the phrase, 'the planting of seek is singular but the harvest comes in multiples.'

"You're saying everyone from Adam to Moses didn't sin. Then why the heck did God flood the world and kill everybody?"

"Because there was no sin."

"Sis, what have you been drinking? Even this dumb fool knows better than that."

Again, the group snickered.

Rance gave them all a discontented gaze. "What's with you? I thought you were going to confront me, but instead, you're telling me weird stuff."

Alyssa stood and paced with her head down and her index finger tapping her lips.

"What?" Rance demanded from her.

Alyssa quoted Romans 5:14, "Nevertheless, death reigned from Adam until Moses, even over those who had not sinned in the likeness of the offense of Adam, who is a type of Him who was to come."

"Okay, explain to this ignorant fool." Rance leaned back in his chair and raised his hands in the air in an act of surrender.

"Before sin was defined, there was only death."

Rance shook his head. Alyssa continued the teaching while she paced. The slurps and crunches were gone, and all eyes followed her every step.

"You see, after Adam and Eve were banned from the perfect Garden God created for them, the dragons were able to weave their deceptions into the minds of man. When it says Adam and Even knew they were naked, it refers to their body but there is also the concept of the goodness of God no longer protected their thinking because now, they knew the existence of evil. And since they knew about it, they could think about it and reason with it, and even commit it. At this point there is no protection against the dragons except trusting God."

"Isn't it the same now?" Rance mocked Alyssa.

"No, it's not, Adam and Eve came from a perfect world of goodness and love. It was all they knew. That is, until—"

"Until a god that likes to use people as pawns in a chess game decided to take away his love," Rance interrupted with arrogant words.

Alyssa bowed her head and shook it. "No, Rance, not until Cain killed his brother Abel."

Rance shook his head and shrugged his shoulders. "So?"

"Evil or the dragons gained power over man. They knew evil thoughts and deeds would cause humans to kill each other. Their power was . . . is to deceive one into evil thinking then destroy others along with themselves."

"You saying a dragon is thinking for me?" Rance said and Mammon laughed.

Alyssa nodded her head, "the only protection we have from the deception of dragons is to know God and trust His word—the Bible.

"That's a bunch of fairy tales. I don't think so." He got up and left.

Alyssa turned to her siblings. "Was it too complicated?" she asked with a tear tracking down her cheek.

Barbara put her arm around her. "We have to trust the Lord's timing. Let the Holy Spirit work on his hard heart."

37

Return

For behold, days are coming,' declares the Lord, 'when I will restore the fortunes of My people Israel and Judah.' The Lord says, 'I will also bring them back to the land that I gave to their forefathers and they shall possess it.''

Jeremiah 30:3

THE TRAIN TRACKS often carried trains through the East edge of Church Creek Falls on the way to somewhere else. When the whistle blew on a bright, crisp Christmas morning, the townspeople took notice. The short blast of three whistles indicated the train would stop and pick up passengers as well as let some off.

Many who heard the whistle, stopped their activities and shouted to other family members, "Let's go see who or what is in town." The community gathered because Santa and Mrs. Claus almost always came to visit, bringing candy and treats for the community. Every child would get a special gift. Every non-believing teen received the latest 45rpm records, and moms and dads received the newest small appliance. This year, every household received a crockpot and forty pounds of beef. They each knew the gifts came from the elevators, gins, manufacturing, and local businesses; the cards were filled with logos revealed the benefactors.

Rance donated a large sum to the community tradition, and he loved being around when the train arrived. Even though his heart felt it had a fifty-pound weight attached, he still arrived at the train station before anyone else, except Zay. This year his drained bank account didn't allow him to support the gift-giving. Unless Jason came through and sent the gifts for which Rance paid his entire fortune to obtain.

The huffing metal engine pulled into the depot to cheers and shouts from the four-thousand citizens of Church Creek Falls. Rance watched the faces of the excited children and the grateful parents. Rance took a deep sigh, *If only Jenny Gale would be my present.*

A large number of people dressed in green and red stepped off the train, carrying large bags of goodies. The children couldn't contain their glee when they saw the brightly wrapped packages peeking out of the bags. The parents balanced young ones on their shoulders, and grandparents stood nearby.

Then it happened. The children came down from the adults' shoulders, and a hush covered the crowd like a blanket. Hands covered mouths, eyes grew wide, and guttural cries held back for years were released.

Stepping off the train were their loved ones—long lost loved ones. Some families didn't immediately recognize their loved ones, but when they did, shouts of joy were mixed with grief.

Rance watched, smiling, hoping.

Jason sent the gifts of recovered loved ones. One after the other came off the train. Then it stopped. Those without a beloved family member were few, but Peggy's mother stood next to Rance, her quivering hands covering her mouth and tears streaming down her face.

Rance put his arm around her shoulders. No words were spoken, none were needed. Jennifer and Peggy weren't among the returning ones.

After several minutes, Santa Claus stepped off the train and began handing out candy and fruit to the children. The anticipation of a gift dimmed by the giving of family members. The once-noisy crowd quieted, and sobs replaced shouts. The departure of families from the platform felt like the Von Trappe family saying good-night and leaving one at a time.

The music of reunited families mixed with the sorrow of missed years. Only four families remained when all was done. The conductor called for loading passengers, Santa boarded the train, and it left, leaving Rance with three other families. His effort to hold back the wailing sobs caused his throat to constrict with the pain of unreleased agony. Peggy's mother turned away from him and left the platform.

Zay came and took Rance by the arm. "Let's go."

In the car, Rance let the dam break, and his gut-wrenching sobs of love lost filled the air.

Zay let him mourn for the fifteen-mile trip to Mom and Dad's house.

"Why . . . here?"

"It's our place., Zay answered and opened the car door for his brother.

Rance nodded and shrugged his shoulders. He didn't want to see his family. He wanted to go home, drink, and sleep. He wanted to stop the pain—an unrelenting type of pain that breaks a heart and ruins lives.

Zay opened the door and motioned for Rance to enter.

Rance growled.

Zay smiled at him.

Buster took the arm of his son and led him into the living room where the family sat in a circle, or rather, two semi-circles because there in the middle of the circle stood Jenny Gale!

Rance stared at her in disbelief. "How . . . when . . ." he stammered.

She smiled. "Jason brought me home."

Rance couldn't move for fear she would disappear.

Jennifer's smile turned to a frown. "I'm sorry." She pulled her shoulders together and tried to hide her body with her hands and arms. She ducked her head.

Rance blubbered something incoherent as he approached her and then took her shriveled, tiny frame into his massive arms, bent his head over her and cried. He whispered in her ear. "I love you, I love you, I love you! I'm never letting you go." He held her arms and pushed her away from him.

The family watched the reunion, dabbing their eyes with tissues.

Alyssa stood and led them to the love seat. "Sit down," she demanded.

They didn't argue.

Alyssa sat on an ottoman in the center facing them. "Now, brother, you must listen." She pointed to Jennifer.

"Every day," Jennifer began, "I faced an ugly green monster telling me the awful things you were doing and accusing you of selling me to my captors. Did he speak truth?" Jennifer didn't allow Rance to hold her hand or touch her.

He pursed his lips and explored her eyes. After several minutes he choked out the words, "I don't know."

Jennifer took his hand and pulled it to her lips. She kissed the back of his hand. "It doesn't matter. The things that happened were meant for evil."

"What does that mean?" Rance asked her.

"The dragon I faced everyday wanted to destroy you and your family. I fought him with prayers. Often, I saw a military man named Davis standing beside the dragon. I would focus on him. You know what he said?"

"No?"

"He told me someday you would understand."

"Well, it's not today," Rance confessed.

Alyssa stepped into the conversation. "That's because you don't know what the phrase means. You will never understand what has happened to you, our family, and Church Creek Falls until you understand the phrase."

Rance twisted his body to face Alyssa. "Okay sis, explain it to me."

The family smiled and joined hands as Alyssa revealed the truth she received in the safety of a cabin. At the same time, each member of the Troye family prayed.

Mammon saw this and roared. He spat his dreadful phlegm over the family. but it disappeared before it hit anyone. He roared and clawed at each member of the family. They would wiggle a bit and return to their prayer.

Then a large bolt of lightning struck Mammon. He roared in pain.

Davis stood in front of the shrinking dragon. "I have orders from the Holy One," he announced.

Mammon growled, "Yeah, what does He say?"

"Go!"

Mammon roared as a powerful force pulled him out of the room. With the motion of Mammon leaving the home, Davis put his hands on Rance's shoulders and whispered to Alyssa, "He's ready."

Barbara came before him first. "My sweet brother, when we left last time, we told you there was only death from Adam to Moses."

Rance nodded, "I don't understand but okay."

Jennifer picked up the thought. "Before today, there was only death in your life."

"I'll say." Rance nodded

"Rance," Daniel said, "The Holy Spirit blessed you with a mathematical brain. You understood the world of finance when no one else in Church Creek Falls did. You were assigned the duty of rebuilding the town's assets."

Rance nodded, stood, and accepted the hug from his brother-in-law.

"Therefore," Alyssa added, "just as through one-man sin entered into the world, and death through sin, and so death spread to all men, because all sinned—for until the Law, sin was not imputed when there is no law." This means there was no revelation of sin or a definition of sin."

"I think I understand. How can you sin, if you don't know what sin is, but you can still suffer the consequences even if you don't know?"

Alyssa tapped her nose. "When the dragon used the phrase, he referred to you as the one seed through which the dragon could bring about his destructive plan."

"Me? Why?" Rance wrinkled his brow.

Buster moved toward Rance. "Remember when we first saw Nisroch?"

Rance nodded and chuckled. "I thought we had oil on our farm, and we were going to be rich."

"That's when the seed of destruction was planted."

"Are you saying I'm responsible for all your encounters with dragons?" Rance asked with some indignation.

"Yes," Alyssa said. "Not through any fault of your own but as God's plan."

"God planned for me to ruin my family and let the love of my life be captured by evil people?" Rance shouted in a rant. "I don't want a God that cruel."

"It wasn't cruel. It's the expression of His love," Alyssa explained

"This oughta be good," Rance mocked. He took Jenny's hand and rubbed it.

"Your Jenny Gale is a gift of life, right?"

"Yes, a gift from Jason, not from God," Rance retorted.

"Yes!" Alyssa confirmed. "It's in Romans 5:15-16, the free gift is not like the transgression. For if by the transgression of the one, the many died, much more did the grace of God and the gift by the grace of the one Man, Jesus Christ, abound to the many. The gift is not like that which came through the one who sinned; for on the one hand the judgment arose from one transgression resulting in condemnation, but on the other hand, the free gift arose from many transgressions resulting in justification."

"Okay, sis, I'm not getting what you're saying."

The family rose from their seats and surrounded Rance and Jennifer. With bowed heads, they prayed for his protection and clarity from the dragons.

Above their heads, a horde of dragons flew like mosquitos on a stagnant lake. They spit fire, growled, and dipped and dove into the crowd.

Mammon roared, "Do not let them have my servant!"

Belial sat above the circling dragons. "If we lose him, you will feel his punishment," He roared.

Nisroch held Buster's shoulder and dug his claws into the throbbing wound, whispering in his mind, "Curse God and die."

Alyssa continued to speak directly to Rance and Alyssa. "Rance, you were the single seed that brought the dragons upon us, but through each of their attacks, we grew in knowledge. We learned how cruel and deceptive the dragons can be, and we learned how powerless they are in the presence of the Holy One. Since the greed in your heart set the stage for our family attacks, you were blinded to the attacks and the goodness of the Holy One as He rescued us—each one of us."

Alyssa continued, "Rance, if one person can bring so much pain and agony to a family then is there any hope?"

Rance shook his head. "I don't think there is."

"Look at Jennifer. She's the answer to your prayer. She was put in a hopeless situation but the battle for her continued. Because our family had faith, we gained peace with God through Jesus Christ who brought the abundance of grace and the gift of righteousness in our lives."

Jennifer took over. "Rance, as hard as it has been, there is hope. You see, after Church Creek Falls experienced the bomb, the city attempted to rebuild itself, and you were the catalyst for that rebuilding. You demonstrated that all the money would not rebuild the town we wanted. Instead, the money only brought more death to the families."

"Where's the grace?" Rance mocked.

"On the train platform today, Here in this room."

"Where's Peggy?" Rance asked.

"Jason took her mother to see her at the hospital in Amarillo. She's in ICU."

"Why?" Rance moaned.

"She took a beating for me."

"What did you do?"

"I talked to you."

Rance groaned and buried his head in his hands. "I'm a curse."

"In a way, yes." Buster answered and groaned. "The dragon Nisroch is digging his claw into my shoulder." Buster bowed his head and prayed, "Please, give me the strength to overcome the pain and speak your Word."

The dragon let go of Buster's shoulder suddenly.

"Son, in this same passage, it says that through one transgression there resulted condemnation to all men, and through the disobedience of one man all were made sinners. The law came in so that the transgression would increase but when sin increased, grace abounded all the more. Son, if you hadn't brought the money-making schemes into Church Creek Falls, we would never have seen the evil going on before our eyes. The selling and abusing of humans has been going on long before you were involved. You were the seed to reveal the sin. Son, you were the law."

"Does that mean what I say goes?" Rance smirked.

The group laughed.

"No," Merilee said. "It means without you; we would never have discovered the wickedness claiming our town. Because of you, it was revealed. Now grace will restore and return families, and our town will be a shining beacon in a dark world of dragons."

A knock on the door aroused everyone. Jason and Peggy's mother came into the room. They joined the group. All scanned them for answers.

Peggy's mother wiped her nose and spoke, "I have a message for you from my sweet daughter."

Jason held her arm and nodded for her to continue. "Peggy said to tell you, 'While we were in the enemy's camp, we were able to bring many hopeless young women to know Christ because of His love and provision in the worse of circumstances." She stopped and wiped her eyes. "Peggy joined our Savior in Heaven tonight with a smile of joy. Her last words were to Rance. She said, 'Your job was to reveal the evil; my job was to keep Jennifer safe. We both succeeded. Now, it's up to you to continue the fight.'"

Rance doubled over and wept. "Jesus help me!"

The dragons fled to their wasteland, and a chorus of angels joined Davis and sang over a new member of the family of God.

Epilogue

For if while we were enemies we were reconciled to God through the death of His Son, much more, having been reconciled, we shall be saved by His life.

Romans 5:10

PEGGY JOINED THE singing angels, marveling at the beauty of their song. "What's happening?" she asked the military man she knew as Davis.

"Rance Troye has just joined the family of God." He smiled.

"Hallelujah!" Peggy shouted. "It's about time."

A beautiful woman stepped up beside Peggy and gave her hug.

"Hello, Mrs. Waithe," Peggy said. "We've seen complete victory over the dragons today."

The two women nodded and watched the scene on earth. "It was worth it all," Peggy said.

Mrs. Waithe agreed.

Patti, Michelle, and Cook joined the Troye family in the private dining room to celebrate the return of Jennifer and Jason to the home front. The private dining room hosted twelve families as they celebrated the return of their loved ones, and Patti, Michelle, and Cook were in the middle of each of them.

"We finally found where we belong," Michelle said.

"And our mission, to reconcile families in joyful celebration," Patti added.

"Food, family, and the joy of the Father who gives." Cook rejoiced as she handed a glass of wine to Christine, "Welcome to the family of Jesus Christ."

There were no dragons present or even close. The monsters stomped around the desert places looking for water.

The military provided security for the tunnels, and the private company, Dragon Wind, lost the contract. A few months later, Long Nguyen was arrested for human trafficking, and his victims from Church Creek Falls inherited the company assets.

Rance and Jennifer married. Even though Jason managed to stop the transfer of Rance's money to the burly man, the couple opted to live in the modest home of Jennifer's parents.

When they drove up in front of the house, Rance said, "I think Barbara's been here."

"Why?" Jenny asked.

"Because it's all clean."

"It's like I remember it," Jenny said with a giggle. "I can't wait to go inside."

At the metal gate, Rance grabbed his Jenny Gale and carried her to the door. Her small frame felt light. He hoped Barbara left them a good meal. The door swung open, and they were greeted with warmth, and a delightful smell of dinner, and a bright shiny new Christmas tree with only one package.

Rance and Jennifer gave Barbara a hug and thanks. She left them alone.

"Do we eat or open the present first?" Rance asked Jenny.

"The present."

Rance felt a bit squeamish. The last present he opened here revealed a dragon bracelet. What would this package reveal?

Jenny sat down on the new couch. "I love the furniture. Did you or Barbara pick it out?"

"Rance did." Barbara smiled at her brother and held the hand of her sister-in-law. "How'd you know?" Jennifer asked him."

"Because you showed me a picture in a magazine." Rance pulled out a well-worn advertisement from his coat pocket. "I looked at this every day you were gone planning for the day you returned and day dreaming of our home together."

Rance sat beside her, and they opened the package. When they saw the contents, tears fell from their eyes.

There in the box were two brand new Bibles with their names engraved on the fronts.

The note read, "Instructions for life."

Buster Troye's family is ripped apart when Hannah Holloway estranges from her mother, Barbara. Buster's dragon wound intensifies as he prays for reconciliation. Then the Dragon Warrior steps forward and allows Buster to witness the defeat of the dragon horde.

A family estrangement threatens Buster Troyes family causing his wound to become unbearable. The window of Heaven opens and Buster sees the work of the Dragon Warrior.

Stones in Clay
PUBLISHING
Available wherever books and ebooks are sold.
Bible Study guide available only from StonesInClay.com

Dragon Series

Buster Troye comes face to face with a horrid Dragon. Will he overcome the dreadful beast?

Barbara Troye is lured by her selfish needs into revolt? Can she be rescued from the Dragon's demon?

Dr. Zay Troye sees a Dragon carrying the secret of hell. Can science find the truth?

Rance Troye's wedding is cut short when the Dragon steals the bride. Will Rance's search save her or destroy him?

The pain of Buster Troye's Dragon bite grows from a family division. His final battle is fought by the Dragon warrior.

During World War II, military "Operation High Jump" explores Antarctica and finds the Dragon's lair.

www.StonesInClay.com

Stones in Clay
PUBLISHING

www.AlongSideYou.org

Available wherever books are sold.